Praise for *Curious Minds*

"The one-liners fly at a ferocious pace.... Evanovich fans will find this closer in style to the Stephanie Plum novels."
—*Booklist*

"Entertaining series launch ... The authors send their odd couple on a harrowing journey that leads, with zany humor, [to] a monstrous conspiracy that promises to be only the first for the duo." —*Publishers Weekly*

"Evanovich's comedic timing and pacing are evident on every page." —*Daily Republic*

Praise for # 1 *New York Times* bestselling author Janet Evanovich

"No less than her plotting, Evanovich's characterizations are models of screwball artistry.... The intricate plot machinery of her comic capers is fueled by inventive twists." —*The New York Times*

"[Evanovich's novels are] among the great joys of contemporary crime fiction." —*GQ*

"Chutzpah and sheer comic inventiveness ... The Evanovich books [are] good fun." —*The Washington Post*

CURIOUS
MINDS

BY JANET EVANOVICH

THE STEPHANIE PLUM NOVELS

One for the Money • *Two for the Dough* • *Three to Get Deadly*
Four to Score • *High Five* • *Hot Six* • *Seven Up* • *Hard Eight*
To the Nines • *Ten Big Ones* • *Eleven on Top* • *Twelve Sharp*
Lean Mean Thirteen • *Fearless Fourteen* • *Finger Lickin' Fifteen*
Sizzling Sixteen • *Smokin' Seventeen* • *Explosive Eighteen*
Notorious Nineteen • *Takedown Twenty*
Top Secret Twenty-One • *Tricky Twenty-Two*
Turbo Twenty-Three

KNIGHT AND MOON
Curious Minds (with Phoef Sutton)

THE FOX AND O'HARE NOVELS WITH LEE GOLDBERG
The Heist • *The Chase* • *The Job* • *The Scam* • *The Pursuit*

THE LIZZY AND DIESEL NOVELS
Wicked Appetite • *Wicked Business*
Wicked Charms (with Phoef Sutton)

THE BETWEEN THE NUMBERS STORIES
Visions of Sugar Plums
Plum Lovin' • *Plum Lucky* • *Plum Spooky*

THE ALEXANDRA BARNABY NOVELS
Metro Girl • *Motor Mouth* • *Troublemaker* (graphic novel)

NONFICTION
How I Write

CURIOUS MINDS

A KNIGHT AND MOON NOVEL

JANET EVANOVICH
AND PHOEF SUTTON

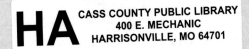

BANTAM BOOKS · NEW YORK

2017 Bantam Books Mass Market Edition

Copyright © 2016 by The Gus Group LLC
Excerpt from *Dangerous Minds* by Janet Evanovich
copyright © 2017 by The Gus Group LLC

Published in the United States by Bantam Books, an imprint of
Random House, a division of Penguin Random House LLC,
New York.

Bantam Books and the House colophon are registered trademarks
of Penguin Random House LLC.

Originally published in hardcover in the United States
by Bantam Books, an imprint of Random House, a division of
Penguin Random House LLC, in 2016.

This book contains an excerpt from the forthcoming book
Dangerous Minds by Janet Evanovich. This excerpt has been set
for this edition only and may not reflect the final content of the
forthcoming edition.

ISBN 9780553392708
Ebook ISBN 9780553392692

Cover design: Carlos Beltrán
Cover photograph: Ditto/Getty (buildings)

Printed in the United States of America

randomhousebooks.com

2 4 6 8 9 7 5 3 1

Bantam Books mass market edition: June 2017

CURIOUS
MINDS

BEFORE THE
BEGINNING

❦

GÜNTER CREPT THROUGH THE DARKNESS, shining his flashlight on the wall in front of him. The light beam reflected back into his eyes so intensely that he had to squint. He moved closer and touched the surface of the twelve-foot tower of solid gold bricks. There were thousands of them, some dented and battered, some pristine and fresh. All of them shining like new, because gold never tarnishes.

There had been a time when Günter loved gold. But that was before he knew the truth. That was before his search for gold led him to this miserable damp cavern. Far off, he could hear the echoing sound of water dripping onto the cave floor. Aside from that steady drip, drip, drip, the silence surrounding him was complete and claustrophobic.

He stood statue-still, awed and horrified by the quantity of gold stacked in front of him. In the all-encompassing silence there was a sigh that didn't emanate from *his* body.

Günter killed his light and waited in the pitch-black, straining his ears for the noise to repeat itself. His heart pounded against his rib cage, and cold fear crawled along his backbone. His testicles had retreated far into his body. Maybe to the point of no return. Not his biggest worry right now. If he was found in the cave it would mean certain death. He caught the faint rustle of cloth and the click of a light switch. Harsh halogen work lamps flashed on and illuminated the grotto.

For the first time Günter was able to see the length and breadth of the storage space. Golden walls had been erected, as if King Midas was building an underground maze. Stalactites and stalagmites, looking like the teeth of some subterranean monster, partially obscured the view.

Günter was overwhelmed with regret. He should never have come here. He'd driven thousands of miles to get to this godforsaken place. What the heck was he thinking? He was just a middle-aged banker with high blood pressure and low self-esteem. He had no business playing amateur detective. He should have gone to the authorities as soon as he began to suspect. Problem was, the authorities were the ones he suspected.

There! He saw a shadow moving among the towering limestone columns. The figure of a short man. A man who moved with the grace of a cat, his footfalls making no sound on the cavern floor. The man stepped into the light, and Günter felt a chill rip through him, felt the contents of his intestines liquefy. The man was bald and had bulging eyes. Günter knew the man. And he knew that the man was looking for him, and that the man was capable of doing terrible things.

Günter was hidden behind a stack of gold bricks. He shrank back and scanned the area, looking for an escape route. He crept to the end of his protective stack, turned a corner, and almost tripped over a body. It was a woman. Her dead eyes were open wide with terror and the top of her head was caved in. A gold bar lay beside her, matted with hair and blood.

Günter gagged and clapped a hand over his mouth to keep from moaning out loud. He recognized the woman. She was Yvette Jaworski. And he knew he was partly responsible for her horrible death. He turned to run and came face to face with the bald man . . . and the shiny scalpel in his hand.

"Günter, you picked the wrong place to go exploring," the man said, in a soft, silky voice.

Günter would have agreed if he'd had the chance.

ONE

—∞∞∞—

RILEY MOON PARKED HER MINI COOPER IN the circular driveway and gaped at the house in front of her. She thought it looked as if it had been designed by the witch from "Hansel and Gretel" after she'd made a killing in the stock market. Its steeply pitched roof, multicolored shingles, odd turrets, and sprawling, ungainly porch made it both inviting and ominous. It was located at the end of a long private drive that wound through a heavily wooded section of Rock Creek Park. It was one of the biggest mansions in Washington, D.C., and it was appropriately called Mysterioso Manor. Emerson Knight, the resident owner, was appropriately known as a nutcase.

Knight had ignored requests that he visit the bank to discuss his recently inherited fortune and to choose a new personal banker, so the bank had dispatched Riley to assure Emerson that his money was in good hands.

Riley maneuvered herself out of the Mini, straightened the hem of her fitted cream-colored Akris jacket, and planted her four-inch Valentino heels on the gravel driveway. It was her second week as a junior analyst at Blane-Grunwald, the mega-bank that made Goldman Sachs look like a mom-and-pop savings and loan. She'd taken the time to get degrees from Harvard Business and Harvard Law, and now at age twenty-eight she was finally ready to set the world on fire. She was going to make her family proud, pay off her gazillion student loans, and carve out a brilliant career. And she was moving closer to her goals on this perfect September morning.

She was two steps from the massive porch when the front door to the mansion burst open and a frazzled woman stormed out, swept past Riley without a word, and headed down the driveway.

A tall, rangy woman in her midsixties stood on the porch and waved at the angry woman. "Danielle, give it one more chance!"

"No! No more chances!" Danielle yelled back. "You're all whacko. And I'm not cleaning up after no damn armadillo."

"At least let me give you a ride home!" the tall woman pleaded.

"I'd rather walk," Danielle said, stomping around the bend in the road, disappearing from sight.

Riley thought that the tall woman looked like she'd

just stepped out of the Dust Bowl. Her hair was mostly gray and piled on top of her head with a bunch of strands escaping. No makeup. Beat-up running shoes, loose-fitting jeans, and an untucked though neatly ironed floral-patterned faded pink shirt.

The woman sighed and turned to Riley. "Sorry you had to hear that, hon, but Danielle had a right to get her tail feathers ruffled."

"Did she say something about an armadillo?"

The tall woman looked at her with stoic resignation. "Yep."

Riley extended her hand. "I'm Riley Moon from Blane-Grunwald bank. I'm here to see Emerson Knight. He's expecting me."

"I'm Emmie's Aunt Myra. Come on in. Nice to see a pretty girl stopping by, even if it is just business. And look at you with all that curly red hair and big brown eyes. And you got a nose that's cute as a button. I bet you work out too."

"I like to run when I get the chance. It clears my mind."

"Well, I'm glad to see you here. Emmie doesn't have many visitors these days."

Riley liked that this woman called Emerson Knight, one of the richest men in the country, plain old "Emmie." Maybe the rumors she'd heard were untrue. Maybe he wasn't as aloof and eccentric as the press reported.

Myra turned back to the door and gave a disgusted grunt. "The dang thing closed behind me," she said.

She tried the handle. Locked. She entered a number

into the keypad beside the door. Still locked. She tried another number. Nothing.

"Shoot," she said. "This is supposed to be a smart house. Why isn't it smart enough to let me in?"

Myra shifted in front of the camera that was part of the keypad, pushed a button, and said, "Hello, Emmie," a little too loud, like Riley's mother did when she talked on a cellphone. "I'm locked out again."

A man's voice came over the intercom. "Aunt Myra? Is that you?"

The man sounded distracted, as if he had just been pulled away from finding a cure for cancer or a marathon binge-watching of *Game of Thrones*.

"Yes," Aunt Myra answered. "Did you change the password?"

"I might have."

"What did you change it to?" Aunt Myra asked, patiently.

"I have no idea. Who's that with you?"

Riley leaned into the camera. "It's Riley Moon, sir. From Blane-Grunwald. You were expecting me, Mr. Knight."

"I received a message that a bank representative would be visiting. I didn't respond. I assumed that indicated disinterest."

"Let us in, Emmie," Aunt Myra said. "*Open the door!*"

There was a faint click, Myra tried the handle, and the door opened.

Inside was all dark wood and high ceilings. A huge

staircase with blood-red carpet rose up the center of the very formal foyer. The banister was mahogany. The elaborate chandelier and wall sconces were crystal. The side chairs, center hall table, and various chests and side tables were antique and reminded Riley of her gram's Duncan Phyfe dining room set. When Gram passed on, the furniture went to Aunt Rose and Uncle Charlie, and it had looked very grand in the small dining room of their doublewide.

"Just head up the stairs. Go down the hall to your right until you hear the weirdo music," Aunt Myra said to Riley. "That'll be the library. I have to go make lunch. You'll be all right. There's nobody here but Emerson and me."

"It's a big house. No . . . staff?"

"No, they keep quitting."

Riley climbed the stairs, and a dark little creature scuttled across the hall in front of her. The armadillo. Riley was from a small, windblown town in Texas, and she was more used to seeing armadillos as roadkill. This one was refreshingly unflattened by an eighteen-wheeler. It trotted along the carpeted hallway like some alien from another planet, its shell bobbing up and down as it moved. Okay, so it's a little odd, Riley thought, but it was adorable all the same.

She'd been anticipating an eerie organ fugue, or monks singing Gregorian chants, or perhaps New Age music played on a pan flute. The music blasting out of the library was 1970s go-go funk.

"I feel like bustin' loose. Bustin' loose!"

Riley entered the library and looked around. The room was gigantic. A lot more dark wood. An intricate parquet floor, inlaid to look like a giant chessboard. A fancy circular wrought iron staircase led up to a balcony. The balcony encircled the entire room and provided access to two levels of towering carved oak bookshelves. A huge domed ceiling loomed above her, featuring an eighteenth-century Italian fresco. A large weather-beaten Coleman tent had been set up in front of a massive stone fireplace.

"Hello?" Riley called, not seeing anyone in the room. "Knock, knock?"

She crossed the room and peeked inside the tent. No one there, but it was very cozy with brightly colored silk prayer flags hanging from the sides and peaked roof. A lightweight sleeping bag was neatly laid out on a camp cot. A small wooden meditation bench and an altar hugged another wall. There were fresh flowers and some photographs on the altar.

Riley turned away from the tent and bumped into Emerson Knight, spearing his foot with her spike heel.

"Crap on a cracker!" she said, jumping away.

"That's an interesting exclamation," he said. "Is that regional to Texas? You have a definite Texas accent."

Whoa, Riley thought. The man was gorgeous. He was about six two and lean. He was wearing loose-fitting gray cords, brown Converse All Star sneakers, and a gray T-shirt that was loose enough to be comfortable and tight enough for Riley to see he was ripped. He had a lot of wavy black hair, and dark eyes that could only be described as smoldering. He looked like the cover of a romance novel come to life. This was a complete surprise, as it wasn't in the bio she'd been given. She'd expected Emerson Knight to look like Sheldon from *The Big Bang Theory*.

"I'm so sorry!" she said.

"It's perfectly all right," he said. "The pain lets me know that I'm alive. Thank you."

"I didn't see you there."

"Entirely my fault. I was exercising my power to cloud your mind, so you couldn't see me."

"You're joking, right?"

"Not at all. In fact, I almost never joke."

"Oh boy," Riley said.

"What does that imply?"

"It implies that I don't believe you."

"Did you see me?" he asked.

"No."

"There you have it."

Riley decided the man was physically a ten, but intellectually he was a certifiable fruit basket. Probably did astral projection to Mars in his spare time. She sucked in some air and did a mental reboot, going into her rehearsed speech.

"Mr. Knight, Blane-Grunwald considers you one of our most valued clients."

"Because I'm really, really rich," Emerson Knight said. Not seeming to brag but simply stating the facts.

"Yes," Riley said. The facts were the facts.

Crossing to a huge wooden library table, Emerson

sat down in a spindly Louis XIV chair and gestured for Riley to join him at the table.

"At the risk of sounding rude, I see no purpose for your visit," Emerson said. "I've repeatedly requested a meeting with Günter Grunwald. Obviously you aren't Günter Grunwald. I find this all quite odd."

Riley perched on a chair across from Emerson. "Mr. Grunwald is out of the office for a few days. Personal leave. I've been instructed to give you any assistance you might need in his absence."

"It's been more than a few days."

"Many days?"

"Yes. That would be more accurate. Günter always managed my family's assets, including our gold holdings. And now that my father's dead and the estate has been settled . . ."

"I know this is a difficult time for you."

Riley's superior had prepared that line for her, knowing that Emerson's father had died just eight months ago.

"Not really," Emerson said. "My father and I were never close. And now that I've inherited the family fortune, I see that it has dwindled."

"The economic downturn has been rough on everyone," Riley said. She'd been coached on that line, too. "I understand you're concerned about the state of your portfolio, and I want to assure you that your personal assets are in competent hands."

"I don't care about my personal assets," he said. "There's more than enough for me. The foundation that controls charitable contributions is in disarray, and I do care about that. The foundation funds several positions at three different hospitals. We support leukemia research at Massachusetts General Hospital. We maintain no-kill animal shelters throughout the country. We run food banks and shelters for the homeless. We support the arts. It's now my personal responsibility that the foundation stays financially healthy."

"Of course."

"For some time now I've been having doubts about the management and security of my assets. These doubts are disturbing my intellectual equilibrium."

"I suppose that's uncomfortable."

"Indeed," Emerson said. "What it comes down to is . . . I want my gold."

"Pardon?"

"My gold," Emerson said. "The family's gold holdings. I want to withdraw them."

"Well, I don't think you mean that literally."

"I do. I mean it literally. Not figuratively."

Emerson looked at Riley with an expectant expression on his face.

"You act as if we keep the gold in a vault in the bank," Riley said.

"Don't you?"

"Yes, of course, but it might not be in the D.C. bank," Riley said.

"Nevertheless, I want it."

"You can't just withdraw the gold. It isn't done."

"Can I look at it?"

"Excuse me?" Riley said.

"Can I look at my gold?" Emerson asked.

"Why?"

"It's my gold. I ought to be able to look at it."

Riley narrowed her eyes and dug in. "It might be too much of a security risk."

"Why? Are you afraid I'm going to steal it? I can't. It's my gold."

"You can't just look at it." Riley was doing her best to speak with authority, but truth is, she was feeling a little out of her depth. Harvard Business School hadn't prepared her for this.

"Why not?" He sat forward on his chair. "You don't know where my gold is, do you?"

Riley met his gaze. "I don't know where your gold physically is. But I can assure you that it is perfectly safe."

"As far as you know?"

"I can't know any further than that."

He cocked his head. "I like that. That's good. I'm going to remember that." Emerson looked at her quite seriously. "Miss Moon, how long have you been working at Blane-Grunwald?"

"Just a short time."

"How short?"

"I started last week."

"Good," he said. "Then we can learn together." He got up and walked toward the doors. "Come on."

"Come on where?"

"To the bank. To get my gold. You have to drive. I forgot to renew my license."

Crap on a cracker, Riley thought. Her assignment was to placate the client, not bring him in to withdraw his fortune.

"I can't just drive you to the bank and give you the gold," she said to Emerson.

"Sure, you can. We'll go see your boss."

"You need an appointment."

"Nonsense. I'm really, really rich, remember? I don't need appointments."

TWO

Aunt Myra handed Emerson a tweedy gray sports jacket as he went out the front door and told him to behave himself.

"Of course," Emerson said, the tone suggesting that he couldn't care less about his behavior.

"It might be a little messy in here," Riley said, leading him to the Mini and unlocking the door. "I wasn't expecting a passenger."

Emerson looked down at the tiny car with the black-and-white checkerboard roof. "What is this?"

"This is my car."

"It's small."

"It's a Mini Cooper."

Riley reached in and cleared the passenger seat of a folder containing random legal documents, a pair of running shoes, a fast-food bag that had held her breakfast sandwich, and a couple crumpled candy wrappers. She was almost sure that her suit skirt was long enough to cover her hoo-ha when she bent over, but she gave the skirt a subtle tug just to be sure.

"Cute," Emerson said.

Riley straightened. "You meant the car, right?"

"What else would I mean?"

"You never know," she said. "Please get in. And watch your head."

Riley neatly slipped behind the wheel, and Emerson folded his six foot two form into the passenger seat as best as he could. He pulled a weather-beaten rucksack in with him and settled it on his lap.

"Sorry about the lack of leg room," Riley said. "I had to get the smallest car I could find. That's the only way I can fit into the little parking space they gave me at work."

"Blane-Grunwald gave you a bad parking space?"

"Well, not bad. It's just . . . well, it is bad, but I'm a rookie, so it's only to be expected. It's okay."

"That's inexcusable. I'll talk to Werner about it."

A bolt of panic shot through Riley's stomach, and she made a silent promise to speak more carefully in the future. It was a promise she made often, with varied results. Werner Grunwald was Günter's brother. He was the Grunwald of Blane-Grunwald. The head honcho. The topmost of top dogs. The last thing she wanted to do was come off to him as somebody who whined to clients about petty things like company parking spaces.

"Thank you, but it's not necessary to talk to Werner about my space," she said. "Honestly, it's *really not necessary.*"

"No problem. Consider it done," Emerson said. He opened his door, planted a foot on the ground, and wrangled himself out of the Mini. "I'm not comfortable in this. We'll take one of my cars today."

Riley did some mental swearing, unfastened her seat belt, and followed after him. The driveway led around the side of the house and ended in a large parking area that backed up to a multi-bay garage. A humongous old Jayco Redhawk Class C motorhome with tinted coach windows was hunkered down in front of the garage. Coming from north Texas, Riley knew her RVs, and she knew this monster slept five and sucked gas faster than you could pump it in.

Emerson walked past the Jayco without so much as a passing glance and rolled one of the garage doors up, revealing a mind-boggling collection of classic cars. Everything from muscle cars, like a '65 Shelby Mustang, to luxury dreamboats like a '39 Rolls-Royce Phantom III Cabriolet, to funky little cult cars like the Zastava 750 were lined up row on row in the pristine garage. Bright overhead pin spots bounced light off the polished chrome and glass.

Riley was mesmerized. Her father, when he wasn't busy being a county sheriff, had spent his weekends tinkering with a '64 Pontiac GTO. He read automotive magazines, was devoted to NASCAR, and dreamed of owning his own fleet of muscle cars. And Riley, her wild red hair bunched back in a ponytail, had been his pit crew, handing him wrenches and nut drivers and ratchets while he operated on the GTO with the precision of a brain surgeon.

She had inherited her father's love of old cars, so she looked at this garage the way some women would look at a display of every Manolo Blahnik shoe in existence.

"Oh man," Riley said.

Emerson dispassionately surveyed the garage. "My father collected things. Wives and cars mostly. Not that he worked on the cars, or even drove them. He just liked to own them. So other people couldn't, I think."

He stopped in front of a '93 Bentley Turbo R. "I guess we could take this one," he said. "What do you think?" he asked Riley.

Riley would rather have taken the '74 Pontiac Firebird Trans Am that was peeking out from behind the '69 Dodge Charger Daytona Hemi, but she was too intimidated to voice an opinion.

"This is a beautiful car," she said, eyeing the butter-soft leather seats and the dashboard of pure, not imitation, walnut.

"It was always Larry's favorite."

"Larry?"

"My chauffeur. He used to drive me to school when I was ten."

When Riley was ten, she was riding her older brother's bike to Bushland Elementary. At least on those days when she could steal it.

Riley got behind the wheel and took a deep breath. "This is a lot bigger than my Mini."

"Everything is bigger than your Mini."

She rolled the engine over, and it purred like an overfed lion. She shifted gears and backed out of the garage, careful to avoid the RV.

"Was that your father's too?" she asked as they drove past the motorhome.

"It's Vernon's. Aunt Myra's son. My father wouldn't have been caught dead in one of those. So, naturally, he was."

"Pardon?"

"Long story. For another day."

He pulled an iPad from his rucksack and touched an app. A blueprint of the house appeared on the screen. He tapped the screen a few times and gave a small grunt of satisfaction.

"That's Mysterioso Manor," Riley said, stealing a glance at the iPad.

"Yes. I was checking my security system. This will inform me, from anywhere in the world, if there's a break-in."

Riley turned off the driveway onto Park Road and then onto Walbridge Place. She thought about calling the office and warning them that Emerson was coming in, but decided against it. What good would it do?

She drove down the Rock Creek and Potomac Parkway and circled around the Watergate complex, skirting along the Potomac River and past the Kennedy Center.

"About the tent in the library," Riley said.

"I was wondering how long it would take you to ask."

"I was trying to be polite."

"And now?"

"Now I'm asking politely."

"It's a very large, complicated house, and I've become a person with simple needs. The tent is a more comfortable scale for me."

"So you basically live in the tent?"

"Correct."

Riley found it hard to believe he was a person with simple needs since he'd *needed* to ride in the Bentley.

"And the name of the house?" she asked. "Mysterioso Manor."

"My great-great-grandfather was something of a Spiritualist," Emerson said. "He claimed the spirit of Christopher Columbus gave him the name during a séance. Originally 'Mysterioso' referred to my great-great-grandfather. When he died, he bequeathed the Mysterioso title to his son."

"Mysterioso Junior?"

"Just Mysterioso."

"And are you the fifth-generation Mysterioso?"

"I suppose I am, although I don't often use it."

"Too mysterious?"

"Too confusing. Vernon took the Mysterioso name as his nom de plume on his blog."

"Why don't you tell Vernon to stop?"

Emerson went still for a moment. "I hadn't thought of that," he said.

She knew from his bio that he'd graduated from Dartmouth, so he couldn't be stupid. Still, she suspected he'd get lost trying to find his way out of a parking lot.

"Truth is, I enjoy Vernon's blog," Emerson said. "It's quite entertaining and every now and then I add my thoughts." He looked over at Riley. "Do you blog?"

"No."

He tapped her name into his iPad. "You have a Facebook page."

"My brother set that up. I don't know how to quit it."

"You can't quit it. It's there forever. That Mark is such a rascal."

"Mark?"

"Zuckerberg. Have you heard of him?"

"Of course I've heard of him. I suppose he's a close personal friend?"

"Not close. It says here that you were born in Bishop Hills, Texas. Your mother is a grade school teacher. Your father is a county sheriff, retired. You have four brothers. You're the youngest. You were a tomboy when you were a child, I think."

"You only *think*?"

"A conjecture. You went to Harvard. On a scholarship, I suppose."

"You suppose right."

"Then Harvard Business School. Then Harvard Law School."

"You're thinking I wasn't in a hurry to get out into the real world?"

"On the contrary. The real world is where you find it."

"Who said that?"

"A very wise man. How do you know the Grunwalds?"

"I got a ten-week internship at Blane-Grunwald last summer."

"Is that hard to get?"

"Almost impossible. And almost impossible to get through. They run you ragged, day and night. You have to get a rabbi or you're sunk."

"A rabbi?"

"A mentor. An advisor. Like Obi-Wan Kenobi. Günter was my rabbi. I wouldn't have gotten through the training program without him."

"And now you're working at Blane-Grunwald."

"Yes, as a junior analyst. I guess I have Günter to thank for that, too."

"Only you haven't been able to thank him?"

"I've been at the firm for a week, and he's been absent."

"And Werner?"

"I only just met him this morning. He told me to visit you and set your mind at ease."

"Why do you think he sent *you*?"

She could lie and say it was because she'd been trained by Günter. But her father had taught her that if you tell the truth, you don't have to remember anything. "I really don't know."

"He probably thought I'd be distracted by a pretty face."

"And?" she asked.

"And what?"

"Were you distracted?"

"Not at all."

Riley slumped in her seat. It would have been nice if he was at least a *little* distracted.

"Not that you aren't pretty," Emerson said. "You're actually very cute. It's just that I'm not easily distracted."

"I see."

There was an awkward silence.

"I'm not especially good with women," Emerson finally said.

"No kidding?"

"I find them confusing."

She turned onto Third Street and circled around to Constitution Avenue where the chrome and glass headquarters of Blane-Grunwald took up almost a whole block of prime real estate. She swung into the parking garage, drove down the loop-de-loops to her assigned space, and stopped just short of pulling in.

"Darn," she said. "I'm not going to fit. Your car's too big."

"Go back to the upper level."

"I can't go up. Executive parking is up."

"Perfect. Go up to executive parking."

Riley went up to where the executive parking spaces were laid out, and Emerson read the names on the parking spaces as she drove by.

"Here. This one," he said.

Riley looked at the name on the curb. "This is Günter's."

"Exactly. And he's not using it."

"How do you know?"

"Because he's not here."

"But he might show up."

"I don't think he will."

Riley pulled into the space and cut her eyes to Emerson. "If we get caught, I'm saying you were driving."

"That would be a fib," Emerson said. "You would be starting your day in a cosmic deficit for fibbing."

"Seriously?"

"Of course you haven't had to fib yet, so unless you've done something terrible that I don't know about, you're on safe ground."

Riley blew out a sigh and got out of the car.

They took the elevator to the lobby, she carded them past the reception desk, and they rode the next elevator to the top floor, the exclusive domain of the senior executives. The average junior analysts had never even seen the seventeenth floor, condemned as they were to spend their days in the rat's nest that was the fourth floor. Riley had visited this floor as an intern. That she had made it up here again, first thing on her second week of real employment, had seemed to her like a significant vote of confidence. That was at nine o'clock this morning, and now a little over two hours later she was thinking this might not have been a good career move.

Emerson left the elevator without the slightest

hesitation, seemingly oblivious to the blindingly white high-arching walls or the huge, expensive abstract art that was hung there. The whole place reminded Riley of the inside of the Death Star after Grand Moff Tarkin had taken over. The interior of the Death Star, like the seventeenth floor of Blane-Grunwald, was designed to awe and subdue.

Clearly it would take more than the Death Star to subdue Emerson, Riley thought. Whether this was due to his privileged upbringing or his own basic weirdness, she couldn't guess, but his attitude gave him an air of invincibility.

Emerson marched straight for Werner's office, and Riley made an end-run around him in an attempt to head him off. She stumbled past Emerson, crashed into the door, and careened into the office.

Werner Grunwald looked up from his desk at Riley's unexpected entrance. "Ah, Riley," he said, with a smile, "did you take care of our reclusive client?"

Emerson breezed past her into the room. "Your client is right here," he said. "And he's concerned."

THREE

I F WERNER WAS DISTURBED BY EMERSON'S appearance, his smiling face didn't show it. He looked to Riley for an explanation.

"He wanted to see you," Riley said.

"Yes, I did," Emerson said. "And, by the way, Miss Moon has a very poor parking space. You should do something about that."

Riley groaned inwardly but kept her professional demeanor. Werner made an effort to look appropriately horrified by the news.

"Of course," Werner said. "I'll personally look into it."

Werner's office occupied the entire west side of the building with a view of the Capitol filling the broad window behind his massive desk. It was furnished in Danish Modern, the only personal touches being photographs of Werner and various political and media celebrities hunting and fishing and generally killing things.

Werner had a full head of gray hair, cropped short on the temples, a little shaggy on the top. Riley knew it took a skilled barber to make a haircut appear that effortless. The result was that he looked like George Clooney crossed with Cary Grant, which, Riley had to admit, was a good cross. Today he was wearing a perfectly tailored dark blue suit, custom white shirt with his initials embroidered on the cuff, and a blue and silver silk rep tie that reeked of good taste and money.

"It's so good to see you, Emerson," Werner said, rising from his executive office chair, offering him a hearty handshake. "Have I told you how deeply your father's death has affected all of us?"

"Yes. At his funeral. Several times. But nice of you to reiterate it."

Emerson took a seat at the round table by the window. The view of the Capitol was breathtaking, but Emerson took no notice of it.

"Mr. Knight has some questions," Riley said.

Werner took the seat opposite Emerson. "Of course he does. And I don't blame him. I'm familiar with the Knight account and would be happy to jump in."

Werner moved into full salesman mode and proceeded to fill the air with such double-talk and gobbledygook that even Riley had trouble following it, and she had a degree from Harvard Business School.

"I'm not interested in hedge funds, venture capital,

or fixed income portfolios," Emerson said, interrupting Werner's dissertation on the world economic system. "I want to see my gold."

Werner leaned forward. "Excuse me?"

"I'd like to see my gold," Emerson said. "I'm thinking of moving it."

"Of course," Werner said. "I'll make arrangements and we'll get back to you."

"Now," Emerson said. "I want to see it now."

"Even *I* need to make arrangements to get into the vault," Werner said. "It's very secure. In the meantime, is there anything else I can do for you? Would you like tickets to a ball game? We have a hospitality suite for the Redskins."

"I'm also interested in Günter. And where he's gone," Emerson said. "I haven't been able to speak with him for some time."

"Günter isn't a typical Grunwald," Werner said. "He's a bit of a free spirit."

"That may be the case," Emerson said, "but I've done a small amount of investigating and the results are intriguing. From what I can determine, Günter has been missing for at least a month. Irene Grunwald filed papers to gain power of attorney for the joint property owned with her husband. She informed the court that said husband, Günter Grunwald, was missing. Oddly, Mrs. Grunwald never filed a missing persons report with the police."

"Irene might have a small drinking issue," Werner said.

"I turned up more missing persons," Emerson said. "Yvette Jaworski, a key Blane-Grunwald employee, went missing two months ago. Hasn't been seen since. Two people in a firm that employs thirty-one thousand seven hundred worldwide? Not statistically significant. But interesting. Also, there have been two suicides of high-profile Blane-Grunwald executives in the past month. One in Tokyo, one in London. Both leapt from their office windows. Both men worked in the division that handled commodities, like gold. As did Yvette Jaworski.

"It's a stressful job," Werner said. "How did you come upon this unfortunate news? Do you have a contact within the firm?"

"I have a contact within the Internet," Emerson said. "And the ability to focus my mind with laserlike precision on any subject."

Riley thought the laserlike focusing was in the ballpark of the mind-clouding disappearing act. A little out there, but what the heck did she know? There were people who could lower their blood pressure and sleep on nails, right? Maybe she should ask Emerson if he could sleep on nails.

"There's something else," Werner said. "I'm telling you this in utter confidence. There have been some improprieties in our bookkeeping."

"You mean embezzlement," Emerson said.

"That's the layman's term. But I assure you, all the misappropriated funds have been identified and replaced."

"And did this misappropriation coincide with Günter's disapperarance?"

"Yes."

"And did it involve Günter's clients?"

"Some of them."

"Me, for instance?"

"Yes, but as I said, as soon as the discrepancy was identified, the money was replaced."

"How long did that take?"

"Six hours," Werner said, his face a mask of remorse.

"That's rather fast."

"We keep a close eye on our clients' portfolios."

"How much was appropriated by the misappropriation?" Emerson asked.

"The culprit took only a small amount from a limited number of clients," Werner said.

"The amount?"

"One hundred thousand dollars from each client."

Riley had to remind herself that she was living in a world where a hundred thousand dollars was a small amount.

"And you're thinking that your brother absconded with these funds and disappeared?"

Werner nodded grimly. "It appears that's what happened."

"How many clients were involved?" Emerson asked.

"Six."

"How much is Günter worth? Conservatively speaking."

"I'm not sure I understand what you mean," Werner said.

"When his wife sued for power of attorney. How much was at stake?"

Riley thought she saw a flash of anger in Werner's eyes. And then it was extinguished.

"Approximately ninety million dollars," he said.

"Ninety?"

"Approximately. Most of that comes from the family holdings."

Emerson focused on Werner's face with what Riley could only call laserlike precision.

"You're telling me that Günter left ninety million dollars behind and ran off with a paltry six hundred thousand?"

"I know it seems strange. But Günter's wealth is tied to this firm, to his family, to his wife. If he wanted to make a clean break, to get off on his own, he might have felt he needed to . . ."

"Misappropriate?"

"There's no telling what he was thinking. Günter had been going through what I suppose you'd call a 'midlife crisis.' He'd been acting strangely, disappearing for days at a time, missing work, going off on his own for long weekends."

"Though we travel the world over to find the beautiful," Emerson said, "we must carry it with us or we find it not."

Werner looked a little uncertain at that. "Yes. I think he just went off the deep end."

"With six hundred thousand dollars? Why wouldn't he take more?"

"Maybe it was all he could get his hands on, on short notice."

"But why the short notice? If he ran off, he could do that at any time, on his own schedule. Was something pressuring him?"

Werner laid his hands, palms up, on the table. "We just don't know."

Riley tried to restrain herself, but the question just couldn't be held in. "Have you gone to the police?"

Werner looked at her. "You're familiar with my family?"

"Of course," Riley said. "Siblings who occupy the highest seats of power in America. You and your brothers are called the Three Musketeers of Twenty-First-Century America."

Werner nodded. "Problem is, there are four of us."

Riley knew the story. The Grunwald brothers had grown up in Washington, the sons of the legendary Bertram Grunwald, the Harvard professor who went on to become chairman of the Federal Reserve and who raised his sons to excel at all costs. Professor Grunwald died seven years ago, having succeeded in pushing his boys beyond his or their wildest dreams.

Werner graduated at the top of his class at Princeton and went on to conquer Wall Street. Scaling up the corporate ladder of the stodgy old banking concern of Blane Brothers, he had transformed it into one of the most powerful investment firms in the world. Before he'd reached fifty, he had added his name to it and made it his own personal fiefdom.

More impressively, there was Hans, who had gone to West Point. He had distinguished himself in the field and became commanding general of the U.S. Army Intelligence and Security Command at Fort Belvoir in Virginia. Two years after he achieved the rank of four-star general, he'd been picked to run the National Security Agency. This was one of the few appointments made by the current administration that had sailed through Congress without a murmur of protest.

As if running the NSA and one of the world's major banks wasn't enough for the Grunwald family, there was Manfred Grunwald, the judge. Manny graduated with honors from Yale Law School. He served as a clerk for Supreme Court Justice Rehnquist before starting his own law firm. Now Manny was about to be sworn in as associate justice of the Supreme Court.

The Grunwalds had conquered America.

Except for the youngest brother, Günter.

Günter hadn't gone to Yale or Princeton or West Point. Günter had gone to Northwestern. He went on to be a successful trader on Wall Street and had been hired by his brother to work at Blane-Grunwald, where he had made millions as head of the Investment Management Division.

Millions, not billions. Head of a division, not head of an empire. A success, not a legend. When Riley googled Günter Grunwald, all she got was information on his brothers.

"You might say that Günter is the black sheep of the family," Werner said with a sigh. "The underachiever."

"And now, apparently, the felon," Emerson said.

"'Felon' is such a harsh word," Werner said. "And this is a very delicate matter. My brother Manny is about to be sworn in as a Supreme Court justice."

"And this would be a bad time for a scandal to break?" Emerson asked.

"The worst time."

"So Günter gets to disappear with impunity."

"Not impunity," Werner said. "We would like to bring him back here, but without the involvement of law enforcement or the press."

"In other words, without anyone knowing about it," Emerson said.

Werner rose, indicating that the meeting was concluded. "Yes, I suppose that covers it."

Emerson nodded decisively. "All right, I'll do it."

Werner looked surprised. "Do what?"

"I'll help you find Günter."

Werner looked around the room. He was apparently so confused he even looked to Riley for clarification.

"I don't think Mr. Grunwald was asking for your help," Riley said to Emerson.

"Of course he was. Why else would he tell me all this? In fact, I'm quite good at finding lost things. Not my keys or the television remote, but other things of more interest. My high school aptitude test scored me very high as a finder of lost objects. And I once found a man bobbing about in the Indian Ocean."

Emerson stood, stuck his hand out, and Werner, looking a little dazed, mechanically shook it.

"If you feel I need to be compensated for my time you can make my payment out to your favorite charity," Emerson said to Werner. "I assume Günter's office is next to yours?"

"Yes," Werner said, puzzled. "How did you know that?"

"He's your brother. You'd give him the second-best office. Nice, but without the view of the Capitol. Not because you like him or feel compelled out of family responsibility, but because one must keep up appearances."

Emerson walked out of Werner's office and into Günter's office. Werner followed him. Riley followed Werner.

FOUR

————✺————

T HE OFFICE WAS NEARLY AS BIG AS WERNER'S. Though Werner's was decorated with austere Danish Modern simplicity, Günter's décor was baronial, with heavy furniture, dark wood paneling, and full brocade curtains on the windows. Riley almost expected to see Rumpole of the Bailey sitting in the embossed leather chair at the monstrous desk.

Emerson stood in the middle of the room, turning slowly around, as if he were a camera, taking it all in.

"There are no mementos, no personal photographs here," he said.

"His wife came in a few days ago and may have removed them," Werner said. "I think she's given up hope that he'll return."

"Did Günter have an assistant?"

"Maxine Trowbridge," Werner said. "She's just one office away."

Emerson gave one last sweeping look around and went to the door. "I'd like to speak to Maxine."

"Of course," Werner said, leading the way.

Emerson paused at the open doorway and looked in at Maxine.

"Emerson Knight, here," he said. "Could I talk with you for a few moments?"

Maxine was in her midthirties. Her hair was blond, pulled back at the nape of her neck, and secured with a simple gold clip. Her makeup was tasteful and perfectly applied but unable to hide the dark circles under her eyes. Her conservative designer suit was a snug fit, as if Maxine had recently gained weight. Stress, Riley thought. She'd seemed close to Günter when Riley was interning, and now that Günter was MIA she had to be worried.

Maxine looked past Emerson to Werner, who nodded his assent.

"Do you have any idea where Günter has gone?" Emerson asked Maxine.

"No," she replied, shaking her head.

"Do you think he embezzled money and ran off with it?"

She shook her head again, more emphatically this time. "No. I know that's what everyone is saying. But I can't believe it. Not Günter. He'd just been given a new responsibility. He'd gotten everything he always wanted."

"Everything?" Emerson asked.

"Well, everything within reason," she said. "He'd just gotten back from a business trip to New York. He said it was going to make or break him. He was on the verge of something tremendous. He wouldn't run out now." She glanced over at Werner, and the line of her mouth tightened. "He is a good man."

"Do you have any further questions for Ms. Trowbridge?" Werner asked Emerson.

"Not at the moment."

Werner stepped away from Maxine's office.

"I should tell you that Günter had not recently been given new responsibilities," Werner said to Emerson. "And the New York trip was one of those long weekends he took. He wasn't on company business."

Emerson nodded. "Understood. I'm off to find Günter. I'll report back when I've located him."

"Wait," Werner said. "Take Moonbeam with you."

"Moonbeam?" Emerson asked.

"That's what we call Miss Moon here," Werner told him. "We all have nicknames."

"What's yours?"

"Everyone but me."

"I'll find a nickname for you," Emerson said.

"Please don't."

"And why would I take Miss Moon with me?"

Werner shrugged. "You could use an assistant. Riley is good with people."

"And I'm not?" Emerson asked.

"I didn't say that. But now that you've said it, no, you're not."

"I can't argue with that. Personal interaction has never been my forte."

"Well, then, this is your girl. She can talk to anybody, can't you, Riley?"

Riley had never before had a panic attack, but she thought she felt one coming on. Werner was giving her away. He was moving her out of the office. Had she just been fired?

"Trust me," Werner said. "She could talk a dog off a meat truck. She'll be a great girl Friday for you."

"I'm not entirely comfortable with this," Riley said.

"*Person* Friday then," Werner corrected himself. "Aide-de-camp."

Emerson turned to Riley. "What do you say, Miss Moon? Do you want to be my amanuensis?"

Riley had no clue what that meant. She made a mental note to look it up when she had the chance. She hoped it wasn't just a fancy word for chauffeur.

"Is this a permanent reassignment?" Riley asked Werner.

"Absolutely not," Werner said. "I'm sure this search will take only a few days, and you'll be back at your desk."

"We'll begin tomorrow morning at seven o'clock at my house," Emerson said to Riley.

Riley made an effort not to grimace. Seven o'clock in the morning? "Sure," she said. "Seven o'clock. Do you want me to drive you home now?"

"Of course."

"I need a moment with Moonbeam," Werner said to Emerson.

Emerson turned on his heel and strode off to the elevator. "I'll be at the car."

Riley followed Werner into his office and waited until the door was closed before she spoke.

"Sir, I'm so sorry," she said. "He insisted we come here."

"You did the right thing. He needed reassurance that his assets were being protected. And now he's going to be occupied by this wild goose chase, so it all worked out perfectly."

"Do you think he can find Günter?"

"Not for a moment. Just keep me in the loop, and we'll all be happy, Moonbeam."

Riley squared her shoulders. She didn't like being called Moonbeam. And she didn't especially like her new assignment.

Werner watched Riley leave his office. He hoped he'd chosen wisely. She had two advanced degrees from Harvard but no street cred. She needed Blane-Grunwald to pay off her loans and push her up the corporate ladder. He had her pegged as psychotically ambitious, and he was counting on her to sell her soul for a shot at the corner office. If it turned out otherwise, he might have to kill her.

• • •

Riley caught up with Emerson at the car. He was leaning against the right front quarter panel, eyes closed, lost in thought. Probably having an out-of-body experience, Riley thought. Or maybe he was convening with aliens from another solar system.

"Hey," she said. "What's up?"

"I'm waiting," Emerson said.

"For?"

"For you."

"Of course."

She unlocked his door and ran around to the driver's side. She plugged the key into the ignition and backed out of Günter's space. "Just exactly what is it you expect me to do?" she asked.

"Drive my car."

"Anything else?"

"I tend to forget details that aren't important to me. I would expect you to remember them. You might even record them, amanuensis style."

Crap, Riley thought. There was that word again.

She drove through the bustling streets of Washington, through the pastoral woods of Rock Creek, and up the long driveway to Mysterioso Manor.

"Would you like to take the Bentley home with you?" Emerson asked.

"Nice of you to offer, but no. The Bentley is lovely, but the Mini gets better gas mileage. It's more environmentally responsible. It's the car I picked out as the wisest for my new life in Washington."

"I thought you bought the Mini because it was the only car that would fit in your assigned parking space."

"That too."

Riley's apartment was on Monroe Street in the Mount Pleasant section of Northwest D.C. It was a tiny one-bedroom flat that occupied the entire third floor of a converted Victorian built in 1907. The plumbing sounded considerably older. The radiator clanged, the water pipes gurgled, and she lived in fear of the toilet exploding.

She stripped off her executive uniform and got into her sweatpants and big, roomy Batman T-shirt. She'd wanted to grow up to be a superhero, and in a left-turn kind of way she felt like she was on track. She was going to be a financial superhero, helping people invest in their future, safeguarding the country's monetary system. At least she had been on track last week. This week she wasn't so sure. This week she was chauffeuring a goofball around town.

She sat at her small kitchen table and unwrapped the turkey breast and Swiss cheese sandwich she'd picked up at Potbelly on her way home. She switched on her laptop and Facebooked her mother and brothers while she ate. When she'd caught up on her family she went into Oracle mode. Oracle had been her favorite comic book character when she was a kid. And truth is, Riley still loved comic books, and especially Oracle.

Oracle was Barbara Gordon, Commissioner Gordon's daughter. She was Batgirl first, but after the Joker put her in a wheelchair she became a computer whiz who could find any information about anyone with just a few clicks of her keyboard.

Riley could do almost the same thing. She typed in "Emerson Cranston Knight," and sources of information flooded her screen. The Knights had been newsworthy for several generations, not just for their wealth but also for their eccentricities.

Emerson was described as an American business magnate, investor, inventor, and philanthropist, the only child of communications and aerospace mogul Mitchell Brown Knight. If Riley read every article on the Net about Emerson's father she'd be up until dawn, so she skimmed Wikipedia and kept her research to articles that addressed Emerson particularly.

The Knight fortune stretched back to Emerson's great-great-grandfather Lamont Knight, one of the legendary robber barons of the Gilded Age. Emerson's father was a confidant to presidents and a close friend of Professor Bertram Grunwald, the architect of the U.S. economy in the post-Vietnam years.

Riley thought it was curious that the Knight-Grunwald connection went back two generations and yet there didn't seem to be any warmth between Emerson and Werner.

Emerson's mother, Sophia Delgado, was a supermodel

from Spain. She and Mitchell separated when Emerson was two, and she went to live in Paris with soccer star Ronaldo Diaz.

Riley scanned some tabloid articles and found that Emerson was raised by a variety of stepmothers and went to a variety of boarding schools.

The most intriguing article was an extended obituary on his father that included a short paragraph on Emerson, the new heir to the Knight fortune. It stated that Emerson was best known for his dramatic disappearances. Following graduation from college he had sailed off on a luxury yacht for points unknown. The world lost track of him completely for a year. After that Emerson would resurface from time to time but always suddenly vanished again. The obit ended by saying that Emerson had returned to his Washington, D.C., home following the death of his father, and that his whereabouts during his absences remained a subject of conjecture.

At the risk of being cynical, Riley couldn't help but speculate that maybe Emerson had been at home all along but in his cloud of invisibility. Or maybe Emerson had removed himself to an alien astral plane. Or maybe he periodically checked himself into rehab.

FIVE

———⟨∞⟩———

A T SIX A.M. RILEY FINALLY GAVE UP HITTING
the snooze button on her bedside clock and
dragged herself out of bed. She had to be at Mysterioso
Manor in an hour. She had no idea why. What on earth
was Emerson going to do so early in the morning?

She took a shower and dressed down in skinny black
slacks, a pin-striped fitted shirt, a little black wool jacket,
and Jimmy Choo ankle boots she'd found on sale. She
chugged a cup of coffee and ate some toast, brushed her
teeth, swiped on some lip gloss, and was on her way.

At precisely seven o'clock, Riley parked in the paved
area behind Mysterioso Manor and hiked her messenger
bag onto her shoulder. The RV was still in the same
location, and a big, impressively muscled guy was
working on the engine. His dark hair was cut into a

mullet, and his T-shirt advertised beer. She guessed him to be around thirty.

He stopped working when she walked by and gave her a big, good-natured grin.

"Howdy," he said, with the same cheerful mountain accent as Aunt Myra. "You here to see Emerson?"

"Yes," she said. "Are you Vernon?"

"That's what they call me. My mom said you were here yesterday, and you were sweet as tea. And she was right. You sure are pretty."

"Thank you. Do you live here with your mom and Emerson?"

"Sometimes, but mostly I live in Harrisonburg, Virginia. That's about a hour from Charlottesville. I come up here when Emerson needs something fixed. I keep all his cars running spit spot." He grinned again. "That's from *Mary Poppins*."

Riley smiled back. "One of my favorite movies."

"Yeah, me too," he said. "I like when that guy dances like a penguin. If you're looking for Emerson, he's probably out in the conservatory at this hour of the morning. Just go around the house till you see the zebras, then turn right."

Before yesterday, Riley would have thought she'd misheard him. Now she went looking for zebras.

Riley counted eight zebras behind a fence. The gate to the enclosure was open, and they could have wandered off, so she guessed they were pretty content where they were. She turned right as directed, and the walkway led to a giant greenhouse. It was a glass and iron structure of intricate design with a big Victorian cupola on top. It looked to Riley like a massive crystal wedding cake.

The glass panes were shattered in spots, and vines grew through the gaps and wrapped themselves around the outside of the building as if they wanted to swallow it whole.

Walking through the open door, she heard the booming seventies funk music that she now associated with Emerson. The interior was humid and crammed with ferns, fruit trees, and flowering plants.

"Hello?" she called. "Mr. Knight?"

No answer. She punched his cell number into her phone, waited while it connected, and heard the phone ringing somewhere on the other side of the jungle. She cautiously crept along the stone path, brushing ferns aside, keeping a watchful eye out for spiders and lizards. She reached an open area that had two pretty white wrought iron benches and a small table. Emerson was sitting cross-legged on the table, eyes closed, his mind obviously somewhere far away.

Riley sat down on one of the benches and watched Emerson. He didn't seem to be breathing, but he was most likely not dead since he hadn't toppled off the table. She checked her email on her cellphone and organized her messenger bag. She went back to watching Emerson and decided he had a nice mouth. Sensuous. And she'd kill for his thick black lashes. Too bad he was so weird. Not that it mattered to her date-wise because she'd decided to put that part of her life on hold while she got a grip on her career. She checked her watch. It was almost eight o'clock. She could have slept an extra half hour.

She leaned forward. "Excuse me? Mr. Knight?"

He didn't respond so she picked a couple kumquats off a nearby tree and pitched them at him. The first one sailed past his ear. The second bounced off his forehead. He opened his eyes, stretched, and came off the table.

"The Siddhar sends his salutations."

"The Siddhar?"

"Yes. Thiru Kuthambai Siddhar, the nineteenth to bear that exalted title. I've studied with him from time to time on Nancowry Island, a tiny spot of land in the northeast Indian Ocean between the Bay of Bengal and the Andaman Sea. Now that my responsibilities dictate that I live here, I've had to discontinue my studies with the Siddhar, but I still commune with him every morning."

"Astral projection?"

"Skype."

Riley wasn't sure if she was relieved or disappointed. "I thought maybe you were talking to him while you were on the table."

"That was a simple yoga relaxation exercise. I find it helpful to periodically clear my mind."

"An excellent use of time," Riley said. "After you get it empty you can pick and choose the information you want to put back in."

"Precisely."

"I was kidding," Riley said.

Emerson snatched a gray sweatshirt off the floor, shook it, and a lizard fell out. "I wasn't. That's why *you're* here. To collect and preserve all the worthless bits and pieces of information deemed too insignificant to be returned to my brain."

"Now you're kidding," Riley said.

"Yes, now I'm kidding, although there is an element of truth to it." He slipped the sweatshirt on over his navy T-shirt and grabbed his rucksack. "Come along, Miss Moon. We'll take the Mustang this time. Larry used to like to drive the Mustang on weekends."

"I'm not Larry and this isn't the weekend."

"More's the pity," he said, and he disappeared behind the ferns.

Emerson's Mustang was a green '68 GT Fastback, just like the one Steve McQueen drove in *Bullitt*. For all Riley knew, it *was* the one McQueen drove. Talk at her parents' dinner table was that McQueen always regretted not driving the Mustang off the set and keeping it for himself. He'd searched for years and never found it, so who was to say where the car resided.

Riley drove the car off the property and headed south through Rock Creek. This was a muscle car, like her father's GTO, and it felt good to be behind the wheel.

"Where are we going?" she asked Emerson.

"To Günter Grunwald's house. I want to ask his wife

a few questions. Take the George Washington Parkway. I'll tell you where to turn."

"Did you call and tell her we were coming?"

"And lose the element of surprise?"

Riley looked at her watch. "It's eight-thirty. Irene Grunwald doesn't impress me as an early riser."

"Do you know her?" Emerson asked.

"I met her once. At the office. Let's just say I'd call first."

"I met her, too. At my father's funeral. She seemed rather distant. You may be right. I'll consider calling."

Riley drove past the golden statues of the improbably muscular horses and riders that guarded the entrance to the Arlington Memorial Bridge. She crossed the Potomac and turned onto the George Washington Memorial Parkway. Riley looked out at the quaint redbrick townhouses of Alexandria, and eventually they gave way to a densely wooded parkway with the broad Potomac River sparkling on her left.

Günter's house was on the riverside, off Southdown Road. It was a large Colonial with black shutters and professional landscaping. Riley parked in the curved driveway and turned to Emerson for further instructions.

"Now what?" Riley said. "Do we get out and ring her doorbell?"

"You suggested we call first," Emerson said. "So you should call."

"But we're already here."

"Does that matter?"

"*Yes*. We can't call from the driveway. We should

have called a half hour ago. It'll be like we're stalking her if we call now."

"Really?"

"Yes. You wouldn't call a girl and tell her you're waiting outside her apartment, would you? She'd think you were deranged."

"That explains a lot," Emerson said, getting out of the car.

He walked to the front door and swung the little pineapple-shaped door knocker. No one answered. He tried the door knocker again, waited two beats, and took off around the side of the house.

"Hey!" Riley whispered, tiptoeing after him. "Psssst! What are you doing? You can't just go wandering around somebody's yard!"

"Of course I can," Emerson said. "Look at me. I'm doing it."

"But what if she sees you?"

"Then my goal will have been achieved."

Emerson reached the back of the house and stopped short, hands on hips, taking it all in. It was a large yard, landscaped into a formal garden that sloped down to the river. There was a dock at the river's edge and a large sailboat tied up to the dock.

Irene Grunwald stood in the middle of the yard with her back to Emerson and Riley. She had a spade in her hand, and she was looking into a freshly dug hole.

"Stupid saint," she said to herself. "I hate these stupid saints."

Irene was silver blond, in her midforties, and

professionally toned. She was dressed in creased tan chinos, a pastel-collared shirt, and fashionable work gloves, presumably to preserve her manicure. Martha Stewart would have approved.

Riley elbowed Emerson and made a gesture to indicate that he should alert Irene of their presence. Emerson cleared his throat. Irene gave a yelp, dropped her spade, and whirled around with her hand over her heart.

"Emerson Knight?" Irene said, squinting at Emerson. "Good Lord, you scared the bejeepers out of me. I didn't hear you drive up."

"Are you digging for buried treasure?" Emerson asked.

"Hardly. My gardener was preparing a flower bed for mums when he dug up a plaster statue of a saint and freaked out. He said it was a bad omen, crossed himself a dozen times, and took off. And it's not the first time this has happened."

Emerson looked into the hole. "Saint Nicholas," he said. "I'd know him anywhere."

"Are you planting the mums yourself?" Riley asked Irene.

"No. I'm filling the hole and selling the house," Irene said. "This is like some kind of weird burial ground. The place is lousy with these stupid saints. God knows how long they've been here or why they're here. We didn't plant them. We aren't even Catholic."

"How long have you lived in this house?"

"Five years."

"Saint Nicholas is in extraordinarily good shape for having been in the ground for at least five years."

"He's a saint," Irene said. "They probably hold up better than the rest of us." She turned her attention to Riley. "I believe we met once before. It's Riley, correct?"

"Yes. I was an intern at Blane-Grunwald this past summer."

"My husband took a special interest in you. He thought you had potential."

"He was a wonderful mentor. And I'm sure he was instrumental in hiring me."

Emerson swung his attention to the boat at the end of the dock. "Nice sailboat."

"I suppose," Irene said. "Günter loved it. He said it was his escape."

"What was he escaping from?"

"Me," Irene said. "He used the boat like a 'men's only' back porch."

"It wasn't your back porch as well?"

"I get seasick looking at it. In all the time we've owned it I think I've set foot on it twice."

"Pity," Emerson said.

"Mr. Knight has a few questions," Riley said to Irene. "He's been engaged to look into Günter's disappearance."

Irene looked shocked. "Who engaged him?"

"Werner," Emerson said.

"So thoughtful of Werner," Irene said. "Of course I want to help in any way. What would you like to ask me?"

"Did you kill your husband?" Emerson asked.

Irene's mouth dropped open, and she blinked three times.

"He didn't mean 'kill your husband,'" Riley said.

"I did," Emerson said. "I very distinctly heard myself ask her if she killed her husband."

"I did *not* kill my husband," Irene said.

"Good to know," Riley said. She gave Emerson a stern look. "Anything else?"

"I understand you filed papers to gain power of attorney for your joint property," Emerson said to Irene.

"My lawyer thought it was prudent."

Emerson rocked back on his heels, hands in his pockets. "But you didn't file a missing persons report with the police."

"I suppose I should do that," Irene said. "Originally I didn't see any reason. We didn't have the perfect marriage, and I thought he was just walking out on me."

"And now?" Emerson asked.

"That's what I still think."

Emerson looked into the hole again. "What will you do with Saint Nicholas?"

"Throw him away. Just like all the others."

"Were they all Saint Nicholas statues?"

"I'm not really up on my saints, but they all looked similar."

"I've always been fond of Saint Nicholas," Emerson said. "Do you mind if I take him?"

"Not at all," Irene said. "Help yourself."

Emerson retrieved the plaster statue, dusted it off,

and tucked it under his arm. "Now I would like to see Günter's study," he said to Irene.

For a split second Irene looked like she wanted to get in her car and not stop driving until she reached California and was far away from Emerson.

"I suppose that would be all right," she said, "but I'm not sure if you'll find anything helpful. Günter didn't spend much time there."

Irene led the way into the house, taking them through a spacious kitchen. The counters were granite, the appliances were stainless and looked professional, the floor was wide-plank hand-hewn oak. The cupboards were faux antique, the breakfast nook was charming, and an empty vodka bottle and the remains of a Lean Cuisine frozen dinner had been stashed in the large sink.

"This is a great kitchen," Riley said.

"Thank you," Irene said. "I don't do much cooking in it, but it's pleasant in the morning when I eat my yogurt." She set her gloves and hat on a sideboard and led Riley and Emerson down a short hall and up a flight of stairs. "The previous owner chose to create a home office over the garage. It's very nicely done, but Günter rarely used it. From time to time I believe he would put documents in the safe."

"Have you checked the safe since he disappeared?" Emerson asked her.

"No. I'm sure there's nothing in it of interest to me. I keep my jewelry in the bedroom. Truth is, I don't even know the combination. I believe our lawyer has the ability to open it should something happen to Günter."

"It sounds as if you expect Günter to return," Emerson said. "Have you heard from him?"

"No, I haven't heard from him. One morning he left for work with his to-go cup of coffee and his briefcase, and he simply never returned."

"You don't seem especially worried," Emerson said.

"I drink a lot," Irene said. "And I smoke dope. It keeps me more or less happy."

SIX

———⊶⊷———

I RENE OPENED THE DOOR AT THE TOP OF THE
stairs, and everyone stepped into Günter's home
office. It was a room much like Günter's office at Blane-
Grunwald, all rich mahogany and plush upholstery. A
few flies buzzed around in the semidarkness. A shaft of
sunlight fell on the ornate partners desk through the
gap in the heavy draperies. The walls were paneled and
lined with bookshelves. The books were for the most
part academic.

Irene opened the drapes. "I really should air this
room. I can't imagine how these flies got in here."

A door chimed downstairs, and Irene looked at her
watch. "That's my housekeeper. I need to talk to her.
And I'm meeting a friend for coffee in a few minutes.
Will you be much longer?"

"Yes," Emerson said. "Considerably longer."

Riley thought Irene looked like she wanted to stick a fork in Emerson's heart. And she didn't blame her.

"Would you mind terribly letting yourself out?" Irene said, forcing a smile. "I really need to run."

"No worries," Emerson said, rifling through Günter's file drawer, not looking at Irene. "We're fine on our own."

Riley settled into an oversized overstuffed chair and watched Emerson search through the room. After fifteen minutes she was tired of watching. She checked her cellphone for emails and surfed some news sites. At the thirty-minute mark she began sighing. Loudly. *SIGH!*

"I hear you," Emerson said. "I would expect better communication skills from you than *sighing*."

"I didn't want to disturb you."

"Rubbish."

"That's very British."

"I went to secondary school in England. Several of them, actually."

"Kept getting kicked out?"

"I was an academic challenge."

"Are you finding anything useful?" Riley asked.

Emerson opened the top drawer on the desk and removed a scrap of paper. "This room is surprisingly sterile. Very much like Günter's office. No personal effects scattered about. And to answer your question . . . perhaps. There's this piece of paper with a quotation from Seneca, the Roman philosopher. *Sometimes, even to live is an act of courage.*"

"What does it mean?"

"It's either a suicide note, or the exact opposite."

"What's the exact opposite of a suicide note?" Riley asked.

"Getting up every day and living. And even better than the quote is the name scrawled on the back. 'Dr. Bauerfeind.'"

"Do you know him?"

"We've met."

"Anything else that's captured your interest?"

"The beetle hanging on the wall. It's a death's head beetle."

Riley crossed the room and examined the beetle. It was perfectly preserved and mounted in a glass frame. The shell was shiny, with two black spots on it. The wings were glossy and golden. Under it was pinned a piece of paper with an inscription, written in a fine scientific hand. SCARABAEUS CAPUT HOMINIS.

While Riley looked at the beetle, Emerson removed a Rembrandt etching from the wall and exposed Günter's safe.

"So predictable," he said. "It really takes some of the fun out of it."

He stared at the digital keypad for a minute or two, punched in a combination, and the safe swung open.

"How did you know the combination?" Riley asked.

"It was obvious. I only doubted it because it was so simple." Emerson pointed to the framed insect on the wall. "What can you tell me about that?"

"It looks fake."

"It is. Someone must have given it to Günter as a joke. It's painted to look like a golden skull. And the inscription on the label, 'Scarabaeus Caput Hominis'—Man's Head Beetle. Clearly, it's an homage to the Edgar Allan Poe story in which a man finds a fabulous treasure with the help of a fantastic insect, 'The Gold-Bug.'"

"'Goldbug,'" Riley said. "That's also a term used in investing. It means an expert who recommends buying gold as an investment."

"Exactly. A person who believes that gold is a stable source of wealth, like it was during the days of the gold standard. So it wasn't hard to guess that 'goldbug' would be Günter's combination. That and the fact that the numbers are written under Bauerfeind's name on the scrap of paper. Of course the numbers are rearranged, but the code is a simple one."

He reached into the safe and pulled out the single object inside. A gold bar. A fly fluttered off the bar and Emerson handed the bar to Riley. She was amazed by the heft of the thing.

"I'm pretty sure this is a Good Delivery bar," she said. "It's the first time I've seen one in person."

"Like you, my knowledge is academic. I know that Good Delivery bars are noted for high purity and large size, weighing in the vicinity of thirty pounds each. Most gold collectors collect coins or small bars of one ounce. Good Delivery bars are much harder to analyze or to trade. They are used in major international markets like Tokyo and London and New York and the gold reserves of major governments. And the International Monetary

Fund. This one was made in Munich. It has the word 'München' carved in it, along with a half moon and crown, followed by the minting date and serial number."

"If this actually is a Good Delivery bar it meets the specifications issued by the London Bullion Market Association, and it would contain about four hundred troy ounces of gold," Riley said.

"A fortune for most people."

"But not for Günter," Riley said. "It's worth hundreds of thousands of dollars, but Günter has more money than he could possibly spend in one lifetime."

"He has ninety million. He could spend that," Emerson said.

"How?"

"If he lived to ninety-five, he could do it."

"I don't see how."

"It could be done."

"I don't think so."

"I could do it."

Riley didn't think she could do it. She came from a culture that clipped coupons and shopped at yard sales.

"What would you buy?" she asked Emerson. "A shark with a laser beam gizmo attached to his head? It would have to be something incredible."

Emerson handed the gold bar to Riley. "Put this in your bag."

"What?" Riley asked.

"Put it in your bag. We're going to take it with us."

"Are we going to ask first? We're going to ask."

"Why should we ask?"

"Because it's a gold bar worth in the vicinity of half a million dollars. That's more than grand larceny. That's great-grand larceny."

"We'll bring it back. We're just going to borrow it. I don't think Irene even knows it's there."

"You don't think?"

Riley dumped her bag onto the Mustang's backseat and slid behind the wheel.

Emerson got in, and Riley put the car in gear and sped out to the parkway before Irene Grunwald could return from her coffee date, peek into her safe, and call the cops. Or the Secret Service. Or whoever they sent after you for stealing gold bars.

"I can't believe I'm doing this," she said.

"Believe," Emerson said.

"Why do you want it?"

"It feels off. The safe had been cleaned out. There were no papers, no stacks of extra cash. None of the things you would expect to find in a home office safe. Why was this gold bar left behind?"

"Maybe it was left in the safe to be . . . safe."

"Maybe. But think back. What was in the safe when I opened it?"

"Just that gold," Riley said.

"Your eyes see, but they do not observe. Cast your mind back to when I opened the safe. What did you see?"

"The gold," Riley said.

"And?"

"A fly."

"Exactly. What kind of fly?"

"A fly with big wings. Almost like a dragonfly, but smaller."

"It was a mayfly. Also called a shad fly or lake fly. An aquatic insect. It only lives for about twenty-four hours after it sprouts its wings."

"And Mrs. Grunwald said no one had been in that room or the safe for days."

"But someone was in that room, and in that safe, sometime in the last twenty-four hours. Someone, most probably, who came from the waterfront and tracked the mayfly larvae in with them. Someone who opened that safe but didn't take the gold. Why not?"

Riley finished his thought. "They took something else?"

"Or they planted this gold inside."

"But you don't know which."

"No, but I intend to find out. That's why we're going to Blane-Grunwald to see Maxine Trowbridge."

"Do you think she planted the gold?" Riley asked.

"I think she has a dislike and fear of Werner and fond feelings for Günter. As his trusted assistant she would know many things, possibly including the combination to his home safe and the code for his security system. When you were working as Günter's intern, what was your impression of Maxine Trowbridge?"

"I thought she was very efficient. The ultimate professional. Always appropriately dressed. Always polite. Günter trusted and respected her, but I never saw anything to indicate that the relationship went beyond the office. She worked for Werner before Günter. That was the one oddity. Working for Günter would have been a demotion of sorts."

"Unless Werner put her in there to spy on Günter."

"Yes. And I suppose I could see him doing that," Riley said.

"Since he asked you to spy on me?"

"It wasn't stated that specifically, but yes."

"And are you spying on me?" Emerson asked her.

"I suppose I am." Riley kept her eyes fixed on the road, looking for the bridge exit. "How did you remember the name of an Edgar Allan Poe story?"

"When the Siddhar was training me, he had me learn all of Poe's Tales of Mystery and Imagination by heart. Along with the first five books of the Bible, the Purva of Jainism, and the tragedies of Shakespeare."

"Just the tragedies?"

"They have all the good lines."

"Why all that memorizing? Don't you have a computer? Or Google?"

"'Wax on, wax off.'"

"You're quoting Karate Kid now?"

"I also memorized a lot of movies from the eighties. But the point was to exercise my mind. The material I memorized was incidental."

"Oh, yeah. Like when Mr. Miyagi from Happy Days had Ralph Macchio wash his car. It was to teach him a greater lesson. I can't remember what."

"Television lessons tend to be fleeting," Emerson said.

"What else did that Siddhar teach you? Did he teach you Kung Fu? I bet he taught you Kung Fu."

"He didn't teach me Kung Fu. Although I know many forms of martial arts."

"Does he have a white beard and bushy white eyebrows? Does he wear a long white robe?"

"No, no, and yes. The robe was terry cloth and I believe he ordered it from Pottery Barn."

"Did he do magic tricks? Walk on coals? Sleep on a bed of nails?"

"I don't think you take this seriously. But I'm enjoying this repartee. You have an agile mind."

"My agile mind is working overtime trying not to panic over the fact that we just committed a felony. Are you sure Irene doesn't know about the gold bar?"

"There's one way we can be sure if she *does* know about it."

"What's that?"

"If we're arrested for stealing it," he said.

SEVEN

RILEY PULLED THE MUSTANG INTO GÜNTER'S parking space at Blane-Grunwald and cut the engine.

"What are we going to do with the gold?" she asked Emerson.

"We'll take it with us."

"I'm not carrying that gold into the building."

"No problem. I'll carry it. I'll put it in my rucksack."

Emerson pulled the bar out of Riley's bag and dropped it into his rucksack.

"Good riddance," Riley said.

They took the elevator to the seventeenth floor, walked the corridor to Maxine's office, and peeked inside. Empty. Riley stepped across the hall and asked a woman if she knew where they could find Maxine.

"At home," the woman said. "She called in sick."

Riley looked at Emerson. "Now what?"

"Now we visit her at her home."

Riley got Maxine's address from Human Resources, they returned to the Mustang, and Riley plugged the address into the maps app on her iPhone.

"It looks like she's about fifteen minutes away," Riley said.

She drove down Pennsylvania Avenue, turned right onto Thirteenth Street, and found herself in the gentrified neighborhood of Columbia Heights. The street was lined with expensive row houses built around the turn of the last century, but remodeled and refurbished and polished like antique jewelry.

"How can she afford a place like this on an executive assistant's salary?" Riley asked as they stepped out of the car.

"Maybe Günter helps her out," Emerson said.

"You think?"

"You're speaking sarcastically as a way of agreeing with me, aren't you?"

"You think?"

"You did it again. I find that endearing."

They walked up the stoop and rang the bell. The door opened and Maxine looked out at them. She wasn't dressed like somebody who was home sick. She was wearing rugged workout clothes and a yellow and gray jacket with a drawstring at the waist.

"Goodness," Maxine said. "This is a surprise. Is something wrong?"

Emerson pulled the gold bar out of his rucksack, and Maxine stared at it, dumbfounded.

"Did you leave this at Günter's house last night?" Emerson asked.

"Of course not," Maxine said. "Why would you think such a thing?"

"Because I'm brilliant," Emerson said. "Can we come in?"

Maxine led them into her living room but didn't invite them to sit.

"I hope you won't think me rude," she said, "but I only have a few minutes. I was on my way out."

The room was nicely furnished with a chunky pale gray sofa and two matching club chairs. The end tables were mahogany and the rug was a deep pile Tibetan.

"About the gold bar," Emerson said.

"I don't know how you came to get that bar," Maxine said, "but something bad might happen if you don't put it back. Does Irene know you have it?"

"She wasn't present when I discovered it," Emerson said. "I would like to know how it got into the safe in the first place."

"You guessed right. I put it there last night."

"How did you manage it?" Riley asked.

"Günter has a sailboat tied up to the dock behind his house. I don't believe he's sailed it in years, but he loved the boat, and he would have his coffee there in the morning, and sometimes a cocktail in the evening.

I knew he kept a spare key with a remote to turn the security system on and off in the cabin, so I went to the boat after dark, got the key, and waited until after midnight, when Irene would be too drunk to hear anything. When I saw the lights go out, I let myself into the house, went up to his office, opened the safe, and left the gold bar."

"Why?" Emerson asked.

"Because that's what I was told to do."

Maxine pulled a plain wooden box off a bookshelf, took another gold bar out of it, and placed it on the coffee table next to the one from Günter's safe. They were identical. Same "München" inscription, same half moon and crown. Same date and serial number.

"A few months ago, Günter heard he was getting a new responsibility—one he's wanted for a long time," Maxine said. "I know Werner told you he wasn't, but Werner lies. He lies about everything."

Riley thought there was a lot of anger in Maxine's voice when she talked about Werner's deceit. Most likely Maxine had some unpleasant personal experience with Werner and his lies. Or maybe she was just feeling protective of Günter.

"Günter was going to be put in charge of all the gold holdings at Blane-Grunwald," Maxine said. "More specifically, the huge underground vault that's built into the Manhattan bedrock below the New York offices. The B&G vault is the biggest privately owned gold repository for central banks, institutions, exchange-traded funds, you name it. It's where all the largest investors store their gold."

"Who was in charge of this prior to Günter?" Emerson asked.

"The senior Grunwald. After he died, the position was simply left open, but for whatever reason the board recently decided to name Günter as overseer. Anyway, Günter went to Manhattan to check it out. He met with Yvette Jaworski, an old friend of his at the New York office, and discussed things. When he came back, he was a changed man. Distant. Uncommunicative. I asked him what was wrong. He wouldn't talk about it.

"Then Yvette disappeared. He became more secretive after that. He would go away for long weekends. Even I didn't know where he went. Finally, he showed up here one night, after work. And he had these two gold bars. They're identical in every way. Down to the serial numbers.

"He told me to keep the one you brought with you, but if anything happened to him, I was to get my hands on the one in his home safe and swap it out. He said if it was found among his effects it would be bad for his wife, for his reputation. So I was supposed to switch them."

Emerson looked at the two gold bars. "One of these is counterfeit."

"I've thought the same thing," Maxine said.

"But which one?" Emerson asked.

Maxine paused and adjusted a wisp of hair. "I don't know," she said. "And I don't care. I've done what he asked me to do. I can let it rest."

Emerson leaned in closer to Maxine. "Did you know that the CIA has identified six primary physical signs of deception, including behavioral delay and grooming gestures? It's true. I read it in a book."

A hint of a smile crossed Maxine's face. "Günter might have also mentioned the one I swapped out would be really, really bad for Werner's reputation."

Emerson nodded and turned to Riley. "Three things cannot be long hidden. The sun, the moon, and the truth."

"Did you read that in a book too?" Riley asked.

"It's attributed to Buddha." Emerson paused. "Or maybe I heard it on an episode of MTV's *Real World*."

"Do you mind if I take these gold bars?" Emerson asked Maxine.

"Why?"

"I want to saw them in half and see what's inside."

Maxine snatched her gold bar from the coffee table. "No! Did Werner put you up to this? Tell him I'm hanging on to this until further notice!"

"I don't intend to tell Werner anything about this until my investigation is complete."

"Well, I'm not giving up my gold bar," Maxine said. "What's really, really bad for Werner could be really, really good for me."

"Possibly," Emerson said, taking the bar that was left on the table. "It's been a pleasure."

"You should put it back," Maxine said. "It belongs in the safe."

"I'll take it under consideration," Emerson said.

Riley followed Emerson down the sidewalk to where the Mustang was parked.

"She's upset," Riley said.

"Indeed she is."

"Well, so much for that question-and-answer session," Riley said. "I'm voting for lunch next. There's a Five Guys on Irving Street. I could really use a bacon cheeseburger with Cajun fries. You ever try that?"

"No. And we're not going to lunch yet."

"Why not?"

"We're waiting to see what Maxine Trowbridge does."

"Can't we find out after lunch?"

"Rise above the hunger. I once went ten days without eating a thing."

"Good for you. Me, I'm hypoglycemic. If I don't eat every three hours I get irritable. You wouldn't like me when I'm irritable."

"I like you fine."

"I'm not irritable yet."

"You're not?" Emerson said with surprise.

"Very funny."

"I wasn't trying to be funny," Emerson said, examining the gold bar. He held it up for her to see. "What do you think? Real or fake?"

"I think she took the real one from the safe."

"Then this is it," he said, tapping the gold bar with his finger.

"What do you mean?"

"I switched them."

"But we were looking at them the whole time."

"I did it all the same."

"I don't believe it."

"It doesn't matter whether or not you believe it," Emerson said. "It is so."

"Well, it doesn't matter whether or not you say it's so. It didn't happen."

"Why would I lie about such a thing?"

"Why, indeed."

His mouth curved into a sly smile for a millisecond.

"And what's that?" Riley asked.

"What's what?"

"The smile."

"I find you amusing."

Two advanced degrees from Harvard and I've got a job amusing a man who steals gold bars, Riley thought.

"The advanced degrees were a waste of time," Emerson said. "You didn't need them."

"How did you know I was thinking about my degrees?"

"It was obvious."

"You're a little scary," Riley said.

"You're not the first person to express that opinion."

The front door to Maxine's townhouse opened, Maxine stepped out, and closed and locked the door behind her. She was still dressed in her workout clothes, wearing Oakley sunglasses and carrying a medium-sized duffel bag. She walked down the sidewalk to a gray Nissan Maxima parked close to the corner, slung her gear in the back, got in, and pulled out.

"Follow that car," Emerson said.

Riley pulled out, hoping Maxine was going somewhere for lunch. She knew that "irritable" was just around the corner. She kept a car between her and Maxine, just in case Maxine looked in her mirror. At least the muscle car Riley was driving was a conservative highland green, not flaming red. Still, a classic Mustang Fastback wasn't the most inconspicuous car on the road.

Maxine turned right on K Street just as the light was changing. Riley had to choose between speeding through the red light and stopping. She stopped. Her father, the sheriff, would have been pleased.

"What do I do now?" she asked Emerson.

"About what?"

"I lost her."

"Figure out where she's going."

"Well, down K Street. Across the Key Bridge."

"She was wearing an immersion jacket."

"And?"

"She was expecting to get wet," Emerson said.

"Car wash?"

"That's a joke, correct?"

"*Criminy!*" Riley said. "You are *so* annoying."

"Yes, but a woman once told me I have excellent eyelashes. Have you noticed?"

Riley had been ready to take a right onto Key Bridge, but she followed a hunch at the last moment and turned left onto Canal Road and drove along the river, past Georgetown University. Soon the city dwindled away.

Trees on her right, the C&O Canal on her left. They could have been out in the country.

She'd been driving for a few minutes when she caught a glimpse of Maxine's Nissan just as it veered off to the left. She maneuvered over to the left lane and took a turnoff by a sign reading FLETCHER'S COVE. Passing a white stone house that looked like it had been old during the Civil War, Riley spotted the Nissan driving down a little road into an old, dark, narrow tunnel carved underneath the canal. She turned to follow.

"This car's pretty wide," she said. "Do you think we'll fit through there?"

"Only one way to find out," Emerson said.

As she drove into the tunnel she found herself inhaling, as if making her rib cage thinner would help her fit between the ancient stone walls of the passageway. They made it through to the other side and Riley exhaled in relief.

The Nissan pulled off the road and parked in a small lot next to a ramshackle boathouse. Beyond the boathouse, the banks of the Potomac looked wild and untamed.

"Hard to believe we're a scarce ten minutes from Georgetown," Riley said, idling just short of the lot entrance.

Maxine got out of her Nissan, collected her duffel bag from the backseat, and walked over to the service window of the boathouse. Rental kayaks were stacked next to the building, and a number of red rowboats could be seen bobbing offshore, the occupants fishing for shad and catfish.

It reminded Riley of fishing spots her dad used to take her to on the Brazos River. She took a deep calming breath of country air with only a whiff of exhaust fumes in it and sighed. So near and yet so far.

Maxine concluded her business at the boathouse and took the path that led through the woods to the dock. The instant she was out of sight Riley pulled into the lot and parked. Emerson was immediately out of the car, following Maxine, with Riley scrambling to keep up.

"Did you know where Maxine was going?" Riley asked Emerson.

"Of course."

"Mental telepathy?"

"Bumper sticker," Emerson said, passing by Maxine's car, pointing to her bumper sticker reading I'D RATHER BE FISHING AT FLETCHER'S COVE.

"That is *so cheating*," Riley said.

They followed the path to the dock, pausing at the sound of men's voices, and Emerson motioned for Riley to follow him into the woods where they'd be lost in deep shadow. They crept closer to the voices, and saw that Maxine stood on the jetty, arms out. A man in a dark suit patted her down, and another man in an equally dark suit looked on, with no visible expression on his face.

When they were done with her, Maxine climbed down into a small canoe. One of the dark suits handed over her duffel bag and pointed downstream. Setting the bag on her lap, she adjusted her sunglasses and paddled off, driving through the water with determined speed.

"Interesting," Emerson said, moving back onto the path, power walking to the boathouse. "We need to rent a boat and follow her."

"All we got left are two-person kayaks," the attendant told Emerson.

Emerson looked at Riley. "Do you know how to kayak?"

"I know how to canoe. It's pretty much like that, right? Except the kayak paddle has two blades, one on either end. That seems one more than necessary."

"We'll figure it out," Emerson said. "How hard can it be?"

EIGHT

———— ✦✦✦ ————

R ILEY AND EMERSON LEFT THEIR SHOES AT
the boathouse, slipped on their rented life jackets,
and climbed carefully into the little lozenge-shaped boat
that was resting in ankle-deep water. Emerson got in
front, and Riley took the backseat. The attendant shoved
them into deeper water, and they bobbed around for a
moment, establishing their balance.

It took a few tries to coordinate their paddling
rhythm, but soon they were cruising off downriver, in
pursuit of Maxine. Moving quickly through the clusters
of red rowboats with their fishing rods dancing above
the water, Riley was struck with how different kayaking
was from canoeing. In a canoe, you felt like you were
riding on top of the water, but in the kayak you felt
like you were sitting right in the water and cutting

through it, like a hot knife through butter. She liked the sensation.

They followed a bend in the river and left most of the fishermen behind. In the woods along the riverbank, a bearded homeless man watched them sail past. Clothes tattered and worn, a slouch hat on his head, a crazy look in his eyes, he stared at them accusingly, a silent reminder that they were still in a metropolitan center after all, pastoral surrounding notwithstanding.

Up ahead, they could see Maxine. Her orange canoe was moving through the water toward an isolated rowboat, where two middle-aged men in fishing vests sat with their casting rods dangling over the side.

Emerson stopped paddling, so Riley stopped too. There were three other rowboats looking strategically placed at intervals around the two fishermen. With their dark suits under their orange life vests, their sunglasses and earpieces, the occupants of these boats looked awkwardly out of place in the idyllic surroundings. They might as well have been wearing big signs around their necks that said PROTECTIVE GOON SQUAD.

All the men in black touched their earpieces and kept their eyes on Maxine as she approached the fishing boat. No one seemed to notice Emerson and Riley.

Emerson steered their kayak toward the riverbank. "Look like you're fishing," he whispered.

"I don't have a fishing pole," Riley whispered back.

"Imagine the fishing pole," he said, pulling an odd pair of glasses from his jacket pocket and slipping them on. They were huge and black and looked like a visor that a robot warrior from space would wear.

"What the heck are those?" Riley asked.

"They're 'zoomies.' They work like binoculars."

"Why don't you use binoculars?"

"These are less conspicuous," Emerson said.

"Are you kidding me? You look like RoboCop."

Emerson sat tall and cocked his head. "Really? I don't usually think of myself in that way, but it's an appealing comparison."

He's sort of charming, Riley thought, in an out-of-the-box, geeky-twelve-year-old-boy kind of way.

Emerson maneuvered the kayak into a stand of cattails while in the distance Maxine steered her canoe up to the rowboat. The two men greeted her in a friendly manner. One of them had a ring of gray hair around a shiny bald head. What hair he had was cut in a military style around his ears, and he carried himself with the bearing of an officer on parade, even sitting in the fishing boat. The other man was smaller and softer. He was wearing a tan brimmed fishing hat and a matching fishing vest. Something about both of them looked familiar to Riley, but they were far away and she couldn't put names to the faces.

Words were exchanged between Maxine and the men, and the mood went from friendly to wary. Maxine dragged her duffel bag out and opened it. The men looked in and recoiled. The man in the hat pulled back and looked around, as if he was worried that the guards could see what was in the bag. The bald man went on the attack, grabbing for the bag. Maxine snatched the bag back, then the man lunged out of the boat and struck her across the face.

Their boats bobbed and lurched about in the water. Maxine righted herself in her canoe and the men in the rowboats converged on her.

"Holy moly," Riley whispered.

"Holy moly, indeed," Emerson said. "Do you recognize him?"

Riley shook her head and Emerson removed the robot glasses and slipped them onto Riley's face.

"The one in the hat. That's William McCabe," Emerson said.

Riley adjusted the focus with a knob on the temple of the glasses. That was McCabe, all right. She knew the face from numerous appearances on CNN and MSNBC. William McCabe, chairman of the Federal Reserve. Like many other central bankers currently working at the Fed, he was also a former employee of Blane-Grunwald.

"The other man is Hans Grunwald," Emerson said.

"I bet she showed them the gold bar," Riley said.

"Most likely."

The men in the rowboats had guns drawn and were almost on top of Maxine. McCabe waved the men off, and Riley let out a breath she didn't even realize she'd been holding. Maxine wasted no time putting distance between her and the men, moving the canoe upstream to the boathouse.

Emerson shoved his paddle into the mud, pushing

their kayak farther into the cattails where they wouldn't easily be seen by Maxine as she cruised past them.

"What's the chairman of the Fed doing in Fletcher's Cove?" Riley asked.

"Fishing," Emerson said.

He poled them out of the reeds, and Riley looked back to where the two older men sat in their boat, peacefully fishing as though nothing had transpired.

Emerson swung the kayak around and in minutes they were past the bend in the river, heading toward the flotilla of red rowboats and, beyond them, the dock.

Emerson stopped paddling and held his hand up for Riley to also stop. The homeless man was still in the woods by the shore, looking out at them.

"Use the magnifying glasses," Emerson said to Riley.

Riley slipped the zoomies back on and focused on the homeless man.

"It's Günter!" Riley said.

As if with one mind, Emerson and Riley changed course and paddled the kayak toward the shore. The boat plowed through the goldenrod that lined the bank and slogged into a foot of muck.

"He's gone," Riley said. "He took off as soon as he realized he was recognized."

"Odd," Emerson said. "He seemed so stable in all my dealings with him."

"At least we know he's alive."

Riley hadn't been close to Günter. She'd known him a short time on a strictly professional level, but he'd been extremely nice to her, generous with both his time and patience during her internship. It was comforting to know he was alive, but disturbing to see him looking like a half-crazed vagrant.

"Should we go after him?" Riley asked Emerson.

"No. He has a good head start on us and we haven't any shoes. We'd never be able to chase him down in the woods."

"What do you suppose happened to him? We should do *something*! I'm sure he needs help."

"I'll make a call and send someone to scour the woods along this stretch of river."

Riley's phone chirped, and she glanced at the caller ID. It was Werner Grunwald. She ignored the call and slipped the phone back into her pocket.

By the time they made it back to the boathouse it was almost four o'clock. They returned the kayak and walked back to the parking lot. Maxine's car was gone, and there were no guys in dark suits hanging around.

Emerson stopped at the spot where Maxine's car had been parked and picked a pair of sunglasses off the pavement. A lens was shattered and an earpiece was askew.

"Oakleys," he said. "Maxine was wearing Oakleys."

"Lots of people wear Oakleys."

"Yes, but not many people carry gold bars around with them in a duffel bag," Emerson said.

"So you think someone conked her over the head and took her gold?"

"I think she's placed herself in a dangerous situation."

. . .

The next morning Riley ate a handful of Cap'n Crunch out of the box, went out to her car, and drove toward Rock Creek Park.

She was two blocks from her apartment when Werner's assistant called.

"Mr. Grunwald needs to see you," he said. "Immediately."

"Tell him I'll be there in a half hour."

Bummer, Riley thought. Now what?

She turned right on Park Road instead of left and cursed the traffic all the way to Constitution Avenue.

Thirty-five minutes later she got off the elevator on the seventeenth floor of Blane-Grunwald and went directly to Werner's office.

"I'm sorry I missed your call yesterday," Riley said to Werner. "I was with Mr. Knight."

"The call wasn't important," Werner said. "I asked my assistant to check in with you to make sure Emerson was comfortable with our arrangement. Unfortunately, the call this morning is of a more unpleasant nature. Maxine Trowbridge has been murdered. I got a call early this morning from the New York office. She was found on Liberty Street, in the Financial District. She was stabbed. Apparently. The details are pretty sketchy."

"That's not possible."

"I know it's a shock."

"No. It's not possible. How could Maxine be in New York?"

"We'll never know. I suppose she went up there yesterday."

Riley sensed movement on the far side of the room and realized there was another man in the office. He'd been sitting quietly in one of the Eames chairs that flanked the window.

"Oh, I'm sorry," Werner said. "This is my brother Hans."

The man stood up, all six foot four of him, massive and imposing in his four-star-general uniform. Hans Grunwald, the director of the NSA. One of the most powerful men in America. The second man in the rowboat.

Riley had a rush of panic, fearing Hans had seen her in the kayak. She'd been wearing the RoboCop visor, and for the most part they were hidden in the cattails. Still, it was hard to miss a woman with red hair.

"Were you close to Maxine?" Hans asked Riley.

"No," Riley said. "I hardly knew her."

"The police think it was a robbery," Werner said. "Her purse, her watch, and her rings were all missing. Such a tragic waste."

The gold, Riley was thinking. The broken sunglasses. The men in the dark suits. *They killed her and dumped her in New York.*

"I never had the pleasure of meeting Maxine," Hans said, "but Günter always spoke so fondly of her."

Riley's mind was spinning. Hans had just lied to her. He'd seen Maxine alive, only yesterday.

"I have to go," she said, moving for the door. "I'm late for a meeting with Mr. Knight."

Werner blocked her way, looking ever so sympathetic. "Of course. But we were wondering. The police, as I say, think it's a simple robbery. But then, they don't know about Günter's disappearance. And they don't know about his . . . special relationship with Maxine."

"Relationship?"

"Surely it was obvious."

"Okay."

"It's possible, some would argue, that they were planning to run off together. And they had a falling out."

Riley took a beat to answer. "You think your brother could have killed her?"

"No, no," Werner and Hans said in the same breath.

"Not at all," Hans said.

"But some might argue that," Werner said.

Hans nodded in agreement. "Some might."

Riley's heart was skipping around in her chest. They were setting Günter up, throwing him under the bus.

"How is Emerson's investigation progressing?" Werner asked Riley. "Has he discovered anything?"

Riley went with her gut reaction to lie. "Nope. Not a thing," Riley said.

Werner studied her for a long moment, and Riley felt her skin prickle.

He took a step closer. "Just tell us what he did yesterday, Moonbeam."

"And where he went," Hans said, closing in on her other side.

These guys aren't so tough, she told herself. I had law professors that could eat them for breakfast. All I have to do is swallow back the panic so I can think on my feet.

"First of all, we went to see Günter's wife," she said. "And then Emerson wanted to talk to Maxine again so we came here, but Maxine was home sick."

Werner and Hans exchanged glances.

Amateurs, Riley told herself. They probably sucked at poker too.

"So we went to Maxine's house," she said.

"And?" Werner asked.

"And she didn't look sick . . . or dead. And then we had lunch at Five Guys. That was it. It was pretty much a waste of time. Between you and me, I think Knight's a little loony."

Hans nodded. "I see."

Werner stepped away and opened the door to his office, indicating the meeting was over. "Keep up the good work, Moonbeam," he said. "And stay in touch."

The two men stood side by side and watched Riley walk down the hall and disappear into the elevator.

"We have a problem with Moonbeam," Werner said.

"We'll fix it," Hans told him.

NINE

⬦⬦⬦⬦

Riley hit the porch of Emerson's mansion
running. She barreled through the front door
and almost tripped over a woman scrubbing the floor.

"Watch where you're going!" the woman said.
"There's capybara doody all over. I didn't even know
what a capybara was when I woke up this morning. Now
I'm cleaning up after one."

An animal that looked like a giant guinea pig hurried
across the hallway and out the front door. Aunt Myra
ran after the animal.

"Emerson's in the dining room," Myra yelled over
her shoulder to Riley. "Down the hall and turn left. Say
hello to Melody. She's the new housekeeper."

"Not for long," Melody said. "I didn't sign on to work
in no zoo."

Riley found the dining room and thought that "banquet hall" would describe it better. It looked like it belonged in Downton Abbey's fancier annex. Huge tapestries depicting maidens in flowing white dresses attending to knights in shining armor hung from the walls. Towering stained-glass windows cast multicolored light on the massive mahogany eight-pedestal dining table where Emerson sat hunched with a power tool in his hand, a protective plastic visor covering his face.

The visor distorted his smile as he looked up at her. "Riley, there you are!" He lifted the little Dremel circular saw to reveal the gold bar they'd taken from Günter's study. It was split down the middle.

"I have to talk to you," she said, walking around the table.

"First things first. Come and see."

The bar had a thin veneer of shiny yellow gold, and under the gold the bar was dull gray metal the rest of the way through.

"It's a golden shell around a tungsten bar," Emerson said. "Tungsten's about the same weight and mass as gold. It makes a good substitute for counterfeiting."

"So it's fake?"

"A beautiful, expert fake. Now, what did you have to tell me?"

"Maxine Trowbridge is dead."

Emerson whipped the visor off his head. "Tell me everything."

"Werner called me into the office so he could give me the news, but I think he was mostly looking for information. He wanted to know if you'd made any progress, and he wanted to know what you did yesterday. And Hans was there. He acted as if he didn't see me in the kayak, but he lied about knowing Maxine, so he'll lie about anything. He said he'd never met Maxine."

"How did Maxine die?"

"Stabbed. She was found on Liberty Street in the Financial District in New York."

"New York? Interesting."

"I think someone in a dark suit grabbed her in the boathouse parking lot, knocking her sunglasses off her face. Then they took the gold, killed Maxine, and drove her to New York to dump her on the street."

"Why would they drive her to New York? That would be unnecessarily complicated. I think after the river meeting Maxine rushed off to New York and was subsequently killed."

"Werner said it looked like a robbery. The killer took her jewelry and her purse."

"No mention of the gold?"

"None."

"What did you tell them about me?"

"I told them that you talked to Irene and Maxine, but that nothing came of it. And I told them I thought you were loony."

"Clever of you to mix a truth with an untruth, but you realize eventually lying will damage your karma."

"What about white lies? Are they damaging?"

"White lies are a gray area," Emerson said.

The big double doors of the banquet hall opened and Melody poked her head in.

"I just want you to know, I quit. Capybara doody is one thing. I'm not cleaning up after no kangaroo. Oh, and there's some strange little man with bulging eyes here to see you."

"Why do you have so many weird animals?" Riley asked.

"My father collected them. He thought owning a private zoo would make him interesting. And I suppose at some level it did."

"What are you planning to do with them?"

"Take care of them. They're my responsibility now. Just as the gold is my responsibility."

"Do you have a zookeeper?"

"I have Aunt Myra."

"Wow. Aunt Myra does a lot. How many animals do you have?"

"I have no idea, but they seem to be everywhere."

Emerson wrapped the two pieces of the fake gold bar in a tea towel and put the package in his rucksack.

"About you, Miss Moon . . ."

"Riley," she said.

"Very well, Riley. You lied to Werner on my behalf. Am I to assume you're no longer working as an informant for him?"

"I never agreed to be an informant. I agreed to be your temporary amanuensis. Whatever that means."

"I thought perhaps you were succumbing to my eyelashes."

Riley took a moment to think about it. "Maybe a little."

A short, muscular man stepped into the doorway. "Mr. Knight?"

The man was dressed in a dark suit, dark shirt, and dark tie. He was bald, with bulging eyes and thick lips. A human goldfish dressed for a funeral.

Emerson turned to the man. "Yes?"

"I'd like a word with you."

The man was soft-spoken, and Riley placed him in his forties. He was excessively pale. His skin was unnaturally smooth. His eyes never blinked. He was followed by a small brown monkey.

The monkey climbed up a chair and jumped onto the far end of the dining table.

"I think your monkey wants food," the man said. "I found it sitting on your porch."

"Is this really your monkey?" Riley asked Emerson.

"I suppose if it's on my property, it's mine," Emerson said.

"My name is Edward Rollo," the man said. "I'm from the NSA."

"I'd like to see your identification," Riley said. "And I'd like to know why you're here."

"Ms. Moon," Rollo said. "We have a file on you, but it doesn't tell us whom you currently represent. Are you representing Mr. Knight or the firm of Blane-Grunwald?"

"Both."

"I fear you'll find that's not possible. You can't have two masters."

"I haven't any masters," Riley said. "I have employers and clients."

"Words with shaded meanings," Rollo said, walking the length of the table to where Emerson was sitting.

"Have a seat," Emerson said to Rollo.

"No, thank you," Rollo said. "This will only take a minute, and standing gives me a superior position over you."

"True. And if I were to stand now it would be in reaction to your behavior, so you would still be in a position of power. But may I remind you that I am sitting at the head of the table, the traditional Feng Shui 'dragon seat,' the place of the leader."

"Oh, for God's sake," Riley said. "Why don't you two just take out a ruler and get it over with?"

Rollo's thick lips pulled back in what might be construed as a smile. "I was building up to that."

"I'll ask you one more time," Riley said. "Why are you here?"

"The NSA is investigating a case. You're interfering with it. We want you to stop."

Riley stared him down. "What case are you investigating?"

"That's on a need-to-know basis. You don't need to know."

"How can we stop interfering with something when we don't know what it is?" Emerson asked.

"Good question," Rollo said. "I see your predicament.

To be on the safe side, why don't you stop doing everything? Stop asking questions. Stop visiting people. Stop leaving the house. Stop using your cellphone. Pretty much stop doing anything but breathing. Do I make myself clear?"

"That sounds like a threat," Riley said.

"Good, then I do make myself clear. One hates to be ambiguous. Now I'd like to examine the contents of the rucksack you have on your lap," Rollo said to Emerson.

"Do you have a rucksack search warrant?" Emerson asked.

"The NSA doesn't need a search warrant," Rollo said, and he snatched the pack away from Emerson.

Emerson batted the rucksack from Rollo's hands. The bag landed with a thud on the table, sliding out of reach on the polished surface. Emerson leapt onto the table, calmly walked to the rucksack, and scooped it up.

"I'm going to have to take that," Rollo said.

"I don't think so," Emerson said, standing on the table like it was the most natural thing in the world.

Rollo had to tip his head back to look up at Emerson. "This is bigger than you."

"I don't know about that," Emerson said. "I'm pretty big."

"Allow me to clarify. This is trouble. The kind of trouble that is resolved by secret NSA courts. The kind of trouble that ruins even eccentric billionaires. The kind of trouble that gets people like Maxine Trowbridge killed."

"Fair enough," Emerson said, moving to the edge of the table. "But I'm not giving you my rucksack."

Rollo produced a switchblade knife. "Then I might have to take it from you by force."

Emerson jumped off the table, snagged one of the huge tapestries hanging on the wall, and flung it over Rollo. He collapsed under the weight of the cloth and struggled to free himself. Emerson hung the rucksack on his shoulder, and in a few long strides was at the far wall.

"Come along," he said to Riley. "Time to disappear."

He pressed a spot on a carved wood panel, the panel swung open, and Emerson and Riley squeezed through a secret door into the space behind it. The secret door clicked closed and they were left in total darkness.

"This is creepy," Riley whispered.

"I was thinking it was comforting," Emerson said. "Like a starless night. And when I stand close to you like this, you smell nice."

"Thank you," Riley said. "What do we do now?"

"I could put my arm around you."

"I was referring to the crazy knife-wielding NSA guy waiting on the other side of the wall. He looks like he might, I don't know, kill you."

"He does, doesn't he? I find that exhilarating. This is obviously bigger than an embezzling banker. A woman has been murdered. And now we have this little man attempting to intimidate us."

"As far as I'm concerned, he's succeeded," Riley said. "It isn't part of my life plan to die here."

"Life is a journey, not a destination," Emerson said. "One must live in the moment."

"I'm not all that happy about this journey and in particular about this moment. It's scary."

"You have nothing to fear. I've had many forms of martial arts training. Ninjutsu, Tae Kwon Do, Inbuan wrestling, Kalaripayattu, Malla-yuddha, Musti-yuddha, and Thang-ta."

"Do you have a knife or a gun?"

"No."

"Case closed," Riley said. "Does this secret space lead somewhere?"

"It opens to a narrow corridor and then stairs."

Emerson put his hand to the panel in front of them, slid the cover on a peephole, and looked into the library.

"He's still there," Emerson whispered. "I'll have to take the back stairs."

Emerson tapped the flashlight app on his smartphone, pulled the Good Delivery bar out of his rucksack, and handed one of the halves to Riley. "Give this to Rollo, and tell him everything. If he's working for the NSA he needs to know. If he's working for whoever is behind all this, he already knows. Either way you can't go wrong with the truth."

"What about you?"

"Places to go. People to see. Rollo isn't one of them. After you've been debriefed by Rollo, you can meet me at Maxine's townhouse. I'm going out the back way. Count to sixty and depress the silver lever in front of you. It will open the door and you can return to the library.

Rollo won't hurt you. He'll assume you're a helplessly confused pawn who can be exploited."

"That's so flattering," Riley said.

"Sarcasm," Emerson said. "I like it."

Riley watched him disappear into the darkness, counted to sixty, and depressed the lever. The secret panel slid open and she stepped out.

"There you are," Rollo said. "I was hoping you'd reappear."

She handed over her half of the fake gold bar. "Emerson thought you would want this."

Rollo examined it. "Interesting. And he has the other half?"

"He does."

"What does he propose to do with it?"

"I have no clue."

Rollo cut his eyes to the wall with the secret passage. "I don't suppose he's hanging out back there."

"He had places to go and people to see."

"Of course. What were his instructions to you?"

"He said I should cooperate with the NSA."

Rollo considered that for a beat. "Tell me everything."

Riley gave him the short version of her life with Emerson.

"So you're sure you saw Hans Grunwald, William McCabe, and Maxine Trowbridge together?" Rollo asked when she finished talking.

"Yes."

"In the interest of national security we're going to rearrange things," Rollo said. "When you walk out of this room you'll be quite sure you didn't see Hans Grunwald or William McCabe at Fletcher's Cove. And you didn't see Maxine Trowbridge there either. Because you were never at Fletcher's Cove at all. Do you understand?"

Riley nodded.

"Good. That way everybody stays healthy." He glanced over at the monkey. "Even Mr. Pip here."

"You know the monkey's name?"

"We know everything. So it's a good thing you told me the complete truth. We were beginning to question your loyalties."

"Who exactly is 'we'?"

"Us," Rollo said. "Keep an eye on Mr. Knight. We want to know exactly where he goes. Exactly what he does." He took out a red cellphone and placed it on the table in front of her. "Call us with a report."

He rose and crossed to the door.

"What's your number?" Riley asked.

"It doesn't matter. Call any number. We'll hear you."

TEN

————◇◇◇————

RILEY CRINGED AT THE SIGHT OF A D.C. police car parked in front of Maxine's townhouse. It was a reminder that the most terrible thing had happened to Maxine.

A uniformed cop was standing on the sidewalk by the cop car. He was back on his heels, hands on his gun belt, looking bored. Two men in rumpled suits were standing on the small front stoop. The front door to Maxine's townhouse was open, and Emerson was in the doorway talking to the two guys in suits.

Riley parked the Mini, hung her purse on her shoulder, and joined Emerson.

"This is Lieutenant Lepofsky and Lieutenant Dannay," Emerson said to Riley. "They're old friends, and they've been kind enough to allow me access to

Maxine's apartment. Come inside. I have something interesting to show you."

Lepofsky and Dannay stayed on the stoop, and Emerson led Riley into Maxine's living room. He pulled the wooden box from the bookcase and opened it so Riley could look inside.

"Check the serial number," Emerson said. "It's different. For whatever reason, someone felt it necessary to substitute this bar for the original."

"That's weird. If they didn't want the bar found, why didn't they just take it?"

"Good question. Maybe they didn't want the fake bar found. Or maybe they wanted a bar found with a different serial number." Emerson closed the box and put it back on the shelf. He took a piece of paper from the desk and put it into his pocket.

"What's that?" Riley asked.

Emerson removed the paper and read it aloud. "'Deliveries to 51. Plan 79.'"

"That's Günter's handwriting," Riley said, looking over Emerson's shoulder. "What does it mean?"

"I don't know. The crime scene unit has already been through the house and removed what they thought necessary. This was left as insignificant."

"But you think it might be significant?"

"Günter wrote it, so it must mean something."

Emerson returned the paper to his pocket and crossed the room to the door. "How did it go with Rollo? Did you tell him you were meeting me here?"

"No. He didn't ask."

"Did he give you a phone?"

"Yes. A red cellphone," Riley said.

"Give him a call and tell him I'm leaving here. Tell him we're going to the Uptown Theater."

Emerson thanked the plainclothes guys on the way out, and looked across the street at Riley's Mini.

"You're still driving that little car," he said.

Riley narrowed her eyes ever so slightly. "And?"

"I suppose we'll have to make do."

Riley reminded herself that she was a professional, and stabbing Emerson with her nail file wouldn't be appropriate. She opened Rollo's phone and saw that there was only one number in the contact list. It had a 410 area code, which meant it was local. She tapped the number and Rollo answered on the second ring.

"Hello, Miss Moon," Rollo said. "How are you?"

"We're leaving Maxine Trowbridge's house. We're on our way to see a movie."

"Which one?"

"I'm not sure. We're headed for the Uptown Theater."

"Splendid. Keep calling in."

Riley disconnected and looked at Emerson. "I feel like I'm in a cheesy spy movie. Now what?"

"Now we drive to the 4300 block of Connecticut Avenue."

"What about the Uptown Theater?"

"That was a fib."

"I thought telling fibs was bad for our karma."

"I've excluded Rollo from my karmic scorecard."

"You can do that?"

"I just did it," Emerson said, crossing the street, folding himself into the Mini. "I removed him from yours as well. Done and done."

Riley pulled to the curb in front of a seventies-style nondescript office building on the 4300 block of Connecticut.

"Pick me up in exactly one hour," Emerson said, maneuvering out of the car.

"Where are you going?"

"I have business at the Mauritius embassy."

"Are you sure you don't need an amanuensis in there?"

"Possibly, but I'm going to risk taking this meeting alone."

Riley watched him walk away. His rigid confidence bordered on arrogance, and was flat-out annoying. It was tempered by an honest simplicity that was charming. Plus he thought she smelled nice.

She put the car in gear and cruised up Connecticut Avenue. She reversed direction and found a parking place close to the embassy. She looked down at herself and gave up a sigh. She had dressed for success, in case today was the day she'd return to her desk. Tailored pale gray suit with a pencil skirt, white silk T-shirt, black pumps. She looked like a junior executive at Blane-Grunwald. She no longer felt like one. Truth is, she felt foolish. She was all dressed up, sitting in her too-small car, waiting to chauffeur some odd guy around while he played detective and got her involved in heaven-knows-what.

The NSA guy was creepy. Maxine's death was sad and suspicious. It looked like the Grunwald brothers had something unsavory going on. And how did Günter fit into all this?

If she had any sense at all, she'd clean out her desk and look for another job. Something safe and sane, like catching alligators or looking for land mines in Afghanistan.

Okay, stay calm, she told herself. You don't want to quit the dream job. It's only been three days. Surely there's a logical explanation for all this. And Werner said this assignment was only for a short time.

Forty minutes later Emerson emerged from the embassy, walked to the corner, and hailed Riley.

"How did it go at the embassy?" she asked him when he was settled in and buckled up.

"It was cordial. I got the information I needed, but we're on a tight schedule. We're going to have to leave for New York first thing tomorrow morning."

"What? I can't do that. Why do you have to go to New York?"

"I need to look around."

"Can't you look around here? Is this about Maxine?"

"It's about gold."

"If it's that you still want to see your gold, I'm pretty sure I can get you a picture."

"A picture won't tell me what I need to know, so we're going to New York to the Federal Reserve gold vault."

"You aren't thinking about *stealing* your gold, are you?"

"That question is wrong on so many levels. First of all, the Federal Reserve Bank holds gold from almost every country, but not from individual citizens. So my gold isn't in that vault. Second, we're not going to steal from it. We're just going to look around. Then, if we have time, we'll look around in the Blane-Grunwald gold vault for Knight gold. And even if I did steal gold from Blane-Grunwald it wouldn't be stealing because it's *my* gold."

"You mean if we have time after serving our sentences in federal prison?"

"You're funny when you exaggerate like that."

"I'm not exaggerating!"

"What can you tell me about the Federal Reserve vault?"

"Not much. I skipped that course when I was at Harvard."

"But you worked for Günter, and he was the Blane-Grunwald gold guru."

"I got him coffee and sandwiches, and copied documents. My knowledge isn't extensive. I know that the Federal Reserve vault holds more gold than Fort Knox. Fort Knox only holds about four thousand six hundred tons of gold. The Federal Reserve vault holds approximately seven thousand. That's a lot of gold."

"Indeed. It's nearly a quarter of the world's gold

reserves. Blane-Grunwald's vault holds nearly that much as well. The gold is stored in New York in vaults resting on bedrock, eighty feet below street level. The walls of the vaults are steel-reinforced concrete. The vaults are impenetrable."

Riley gave him a single raised eyebrow. "But you're going to penetrate it?"

"Yes. The countries let us keep their gold because they trust the United States government. They started storing it there during and immediately after World War Two, when it looked like America was the safest place on the planet. So they keep it all in tidy lockers."

"Lockers? You make it sound like high school."

"The vault lockers are a bit bigger."

Riley thought he was probably cute but nonconforming in high school. He wouldn't have been one of the Goth kids. He would have been the kid who spoke Klingon and ignored his homework because it was tedious.

"Getting back to the gold, it makes sense to have it all in one place, after all," Emerson said. "If country A wants to make a monetary deal with country B, all it has to do is shift the gold from one locker to another. It's like the world map in a single vault."

Riley nodded. "I get that."

"Recently, the trust has been shaken. And Germany's Bundesbank asked to repatriate their gold."

"Repatriate?"

"They want it back. In Germany. But the Fed is dragging its feet. To date they've only given back a portion of it."

"Why won't the Fed give it back?" Riley asked.

"Logistics, they say. But what if the gold isn't there? What if someone has been replacing it with fakes like the one we found in Maxine's apartment?"

"That would take years."

"What if it *has* taken years? What if it's the longest and largest con in the world?"

"That's pretty far-fetched."

"The farthest. Tell me, do you know what the largest *private* gold vault in the world is?"

"Blane-Grunwald in Manhattan?"

"Excellent. It's rumored to have five hundred billion dollars' worth. That's half a trillion dollars in bullion. Including my paltry amount."

"That's a lot of . . . you know."

"I know. And do you know where the Blane-Grunwald bank in New York is located?"

"Sure. One Chase Manhattan Boulevard."

"Right across the street from the Federal Reserve," Emerson said.

"And?"

"The diabolical possibilities are endless."

"Here's the thing," Riley said. "I'm not really into diabolical possibilities. I'm more into logical explanations."

"Maxine's body was found on Liberty Street. Just a block from the Federal Reserve. The logical explanation is that Günter and Maxine uncovered something big in New York. And it involves the world's gold supply."

Riley's heart skipped a beat. "Involves?"

"Someone is stealing the world's gold supply and substituting it with counterfeits."

"Someone?"

Emerson shrugged. "Mystery creates wonder, and wonder is the basis of man's desire to understand."

"Buddha?" Riley asked.

"Why would Buddha steal the world's gold supply? He believed that material possessions were the root of unhappiness."

Riley did an exasperated eye roll. "I meant, who said 'Mystery creates wonder'?"

"Oh, that was Neil Armstrong. He didn't steal the world's gold supply either." He leaned into her and whispered, "He's dead, you know."

"I don't want to hear any of this. You're a good client and probably a nice guy, but it has to end here. I'm going to take you home, and I'm not coming back."

"Of course you're coming back. You're on loan to me, and I need you to drive me to New York. How else will I get there?"

"The train."

"The train doesn't fit into my plan."

"Then have someone else drive you to New York. Your aunt or your cousin."

"I'd prefer not to involve them in this."

"And me?"

"You're already involved. And you're an excellent driver."

ELEVEN

T HE HICKORIES AND OAKS THAT SPANNED
Rock Creek Park formed an arch framing the
many gables of Mysterioso Manor. When Riley pulled
up the next morning the sun had just risen and the
world looked dewy and fresh. She'd spent the night
telling herself she absolutely was not going to drive
Emerson to New York. She'd dressed for the office in
black heels, a simple white silk T-shirt, and a black suit
with a short fitted jacket. She'd pointed her Mini toward
Blane-Grunwald. And somehow she'd ended up here.

"Stupid, stupid, stupid," she said out loud in the
privacy of her car, referencing herself, and Emerson, and
the world in general.

She parked and watched Emerson and Vernon
wrestling what looked like a tank of compressed air into

the trunk of a vintage cream-colored Rolls-Royce Silver Shadow. They slammed the trunk lid closed and turned to look at her. Vernon smiled and waved. Emerson was stoic.

Riley grabbed her messenger bag, left her car, and walked over to the men.

"You look darned pretty with your hair pulled back," Vernon said to Riley. "And I like that you're always so dressed up in heels and everything. You look like you could be president of the United States."

"I like it too," Emerson said. "Very professional. Although it's entirely unnecessary when you're working for me. Perhaps I never mentioned that."

"I'd planned to be at my desk at Blane-Grunwald today," Riley said.

"But you're here instead," Emerson said. "You made the correct choice." He tossed his rucksack into the Shadow's backseat and handed Riley the car keys. "Drive carefully. We have a science experiment in the trunk."

The first stop in Manhattan was on East Forty-Third Street. The Mauritius Permanent Mission to the United Nations.

"Mauritius again?" Riley asked.

"I have a helpful contact," Emerson said.

"Is this contact going to get you into the vault?"

"Yes. He's going to get us into the vault."

"No, no, no. There's no 'us' in the vault. I'm the innocent driver. *You* are the guy in the vault. I don't even want to talk about it. I don't want to know any details."

"Actually, you brought the subject up. I merely gave you an address."

"Good point. Won't happen again. I swear I won't ask another question."

"That places the burden of imparting information squarely on me," Emerson said. "So I should tell you that I'll be in this building for exactly thirty-five minutes, at which time you can pick me up and take me to the Carlyle hotel."

Emerson went into the building, and Riley circled the block with the Silver Shadow creeping along in heavy traffic. Her Mini would have been much easier to maneuver, especially on the cross streets. Emerson reappeared on Riley's third swing. He jumped into the car, and they headed uptown.

The Carlyle is located on Madison and Seventy-Sixth Street. It's an intimate luxury hotel and an iconic model of discretion where presidents have had clandestine trysts and movie stars have entered and exited through a system of secret tunnels. The building is art deco, and the service is impeccable. The bathrooms were state-of-the-art when the hotel was built in 1930.

The receptionist behind the front desk greeted Emerson like the prodigal son. "Mr. Knight! How good to see you. It's been too long!"

"Always good to be here, Maurice. Is my suite available?"

"Of course. And Jane is playing in the Café Carlyle tonight. Shall I book your table?"

"Absolutely. A table for two." Emerson gestured to Riley. "This is Riley Moon. Miss Moon is my amanuensis. She'll be staying with me."

"Welcome to the Carlyle, Miss Moon," Maurice said. He turned his attention back to Emerson. "I'll have James bring your bag up immediately."

Emerson nodded, turned on his heel, and took off for the elevator with Riley tagging behind.

"Hold up," Riley said. "What was that all about back there? I'm not staying with you."

Emerson stepped into the elevator. "Of course you are. Where else would you stay?"

"I assumed I'd be going home."

"You assumed wrong. I need you to drive me to the Federal Reserve tomorrow."

"I'm not prepared for this."

"I've prepared for both of us."

The elevator doors opened to the thirty-first floor and Emerson stepped out.

"I have no clothes," Riley said. "I haven't got a toothbrush. I don't want to be here."

Emerson unlocked the door to his suite. "Why wouldn't you want to be here? It's very comfortable."

Riley looked into the suite and had to agree. It was very comfortable. It had a view of Central Park and beyond that the West Side skyline. There was a baby grand piano, a dining room table, assorted couches and chairs, fresh flowers on the side table, and fresh fruit on the coffee table.

"This is lovely," Riley said.

"My father used this quite a lot, and I have to admit that I find it convenient, although I use it sporadically. Your bedroom with bath en suite is down that short hall. I'm going to my bedroom for a moment of meditation, and then there are things I need to discuss with the Siddhar. Dinner is at seven."

Hans Grunwald stood at parade rest with his back to his brother. He was staring out the window in Werner's office, looking at the Capitol, and he wasn't happy.

"They're in New York," Hans said. "This has gone too far."

"It's a harmless wild goose chase," Werner said. "He's a complete flake. If it wasn't for Moonbeam he couldn't find his way home."

"He found the gold, and he found us at Fletcher's Cove."

"This is an entirely different situation. Plus we have Rollo on the scene."

Hans turned and looked at Werner. "You'd better be right. The old man will have your head if this goes south . . . literally. And I'll be the one to carry out his orders."

• • •

Riley sat at the writing desk in her room and googled Mauritius on her smartphone. There were a lot of pictures of a beautiful island nation about twelve hundred miles off the coast of Africa. A picturesque jewel of white sandy beaches in the Indian Ocean, mostly known for being the home of the dodo bird before it went extinct. Mauritius was now a model democracy with a booming economy and a population consisting of a homogenous blend of Indians, Africans, Chinese, and Europeans. There was an awful lot of stuff about banking hours on its official site, but other than that, and the fact "nudism and topless sunbathing are frowned upon on our public beaches," it looked like a pretty fun place.

Next up for Google was the name on the note they'd found in Günter's office. Dr. Bauerfeind. Riley found three listings. An anesthesiologist in Augusta, Maine. A gynecologist in Lucerne, Switzerland. A chemist in Frankfurt, Germany.

She read the information on the anesthesiologist and the gynecologist and was about to check out the chemist when there was a knock on her door.

"Fortunately, this hotel has an excellent personal shopper," Emerson said, handing over several boxes. "This should get you through the next twenty-four hours."

Riley looked at the boxes. "How did the personal shopper know my size?"

"I gave her the information. I have an excellent eye. And I personally made the decision on the dress. I think it will be perfect."

"Did the Siddhar tell you to do this?"

"Perhaps telepathically. I haven't had a chance to speak to him yet."

Emerson left and Riley brought the boxes into her room and opened them. Silky pajamas, lingerie, basic toiletries, jeans, T-shirt, sneakers, fleece hoodie, and a little black dress. She stripped her suit off, dropped the dress over her head, and looked in the mirror. Emerson was right. The dress was perfect. Better than perfect. It was the dress of her dreams. Simple, classy, sexy, flattering. She was Anne Hathaway after the transformation in *The Devil Wears Prada*.

The Café Carlyle is an intimate dining room with a tiny stage, low-key lighting, and wall murals that look like Matisse and Picasso painted them after they'd been out together on a bender. The waiters are elderly gentlemen who take their jobs seriously. There was no barbecue on the menu and no room on the floor for the Texas two-step, but Riley thought it was wonderful all the same.

She looked at Emerson sitting across from her. He was wearing a black Tom Ford blazer over a black T-shirt. He was getting a five o'clock shadow, and his teeth were exceptionally white in the dimly lit room. Riley was reminded of the wolf in "Little Red Riding Hood."

Riley took in the candlelight, the wolf, and the glass of champagne that had magically appeared in her hand.

"This isn't a date, is it?" she asked Emerson.

"Between you and me? I don't think so. Do you?"

"I don't think so."

"I don't think so either."

She sipped her champagne and looked around the room.

"Is that Al Roker at the next table?" she asked Emerson.

"Yes. He's a nice man. And surprisingly funny."

"You know him?"

"I did him a favor once."

"You do a lot of favors."

"Opportunities arise," Emerson said.

"I bet. Tell me about Dr. Bauerfeind. I ran out of time before I could research him."

"He's a German chemist who has developed a technique for reading the fingerprint of gold even after it has been recast."

"Fingerprint?"

"Precise chemical composition."

"And this fingerprint reading is a big deal?"

"It's unique to him."

"And we care about this, why?"

"On a personal note, someone could be stealing my gold, melting it down, and putting it into some other form. Ordinarily it would be untraceable. On a global scale the theft and transformation of the world's gold could bring about economic chaos."

"Wow."

"Exactly."

"So have you done Bauerfeind any favors?"

"Not lately."

"About tomorrow," Riley said.

"It should be a fascinating day. I have a plan in place."

"I'm not part of the plan, am I?"

"Yes."

"No."

Emerson glanced at his menu. "I'm very fond of the chicken hash."

"I'm going with the prosciutto-wrapped monkfish," Riley said. "I'm all about anything related to bacon. Although it's sort of a bummer that it's wrapped around fish."

"You don't like fish?"

"I like to catch them. I'm not crazy about eating them unless they're fried and smothered in tartar sauce."

"I'm sure if we give those instructions to our waiter it can be arranged. The chef is very accommodating here."

"About the plan, and the fact that I'm not participating in any way other than driving you to the Federal Reserve."

Emerson reached behind him, grabbed the champagne bottle from the ice bucket, and refilled Riley's glass.

"Thank you," Riley said, "but I still want to make my role in the plan perfectly clear."

"We can talk about it tomorrow," Emerson said.

Riley narrowed her eyes. "Now."

"No."

"Yes."

"You're going to ruin the moment," Emerson said.

"I thought we weren't having a moment."

"We aren't having a *date*, but we could have a moment."

"Would it be a romantic moment? A romantic moment might be awkward."

"It could be a chicken hash moment," Emerson said.

"I suppose that would be okay."

"And you can have a prosciutto moment."

"I owe it to the dress to have a moment," Riley said. "It's wonderful. Thank you. But just to state my position one last time before the moment begins, I'm dropping you off tomorrow morning and going home."

Emerson was already at the breakfast table when Riley came out of her room dressed in the new jeans and sneakers.

"I took the liberty of ordering for you," Emerson said. "Cheese omelet, hash browns, multigrain toast, a side of fruit, a short stack of pancakes, and extra bacon. I didn't know what you normally ate in the morning, so I ordered everything."

Riley started with coffee and worked her way around the table. "Are you eating any of this?" she asked Emerson.

"I've already eaten." He checked his watch. "We need to be downstairs in thirty minutes. I've called for the car to be brought to the back door."

"Why the back door?"

"I thought it would make the day more interesting for Rollo."

"You think Rollo knows we're here?"

"Yes. You're carrying his phone. And while we're on the subject, I'd like to see the phone."

Riley gave him the phone, and he locked it in the suite safe.

"This should make Rollo's job a bit more challenging."

TWELVE

———◆◇◆———

R ILEY AND EMERSON EXITED THROUGH A side door and found the Silver Shadow on Seventy-Seventh Street. A bellman handed them the key and wished them a nice day. Riley got behind the wheel and cranked the engine.

"I assume we're going to the Federal Reserve building," she said.

"Correct."

"I studied the route yesterday, but I'm going to need help when we get to the Wall Street area. Streets and avenues are in a grid all through Midtown, but they make no sense in lower Manhattan."

"No problem. I can find my way."

Thirty-five minutes later Riley drove up to the massive Federal Reserve building. It occupied an entire block on Liberty Street, and it looked to her like a limestone fortress, a positive citadel of finance.

"We need to find a parking place on this block," Emerson said.

Riley scanned the street. "There aren't any."

"Then we'll have to wait for one."

Riley circled the block four times, and on the fifth pass found a vacant space in front of Blane-Grunwald's New York office.

"Perfect," Emerson said, opening the glove box and pulling out what looked like a remote control timer for a camera. He set the timer and returned it to the glove box.

"What was that all about?" Riley asked.

"It's part of my plan."

"You aren't going to blow something up, are you?"

"I thought you weren't asking questions."

"Right. I don't want to know, but it would be bad if you blew something up. And it wouldn't be good for your karma."

"I'm touched that you care. Rest assured, my karma will stay intact."

"Okay then. Have a nice day. Adios. Goodbye. Arrivederci."

"The 'arrivederci' is premature. We're not parting yet."

"The deal was that I drive you to the Federal Reserve building, and then I get to drive home."

"Not exactly," Emerson said. "The Silver Shadow stays here."

"How am I going to go home?"

Emerson got out of the car. "I've made arrangements. Follow me."

Riley grabbed the key out of the ignition and scrambled to keep up with Emerson. "Where are we going?"

"That's a question again," Emerson said, crossing Nassau Street.

"I'm not going to just blindly follow you around."

"Of course not. You're going to keep your eyes open. And if you must know, we're going to the subway stop on Broadway."

Okay, that might be promising, Riley thought. The subway could lead to Penn Station. "Are we heading toward Amtrak?" she asked him. "If I get an early train, I might be able to check in at the office before everyone leaves for the weekend."

"Unlikely," Emerson said. "We aren't taking the subway. It was a point of reference. Once we get to the subway stop, we need to walk two blocks on Cedar Street to meet our ride."

"Why are we meeting our ride on Cedar Street? Why didn't he just pick us up on Liberty Street?"

Emerson walked past the subway stop and turned onto Cedar. "We're meeting them on Cedar Street because they always stop at a little shop on Cedar for coffee when they're in the neighborhood. It seemed like the convenient thing to do. A pickup on Liberty might raise red flags."

An armored truck was stopped on the second block

of Cedar. An armed guard stood at the back of the truck. Another armed guard, carrying a white bakery bag and four cups of coffee in a cardboard box, stepped out of a shop and moved toward the truck.

Riley stopped in the middle of the sidewalk. "Tell me that isn't our ride."

Emerson took her hand and tugged her forward. "I'm told it's quite comfortable inside."

"No way. No how. I am not getting into that armored truck."

The back doors to the truck opened, the man carrying the coffee got inside, and two men in black Kevlar vests sprang out.

Someone inside the truck called out, "Good morning, Emerson."

"Good morning, Wesley," Emerson replied.

The two men in Kevlar scooped Riley up and swept her into the truck. Emerson followed, and the doors were slammed shut. When Riley lunged for the door handle, one of the men attempted to restrain her and she kneed him in the groin.

The man yelped and doubled over. "I'm guessing you didn't tell her about this part of the plan," he said to Emerson.

"Actually . . . no," Emerson said.

The truck lurched forward, and Riley put her hand to the door to steady herself. "This truck had better be taking me to Washington, D.C.," she said. "And what's under the blanket in the middle of the truck? Have you boxed up another kidnap victim?"

A man leaned out from the shadows. "I'm Wesley Bachoo, Ministry of Finance and Economic Development of the Sovereign Republic of Mauritius. Allow me to put your mind at ease." He stepped forward, pulled the blanket off the cargo, and revealed a small stack of gold bricks. "This is part of the treasury of the Republic of Mauritius."

"Lovely to meet you," Riley said. "I'm Riley Moon of Blane-Grunwald. Sorry I kneed your guy in the groin. I might have overreacted."

"Perfectly understandable," Wesley said. "You were caught by surprise. Still, it's very good of you to help set Emerson's mind at ease that his gold is secure. I know this is something of a covert operation, so our lips are sealed. However, I will make sure your employer understands that we are favorably impressed with your assistance in all matters. After all, we owe Emerson a huge debt. He was instrumental in discovering who was responsible for putting ricin in the prime minister's morning coffee and nearly killing him. If it hadn't been for Mr. Knight, we might have gone to war over it."

"Was it a terrorist organization?" Riley asked.

"No. It was our prime minister's wife," Wesley said.

"They were having marital problems," Emerson said.

"No doubt," Riley said. "What happened to them?"

Wesley smiled. "They went to couples therapy. They're doing fine now."

"Good to know," Riley said. "Attempted murder is something a lot of couples can't get past."

She looked at the rearview monitor attached to the wall and saw that they'd picked up a police escort.

"I don't suppose they're here to rescue me," Riley said.

"They're a courtesy afforded to us by the city," Wesley said.

Riley sucked in her anger. Get a grip, she told herself. Punching Emerson in the face won't make the situation any better.

"We're going into the Federal Reserve vault, aren't we?" she said.

"We are."

"Why?"

"Mauritius is making a deposit," Emerson said. "And I'm going to look around."

Damn! "Okay. We're going to look around and then we're going to leave, right?"

"Absolutely."

"And just looking around wouldn't be considered a felony?"

"We're going in as a part of the Republic of Mauritius's security team to make sure their gold is deposited safely," Emerson said. "We have the permission of the minister of finance, don't we, Wesley?"

"Indeed," Wesley said.

"And we are all citizens of Mauritius," Emerson said.

"I'm not," Riley said.

"Wesley, could you make her an honorary citizen of Mauritius?" Emerson asked.

"Consider it done," Wesley said, handing over Kevlar

vests and black polo shirts. "Both of you need to put these on."

Emerson pulled his polo shirt over his existing shirt and slipped into a Kevlar vest.

Riley stared at the vest and polo shirt. "Is this necessary?"

"Protocol," Wesley said.

Riley tugged the shirt over her head and shoved her arms into the vest. "This isn't going to be dangerous, is it? The vest is just a formality, right?"

"Right," Emerson said. "There's nothing to worry about."

One of the men handed Riley an AR-15 assault rifle. "Just in case," he said.

"In case of what?" Riley asked.

"In case someone expects you to follow protocol," Wesley said. "I hope you aren't afraid of guns."

"I'm from Texas," Riley said. "And my daddy was the county sheriff. I can shoot the eyelashes off a roach half a football field away."

"Beats me," one of the men said. "I couldn't hit the side of a barn."

Riley turned to Emerson. "You knew Mauritius was making a deposit this week?"

"Serendipity," Emerson said. "Mauritius is an emerging force in the banking industry. You might say Mauritius is the Cayman Islands of Africa."

"Not yet," Wesley said, modestly. "In time."

The truck stopped and went into reverse. The bands of sunlight from overhead louvers vanished from Wesley's face. The truck was plunged into semidarkness and came to a halt. The guards stood, rifles at their hips. One of them moved forward and opened the back door. They were met by more men in black with more assault rifles.

Wesley stepped out and was greeted by his opposite number, a drab-looking portly man in a Brooks Brothers suit. "Wesley Bachoo? I'm John Varnet, vault auditor with the Federal Reserve. What do you have for us?"

"A ton of gold, give or take a few ounces."

One of the Federal Reserve guards rolled a reinforced dolly up to the back of the truck and the gold was off-loaded. Riley counted out seventy gold bricks. The dolly was pushed down a long corridor to an elevator, and all the guards, along with Emerson and Riley, crowded in with it. The doors closed and the elevator began its descent.

"For those guards who haven't been into the vault before, we're going eighty feet down, into the substratum of Manhattan Island," Varnet said.

The elevator doors opened onto a small green hallway. More guards greeted them at this floor, and the dolly was pushed a short way to a massive vault door. It looked like a cartoon version of a safe. Riley expected to see Yosemite Sam come out from behind it, guns a-blazing.

Instead of one dial in front, there were two on either side. One guard turned the right wheel a few times. Another guard turned the left wheel about twenty times, and the door spun slowly around, like a huge childproof top on a bottle of golden pills.

"That's a steel cylinder, weighing ninety tons," Varnet said, still in tour-guide mode. "It revolves in a hundred-forty-ton steel and concrete frame. When it rotates, it drops three-eighths of an inch. This creates a seal that is both airtight and watertight."

The transport dolly was pushed rattling and clinking through the open door, down a corridor, and into a dingy waiting room with floor-to-ceiling metal bars at the far end.

"It takes three separate keys to unlock the gate that will take you past this last barrier," Varnet said. "The keys are assigned individually to two vault custodians and the auditor, me."

The three men with the three keys unlocked the three locks and the gate swung open. Beyond the gate, lockers with iron cage doors were filled to the ceiling with gold bricks.

"There it is," Varnet said. "One-quarter of the world's gold reserves. Approximately seven thousand tons, worth approximately two hundred fifty billion dollars."

Riley and Emerson exchanged glances, and Riley suspected Emerson was thinking the bricks in the vault might be worth a lot less than two hundred fifty billion. She suspected he was thinking some of those bricks could be fakes.

"A little safety tip," Varnet said, crossing to a large cabinet, opening the doors. "When you're working with gold bars you have to wear these."

The cabinet contained rows and rows of what appeared to be bedroom slippers made of metal.

"These shoe covers are made of magnesium. They might seem silly, but if you drop one of those bars on your foot you won't be laughing."

Everyone slipped the covers onto their shoes and walked, with clinking Tin Man–like feet.

Labels on each of the gold lockers had the names of the countries of ownership on them.

THE FRENCH REPUBLIC

THE KINGDOM OF SPAIN

JAPAN

THE DEMOCRATIC REPUBLIC OF THE CONGO

They appeared to be in no order. Some of them, like the United Kingdom of Great Britain and Northern Ireland or the Federal Republic of Germany, were piled high with gold and filled up two or three lockers. Others, like the Republic of Mauritius, had a more modest stash.

The dolly was rolled up to a gigantic balance scale.

"We have to weigh the gold because each gold bar is unique," Varnet said. "We have to know precisely what we have here, before we can enter it into our records."

They loaded twelve gold bars at a time onto a metal disc at one end of the scale. Large counterbalances were placed on the opposite end, and the two ends of the scale shifted into place like a child's teeter-totter.

"This might seem old-fashioned," Varnet said while the vault custodian carefully observed the needle moving in the middle of scale, "but it's very accurate. We've been doing it this way, with this exact scale, since the vault first opened in 1924."

A red light flashed and a siren blared. Everyone froze. Varnet's face turned ashen.

"We're under attack," Varnet shouted. "Everyone out of the vault. We need to lock it down."

There was a mass exodus to the gate, and down the corridor to the door. The two custodians spun the wheels and the massive door slowly rotated shut.

Varnet looked around. "We're missing two people," he said. "The woman isn't here. And one other."

THIRTEEN

FIVE MINUTES BEFORE JOHN VARNET ANNOUNCED
that the building was under attack, Hans Grunwald's
town car pulled up to the front of Blane-Grunwald's
New York office. Hans and Werner got out and stood on
the sidewalk while Werner shrugged into his suit jacket.

"I hate these monthly meetings with the old man,"
Werner said. "Sometimes I leave thinking he's a genius,
and sometimes I leave thinking he's a bloodthirsty
sociopath."

"Despotic fascist would be closer to the truth," Hans
said. "And we're irrevocably tied to him."

Werner buttoned one button, took the briefcase the
driver had been holding for him, and the classic cream-
colored Rolls parked two cars in front of them exploded.

The noise was deafening. *BAROOOM!* Black smoke

poured out of the Rolls, clogged the street, and billowed into the sky.

The three men froze for a beat.

"What's happening?" Werner asked.

"Fucking terrorists," Hans said. "They're everywhere. You can't throw a stick without hitting one of them."

"Get off me!" Riley yelled at Emerson, struggling to be heard above the screaming siren. "What the heck are you doing?"

"I'm restraining you," Emerson said.

Riley was flat on her back with Emerson on top of her.

"You tripped me!" Riley said.

"Actually I wrestled you to the ground," Emerson said, "but I suppose that's splitting hairs."

The siren stopped wailing, there was the sound of rushing air, and then *phunnf.* Total silence.

"Omigod," Riley said. "Did we just get locked in the vault? Tell me we're not locked in."

She looked around. They were alone.

"Crap on a cracker," she said. "We're going to die."

Emerson rolled off her and helped her to her feet. "You have nothing to worry about. It's all part of my plan."

"I *hate* your plan."

"Nonsense. It's a brilliant plan. We have five minutes until they figure out the explosion was harmless and come in after us."

"Explosion?"

"The car. Why else do you suppose we left it parked on the street?"

"You didn't tell me there'd be an explosion."

"Are you sure I didn't tell you?"

"*Yes!* I would have remembered a plan to blow up a Rolls-Royce Silver Shadow."

"Well, at any rate, it was harmless. A lot of noise and a smoke bomb. I can't take full credit for it. Vernon made the bomb, which wasn't truly a bomb. It was more of a delivery system."

"That was your car!" Riley said. "Everyone will know you were responsible. You'll be investigated as a terrorist."

"Vernon and I have the explanation all worked out. It was all a simple miscalculation. This is the advantage to being an eccentric. Everyone expects you to be eccentric."

Emerson crossed to the Republic of Germany locker and opened it.

"They don't have locks on the doors?" Riley asked.

"Why should they? Who could get in here?"

"We did."

"Yes, but we're special."

Emerson took a small battery-operated drill from his pocket, selected a gold bar from the locker, and drilled into it.

"Just as I suspected," Emerson said, examining the bar. "As you can see, there's a thin veneer of gold covering a block of tungsten."

"Crap."

"You say that a lot."

Emerson drilled into twenty more bars. All of them fake.

"You should stop drilling holes," Riley said. "The bad guys are going to get mad that you're ruining their stuff."

Emerson lined the bars up and shot video of them with his smartphone. He tried to send it to his email, but there was no signal eighty feet down.

"Crap," Emerson said.

He restacked the bars, made sure the drilled sides faced down, and pocketed the drill.

"Now what?" Riley asked. "Are we done?"

"Hardly. I told you when we first met that I wanted to see my gold, and all I've seen so far is a vault full of worthless counterfeits. The real question is, where is the real gold, and how can we bring the thief to justice?"

Riley's heart was beating so fast she thought it was about to burst out of her chest. "Well, for the love of Mike, just how do you intend to do that?"

"We're going to find the real gold and match the serial numbers with the serial numbers on the fake gold stored in this vault."

"They're opening the vault," Riley said. "I can hear the door beginning to rotate."

Emerson checked his watch. "It took them longer than I thought."

"You have a plan, right? Something that doesn't involve us getting shot or rotting in prison?"

"I don't think they'll shoot us," Emerson said.

"You don't *think*?"

"It's not part of my plan. My plan is to have them rescue us."

An armed guard was the first to reach them. Varnet followed with Wesley.

"What are you doing in here?" he asked.

"Waiting to be rescued," Emerson said. "My partner tripped on the way out, and by the time we got her to her feet the vault was sealed."

Varnet stared Emerson down for a full minute before turning to Wesley.

"We need to finish processing your gold," Varnet said to Wesley. "And then we need to address this security breach."

Werner looked down from his office window and watched the police cordoning off the street around the Silver Shadow. The office was an exact replica of Werner's office in Washington. The only difference was the view. Sometimes Werner had to look out the window to remember where he was. If he saw the Manhattan skyline instead of the white dome of the Capitol, he knew he was in New York.

"Who do you think is responsible for this?" Werner asked Hans.

"Someone wanting to go viral on YouTube," Hans said. "International terrorist organizations don't usually use stink bombs."

"That's a classic car down there," Werner said. "Maybe one of a kind. And it had a classic plate from the District. I'm going out on a limb and guessing it belongs to Emerson Knight."

Hans gave a bark of laughter. "You think Emerson Knight stink-bombed Blane-Grunwald? The old man would love it."

There was a knock at the door, and Werner's New York assistant looked in.

"Sorry to bother you," he said, "but I thought you should know there was a security breach in the Federal Reserve vault that coincided with the car bomb. It seems it was an explainable incident, but I thought you'd want to be informed."

"What sort of a security breach?" Werner asked.

"When the alarm was raised and the vault was cleared, two foreign nationals were locked inside." He referred to his notes. "They were from the Republic of Mauritius. Mauritius was making a deposit at the time."

"Do you have a description?"

"A young man and a young woman. The young man was tall and lean. The young woman had red hair."

Hans and Werner turned from the assistant and looked down at the Silver Shadow. Werner blew out a sigh, and Hans tapped a number into his cellphone.

"Thank you," Werner said to his assistant. "That will be all."

"Detain the two Mauritius nationals who were involved in the security breach at the Federal Reserve,"

Hans said into his phone. "My man will want to speak with them."

The gold was weighed and stored, and everyone solemnly filed out of the vault and walked down the narrow corridor to the elevator. Doors opened onto a second elevator, and several men in gray suits got out. They pulled Varnet aside, whispered to him, and Varnet nodded his consent.

Emerson and Riley were culled from the group, their rifles were confiscated, and they were ushered into the second elevator.

"What is this about?" Riley asked.

"Protocol," one of the men said. "Standard security debriefing."

Riley saw him punch in a code and press the DOWN button, and she fought back panic. They were already eighty feet below the surface. How much lower could they go?

After a long descent, the door opened, and they were led through another long, narrow corridor. They reached a spot where the hallway split in two, and Riley was alarmed to see Emerson led down the left while she was led off to the right. She was shown into a room that was empty except for three straight-backed chairs and a small table with a couple disposable plastic cups and a pitcher of water on it.

"Someone will be in shortly," a suited man said. "Make yourself comfortable."

The door was closed and Riley was alone, the silence disturbed only by the beating of her heart. As a teenager, when she'd yearned for something more exciting than her north Texas town, this hadn't been what she'd imagined.

She sat in one of the chairs and waited. She looked at the water. No way was she drinking it. It could be laced with truth serum. Not that it would make a difference. She was going to spill her guts. She was going to tell them whatever the heck they wanted to hear. Whatever it took to get her out of the room, out of the building, out of New York . . . that's what she was going to say.

Anyway, she was just doing her job. Following Werner Grunwald's orders. She was an innocent pawn. What was the worst they could do to her? A long list of hideous possibilities flew through her mind. Good thing she was sitting down, because suddenly she wasn't feeling all that great. Her stomach was sick, and her heart was thumping in her chest.

She was debating the wisdom of waiting as opposed to trying to find her way out when the door swung open and Rollo walked in.

Riley jumped up. "You!" she said.

"You're looking pale," Rollo said, closing the door. "Maybe you should have some water."

Riley looked at the water but didn't make a move.

"Not thirsty?" Rollo asked.

Riley shook her head.

Rollo poured himself a glass and drank it. "It's

excellent water," he said. "Why didn't you keep me informed as to your whereabouts?"

"I assumed you were following me with the phone. And half the time I didn't know my whereabouts until I was there. Besides, you're the NSA spy. The NSA knows everything. They don't need someone phoning information in. That's so low-tech."

Yeah! Riley thought. Score one for Harvard Law. The best defense is always an aggressive offense. Especially when you might not have a very good defense.

The door opened, and Werner Grunwald stepped into the room. William McCabe and Hans Grunwald were standing a step behind Werner. McCabe looked far more imposing in his custom-made suit than he had in his fishing gear at Fletcher's Cove. Hans Grunwald in his uniform was even more impressive. Riley thought they were the nightmare version of the Scarecrow, the Tin Man, and the Cowardly Lion.

"I don't think we'll be needing you just yet," Werner said to Rollo. "You're excused too, McCabe."

Rollo nodded subserviently and left the room. He was followed by an obviously sullen William McCabe.

FOURTEEN

"**F**ANCY MEETING YOU HERE," WERNER SAID TO Riley.

"Just doing my job," Riley said. "You told me to assist Emerson, and that's what I've been doing."

"Understood," Werner said. "You were working as an operative for Blane-Grunwald. You obviously are everything we hoped you would be."

Riley wasn't so sure that was a good thing.

"Emerson clearly went to a great deal of effort to get himself into the Federal Reserve vault," Werner said. "Why was that so important to him?"

"He wanted to look around," Riley said. "He wanted to see his gold."

"And did he see his gold?"

"No. He couldn't find it."

"He couldn't find it because he was in the wrong vault," Werner said. "His gold is in the Blane-Grunwald vault. Surely he knew that."

"Sometimes it's hard to tell what he knows," Riley said.

Even as she said it, she knew she was in trouble. She was being evasive with Werner because she didn't like and didn't trust any of the men who were in the room with her. In her heart she knew there was something bad happening to the world's gold supply, and the Grunwalds were tied to it somehow. And there was a good possibility that people were getting killed over it. Bye-bye, dream job. Hello, unemployment.

Werner reached for the water, thought twice about it, and withdrew his hand. "As you know," he said to Riley, "our brother is about to take his seat on the Supreme Court next week. His seating will coincide with the Red Mass being held at the Cathedral of Saint Matthew."

"I'm not familiar with the Red Mass," Riley said.

"The Red Mass is celebrated annually by the Catholic Church to request guidance from the Holy Spirit for judges, attorneys, law school professors, students, and government officials. Needless to say, the last thing we need is a scandal disrupting the proceedings. It doesn't matter if it's a genuine scandal or a bogus rumor started by a conspiracy theory nut."

"Like Emerson."

"Exactly. Like Emerson."

"Have you spoken to him yet?" Riley asked.

"Yes, and he didn't have much to say. We were

hoping you would have an explanation for his behavior. We know he set off the bomb in front of the building."

"I don't know anything about a bomb, but we did park his car in front of Blane-Grunwald. Emerson said it was equipped with a special delivery system."

"Indeed," Werner said. "And when Emerson was in the vault alone, he did nothing more than look for his gold?"

"So far as I know. I wasn't with him the entire time. I waited in front of the Germany locker."

Riley resisted the urge to scan the room for security cameras. Hard to believe they wouldn't have any. Her hope was that she'd have a chance to escape before they reran the tape.

"We found a drill on him. What did he expect to do with the drill?" Werner asked.

Riley did a palms up. "Don't know. He's odd. And he doesn't talk a lot. Maybe he was going to drill into his gold when he found it. He's worried that his gold is fake."

Werner and Hans exchanged glances.

"His family has a long history of crazies," Werner said. "My father was very close to Emerson's father, so we feel somewhat *protective* of Emerson. Still, there's a limit to what we can tolerate."

"Sure," Riley said. "I get that."

The Grunwalds stared at Riley for a beat, and Riley stared back.

They're trying to decide if I'm a team player, Riley thought. They've been using me to keep an eye on

Emerson, but now they're worried I might know too much. And they're not sure where my loyalties lie. And it's possible they're trying to decide whether they need to kill me. And who knows if they've already killed Emerson?

Werner took a step back. "I think our business is concluded here. Emerson won't be needing your assistance any longer, Moonbeam. You can report to work as usual on Monday. Wait here and I'll send someone to escort you out."

The three men left the room and the door clicked closed.

Riley had no confidence that someone would escort her out. In her gut she felt like the escort would be Rollo, and he'd escort her out tortured and dead. She supposed there was a slim chance that Werner had decided she'd come over to the dark side and was usable, but she wasn't going to count on it. She was going to sneak out like a thief in the night, and she wasn't going to stop running until she was safe at home in Texas.

She tried the door and was relieved to find it unlocked. She poked her head out and looked up and down the hall. No one there. She retraced her steps down the empty corridor and came to the intersection where she and Emerson had gone in separate directions. The elevator was in one direction. Emerson was in the other.

Riley moved toward the elevator, got about twenty feet, and stopped. She couldn't do it. She couldn't leave Emerson behind.

"Crap!"

She put her head down and marched back to the other corridor. The first four doors she came to had labels. MECHANICAL ROOM, HOUSEKEEPING, WOMEN, MEN. There was a chunk of hall without doors and then there were doors without labels. Someone was whistling behind one of those doors. It sounded like the stuff Emerson listened to when he meditated.

Riley crept down the hall, stopping at every door until she found the room with the whistler. There was no one else in the hall, and no sound from behind the door other than the whistling. If she opened the door and Emerson wasn't alone, it might be ugly. She'd have to deal with it, she thought. Go into commando mode. She didn't have self-defense training, but she thought she could improvise. She was up for sucker punching and eye gouging. She could probably even execute a crotch kick. She counted to three, sucked in some air, and opened the door.

Emerson was alone in the small, sterile room. He was sitting in a straight chair with his hands cuffed behind him. His face was bloody, his lip was split, and his left eye was starting to blacken. He stopped whistling when Riley entered.

"Ah, Riley," he said. "There you are. Could you untie me? I have an itch right above my left eyebrow that's driving me crazy."

"My God," Riley said. "What have they done to you?"

"Beat me, somewhat. Nothing serious."

"It looks horrible! Doesn't it hurt?"

"I've risen above the pain."

Riley looked at the cuffs. "They've got your hands bound by plasticuffs. My dad used them all the time. I could cut them off if I had a knife or shears."

"I think Rollo left some tools on the table."

Riley looked over at the small black case holding surgical instruments. Scalpels, stainless steel pliers, and long metal rods.

"Rollo was here?" Riley asked. "With those?"

"Yes, but I think they were meant to simply intimidate me, not to flay. At least he hasn't used them yet."

"Where is he now?"

"He went to get some first aid."

"For you?"

"No, for himself. When he leaned to whisper something threatening in my ear, I gave him a head butt that made a gash in his chin."

"Are we talking about a gash that needed stitches or a gash that needed a Band-Aid?"

"Hard to say. There was a lot of blood."

Riley studied the display of torture tools and chose a scalpel. "Why were you whistling?"

"To lead you to me, of course."

"Of course," Riley said. "Hold still so I don't slit your wrist when I cut this plastic band."

A moment later Emerson was on his feet, shaking his hands to aid circulation.

"We need to get out of here before Rollo returns," Riley said, sliding the scalpel into a leather sheath.

"Agreed. He mentioned vengeance as he was leaving. He said it would be unpleasant."

Riley thought that if Rollo used the instruments in the black case, the results would be beyond unpleasant. She squelched a grimace and stuffed the sheathed scalpel into her vest. It wasn't big, but it was deadly sharp and it might come in handy. They hurried to the elevator and stepped inside the instant the doors opened. Emerson tapped a code into the keypad beside the door and pressed the B3 button.

"No!" Riley said. "That takes us down."

"Exactly," Emerson said. "It's all part of my plan. It's working perfectly."

"Working perfectly? You have a black eye and a split lip. We're being pursued by a psychopathic madman. And we're probably on television." Riley looked around the elevator for a security camera.

The elevator doors opened and Emerson stepped out at B3.

"You are really self-destructive, you know that?" Riley said to Emerson's back as he headed down a corridor.

"Not at all," Emerson said. "I'm inquisitive and I'm being proactive. You should be pleased that I'm assuming a leadership role. I'm very well suited for it. My analytic abilities and sensory instincts are superior."

"You are *so annoying*."

Emerson stopped at a door with a keypad, fed it the

code, and pushed the door open. "If my calculations are correct, there should be another door at the end of this corridor to the right."

The corridor was long and dimly lit. More of a tunnel than a corridor.

"We haven't much time," Emerson said, breaking into a run. "I'm sure they're scrambling by now, trying to find us. And most likely there will be an alarm going off in a control room somewhere when we open the next door."

They approached the door, and Riley was chilled to see the Blane-Grunwald logo stenciled on it. The labyrinth of corridors under the busy Manhattan streets had led them to Günter's "backyard."

Emerson eased the heavy door open, and they blinked at the glare off the gold bricks that were stacked waist high in the large storeroom.

Emerson took a brick from the stack in front of him and examined it. "I believe this is newly minted. New gold from old. I imagine there's another room in close proximity where they melt the original bricks down and re-form them into new untraceable bricks."

"That's ridiculous. How could they possibly get away with such a thing?"

Emerson looked around. "This is private property, and I'm sure access is complicated."

"We walked right in!"

"Yes, but first we had to break into the Federal Reserve and get arrested."

"This is a big operation," Riley said. "People are

needed to move the gold and melt the gold and protect the gold. Where do these people come from? How are they kept quiet?"

"This would be no different from other conspiracy movements. Intimidation, reward, elimination of problem employees . . . like Maxine Trowbridge. Many of the people involved will be enamored with the cause. Whatever that cause might be. Blind ideologues. And this is probably the tip of the iceberg. I suspect they periodically move the gold to a more obscure holding facility."

"Holy moly."

"I had expected 'crap on a cracker.'"

"I thought you were getting tired of 'crap on a cracker.'"

Emerson grinned. "'Holy moly' is refreshing, but it's hard to top 'crap on a cracker.'"

"What do we do now?"

"We leave as quickly and as stealthily as possible. I'm hoping it will be easier to get out than to get in. Codes and keys are necessary to go down in the elevator but I'm thinking it's like staying on the concierge level of a hotel. Nothing special is needed to exit."

They stepped into the elevator on the far side of the room, but the elevator refused to move without a code.

"This is getting tiresome," Emerson said, tapping a code in and pushing the only button.

Riley stopped holding her breath when she felt the elevator moving up.

"How do you know the door and elevator codes?" she asked Emerson.

"I watched the first guard when he gave the elevator his code. Foolishly all the doors work off the same code. I'm sure it's his personal code but it's still a poor practice."

The elevator stopped and opened onto a small foyer with an armed guard at a desk. Beyond the guard was another elevator.

Emerson approached the guard and said something in French. The guard took in their uniforms and nodded. Emerson signed the logbook, smiled pleasantly, and motioned Riley to the elevator.

They stripped their guard uniforms off in the elevator and were relieved to see a deserted hallway when the doors opened. They dumped the Mauritius shirts in a trash receptacle, walked toward an exit sign, and found themselves in the main lobby of Blane-Grunwald.

The front door to the building was roped off with crime scene tape, and beyond the big double-glass windows Riley could see police milling about in bomb disposal gear.

"Back door," Emerson said.

Riley was way ahead of him, already having done an about-face. In less than a minute she was out of the building, walking toward the subway stop, and Emerson was matching her strides. She was on the platform for twenty seconds when a train rolled in, and she took it with no knowledge of where it was going. She just knew it was going to move her away from Blane-Grunwald and the Federal Reserve.

"I have a plan," Emerson said, swaying with the motion of the train.

"Oh boy," Riley said. "Another plan."

"I'm going off the grid."

"Good plan. What about me?"

"You should go back to your life."

"Which life would that be?" Riley asked.

"Life is a series of natural changes. Resisting change only creates sorrow. Let reality be reality. Let things flow naturally forward in whatever way they like."

"Gee, that's really helpful...whatever the heck it means. Thanks a lot."

The train eased into a station and Emerson pulled a wad of money from his pocket. He handed the money to Riley and moved to the door. "I'll contact you."

"No! Do not contact me. Erase me from your memory bank."

Emerson stepped onto the platform, the doors slid closed behind him, and the train lurched forward. Riley got off at the next stop and studied the route map on the wall. She was in Brooklyn.

FIFTEEN

━━━ ⋙⋘ ━━━

IT WAS A COUPLE MINUTES AFTER MIDNIGHT WHEN
Riley retrieved the key she kept hidden in a fake rock
near a shrub next to the front steps and let herself into
her apartment. So far so good, she thought. She hadn't
been stopped by the NSA. No sign of Rollo. No SWAT
team waiting for her on the sidewalk in front of her
building. If her apartment had been searched at least
they'd been neat about it, because nothing seemed out
of place. She poured herself a glass of wine, took two sips,
and decided she was too tired to drink the rest of it.
The day had been mind-numbing. Confusing, terrifying,
exhilarating, and exhausting. Her purse had been left
behind, so tomorrow she was faced with the chore of
replacing her driver's license, smartphone, and credit cards.
She hoped she lived long enough to do it. She had no

clue how she stood with Werner but she took it as a good sign that her apartment hadn't been booby-trapped.

She had a nervous flutter in her stomach when she fell asleep and it was still there when she woke up in the morning. Her life was a mess. One day everything was on track and then *WHAM!* Emerson Knight.

Riley checked her email while she downed two cups of coffee and a bowl of cereal. Her mother had sent her a picture of the cake she'd made for Uncle Mickey's birthday party. It was followed by a picture of Uncle Mickey eating a slice of the cake and a message that everyone misses Riley but is excited that she has her dream job in Washington, D.C.

Crap on a cake, Riley thought.

Her oldest brother, Lowell, usually sent her a conspiracy-laden tirade about the government being in cahoots with Big Oil, the Russians, and the Taliban, in no particular order. Today Lowell was going on and on about the Treasury Department and Big Gold. He said a rumor had appeared on the Internet just last night, claiming that the gold treasuries at the Federal Reserve were all fake. Bogus. Counterfeit. Nothing but hollow shells filled with tungsten.

Riley broke out in goosebumps. It was unusual for Lowell to strike a note so close to reality. Usually, he favored the black-op-helicopter-time-machine-was-behind-the-Kennedy-assassination type of theory. Lowell was part conspiracy theorist and part aspiring author. Sometimes it was hard to tell where his political rants stopped and his thriller plot took over.

Riley scrolled through the endless text where Lowell seamlessly floated between fact and fiction and finally gave credit to the origin of the fake gold disclosure. Lowell stated that his information came from an unimpeachable source, the well-known philosopher and mystic Mysterioso.

More goosebumps. Emerson had "outed" the Grunwalds through the blog he shared with Vernon. Riley clicked over to the Mysterioso site and read down. It was all there with names omitted. Emerson and Riley had become Mr. K. and Miss M., but the rest was there, in all its unbelievable glory. The car bomb, the infiltration of the Fed vault, drilling into the gold bars, finding the tungsten, escaping. It sounded like the ravings of a madman.

And it was all true.

If she hadn't been there, she'd never have believed it, not for a second. No one would. Except nuts like her brother Lowell. She closed her computer and sat for a moment in numb disbelief before trying to continue on with life in its normal rhythm. She rinsed the dishes and put the cereal box back in the cupboard. She moved on to the bathroom.

She took a shower, applied minimal makeup, and stared into her closet. Now what? She asked herself. Do I put on jeans and a T-shirt and go home to Texas? Or do I get dressed in a suit on Monday, march into Blane-Grunwald, and act as if nothing unusual happened and I still work there? None of the above, she decided.

It was Saturday. Blane-Grunwald was mostly closed.

There would just be a skeleton crew in the building, tending to emergency transactions. She'd retrieve her Mini Cooper from Emerson's house. Then she would calmly and casually stroll into Blane-Grunwald, clean out her desk, and sneak off. By the time Monday rolled around she'd have figured out the next step.

Riley flagged down a cab two blocks from her house and directed the driver to Mysterioso Manor. Aunt Myra was on the front porch when Riley arrived.

"Were you going out?" Riley asked Myra.

"No. I was just coming in from feeding some of the critters. They're scattered all the heck over the place. Sometimes I think I should just let them eat each other and be done with it."

"I came to collect my car and to talk to Emerson."

"Emmie's not here, hon. I thought he was with you."

"No. We got separated in New York. He said he was going off the grid. I wasn't sure how *off* he was talking about."

"Well, he'll find his way back. I remember when he was nine years old and ran away to join Greenpeace."

"Really?"

"Oh, yes. We were very worried. But he was back two days later, ready to eat everything in the fridge. He's got some homing pigeon in him."

Riley glanced at the monkey curled in a rocking chair. "Looks like the monkey is still here."

"Seems like he comes and goes. Already had a

runaround with the armadillo this morning," Myra said. "Truth is, I'm not sure it's always the same monkey. I think we might have a pack of them."

Riley wondered if Rollo was coming and going too. Hiding out there somewhere, watching, waiting to pounce on Emerson. And maybe on her as well. It was a chilling thought. It reminded her that she needed to stay vigilant.

"Have you seen Emerson's and Vernon's blog?" she asked Myra. "Why the Sam Hill would he provoke the Grunwalds?"

"Emmie wants to expose the gold stealers. He said if he couldn't bring Muhammad to the mountain, he'd bring the mountain to Muhammad, or something like that. Guess that's his way of saying if he can't get to the bad guys, he'll have the bad guys come to him."

"That sounds like Emerson."

Riley moved off the porch and walked toward her car. "Tell Emerson to call me when he comes home."

"I'll have him call you first thing," Aunt Myra said.

Twenty minutes later, Riley was at the Blane-Grunwald building on Constitution Avenue, circling it repeatedly, trying to decide whether to pull into the garage or to get on I-66 and go back to Texas.

Her dad would tell her to hitch up her jeans and just get on with it, so she turned in to the garage and drove down to her space, feeling like she was driving down the Nine Circles of Hell. Plus a few more. She parked, took the elevator to the lobby, and was relieved to see a familiar face at the reception desk. She was waved through to the bank of elevators, took one to the fourth floor, and made her way through the maze of desks to her cubicle. She could hear someone working on the far side of the room. Eager beaver, she thought. Someone going the extra mile to impress, hoping to move up the food chain. That would have been her if she hadn't gotten involved with Emerson Knight.

She put her few personal belongings in a tote bag she'd brought. A couple granola bars, a roll of peppermint Life Savers, a Starbucks coffee mug, Burt's Bees lip balm, and a picture of her family standing in front of a Christmas tree. She hadn't occupied the desk long enough to really take possession. She would have left all but the picture.

Werner was on the golf course when a text message came in from office security, alerting him that Moonbeam was in the building. Ten minutes later he received a text that she had removed personal items from her desk and was offsite. He couldn't care less except that he knew the message had also been sent to the old man. The old man was informed of everything. And the message would trigger a phone call. The one phone call he couldn't ignore. Ever.

Werner's phone dinged and he pushed down the panic that always arose in his chest whenever he heard the telltale ringtone.

"It's under control," Werner said on answering. "He'll be taken care of. And so will she."

There was a long pause before the sound of labored breathing came through the line. "I hope so. For your sake."

Riley drove back to her apartment and parked in the space allotted to her in the alleyway behind the Victorian. She hiked the tote bag onto her shoulder, locked her car, and crossed the small yard to the house's rear entrance. She had her house key in hand when a man rounded the Victorian from the street side.

"Stop!" he shouted at Riley. "You need to come with me."

He was big. Over six foot tall and built like an NFL linebacker. In his late fifties, Riley thought. Used to giving orders and being obeyed. He had a scar running down the side of his face and a military-style buzz haircut.

Riley's assessment was that he was scary as hell and made Rollo look like a choirboy. No way was she going *anywhere* with him. She rammed the key into the lock, pushed the door open, and rushed inside. She threw the bolt, ran down the short hall to the front foyer, and ran up three flights of stairs to the safety of her apartment. She let herself in, locked her door, and looked out a back window at the man standing in the yard.

He looked confused. Unsure what to do. Less threatening from this vantage point. He looked up at her and she jumped away from the window. When she returned moments later, he was gone.

I'm in big trouble, Riley thought. And I don't know

where to go for help. I could trust my dad but I don't want to drag my family into this. Going home to Texas is no longer an option. I can probably trust Emerson, but he's weird and I don't know how to get in touch with him. Government agencies are out. I don't know how far the Grunwald tentacles reach into those agencies.

She set the tote bag on a kitchen chair and checked the time. Almost noon. She should have lunch. Keep up with the normal activities, and maybe everything would eventually fall back into place. She stared into her fridge and let the cold air wash over her while she scanned the contents. White bread, strawberry jelly, mustard, a carton of eggs, 1 percent milk, provolone cheese slices, some deli ham, a jar of olives, a bag of baby carrots.

She was contemplating a cheese sandwich when she was grabbed from behind. An arm crooked around her neck, and her head was pushed forward in a choke hold.

It was Rollo.

"Memo to Riley," Rollo said. "Check for killers hiding in closets when entering your apartment. Oops, guess you won't be able to use that advice since you'll be dead. I'm going to slit your wrists after you pass out, and you'll just be another unstable woman who was driven to suicide over losing her dream job."

Riley grabbed at the arm around her neck and kicked back with her foot, but she was already too oxygen-deprived to be effective, and she slipped into unconsciousness.

. . . .

Emerson and Larry Quiller took the stairs to Riley's apartment two at a time.

"I tried to stop her," Larry said, struggling to keep pace with Emerson. "I told her she needed to come with me, but she ran into the house."

Emerson reached Riley's apartment and found the door locked. He stepped aside and Larry kicked the door open, splintering the doorframe, sending the door crashing against the wall.

Rollo was on one knee, bent over Riley with a knife in his hand.

"Mr. Knight," Rollo said. "We meet again."

Larry lunged at Rollo. Rollo jumped to his feet and hurled himself through a kitchen window, shattering the glass. He landed on a narrow metal fire escape, shook off the glass shards, and scrambled to the ground.

"Agile little bugger," Larry said, looking down at Rollo, who was limping away, dripping blood.

Riley struggled to breathe, to open her eyes, to rise out of the suffocating darkness and into the light. The first face that swam into view was Emerson's. The second face she saw was the big guy with the scar.

"What? Who?" Riley asked.

Emerson leaned close and shouted at her. "I AM EMERSON KNIGHT!"

"Crap on a cracker," Riley said.

Emerson moved back. "Precisely. And the large man to my right is Larry Quiller. Larry was my chauffeur when I was a child."

"Very pleased to meet you," Riley said to Larry.

"Likewise," Larry said.

Riley looked at her wrists. Not slit. Good deal.

"Rollo was going to kill me," she said.

"Fortunately we arrived in time to prevent that," Emerson said. "We were parked across the street waiting for you when we saw Rollo go into your apartment house. We thought it more prudent to intercept you rather than try to root Rollo out before you got home. I was on a phone call when you drove past us and parked in the back, so I sent Larry to retrieve you."

Riley pushed herself up to a sitting position, and Larry helped her to her feet.

"Larry scared the bejeepers out of me," Riley said. "I thought he was one of Werner Grunwald's henchmen."

Emerson glanced at Larry. "He does have an imposing presence."

"I try to keep fit," Larry said.

"Now what?" Riley asked.

"We're disappearing," Emerson said. "And we're going on the hunt. I intend to find the missing gold. Larry has agreed to help us."

"Yep, I'm coming out of retirement to do some chauffeuring for Emerson. Just like old times."

"*Us?*" Riley asked Emerson. "Like, you and me?"

"Of course," Emerson said. "You can't continue at Blane-Grunwald. They're trying to kill you. And since you're unemployed, I'll hire you. You can be my apprentice."

"Your apprentice *what*?"

"Whatever I am."

"Criminy."

"Ask him for two weeks' paid vacation," Larry said.

"Vacation is a dated concept," Emerson said. "No one of any consequence takes a vacation."

"What about all those trips you took to commune with the Siddhar?" Riley asked.

"I didn't have a job, therefore they weren't vacations. They were extensions of my life experience."

Riley returned to the refrigerator and pulled out the loaf of bread, the ham, the cheese, and the mustard. Her life experience told her she was hungry.

"Were you able to retrieve any of my things?" Riley asked Emerson. "My phone? My wallet?"

"All safely locked away at the Carlyle. If we're going to go off the grid we must do so completely. No more cellphones. No more Internet. No more credit cards. Nothing that can leave a footprint in cyberspace."

"I feel like a fugitive."

"Quite the opposite, but I see the comparison," Emerson said.

Riley made three sandwiches, wrapped them in aluminum foil, and handed them over to Emerson. She went to her bedroom, threw some underwear and other basic essentials into a small backpack, and returned to the kitchen.

"What about my broken window?" she asked.

"After I do my chauffeuring I can come back and fix the door and the window," Larry said.

SIXTEEN

⟨※⟩

LARRY STEERED HIS HONDA CIVIC DOWN A back road that ran parallel with Rock Creek Park and turned in to an isolated cemetery. It was a boneyard straight out of an old black-and-white horror movie, filled with mausoleums, tombstones, and weird statues. It was built on a slope that dipped down into the wilderness of the park, and Larry drove down the rutted, bumpy road to the furthest edge of the burial ground.

They stopped in front of an old, lichen-covered monument that read KNIGHT in bold letters.

"Holy moly, it's a family crypt," Riley said.

"Yes, but I don't plan to be buried here," Emerson said, getting out of the car. "I'm going to be stuffed and put on display in my parlor."

"You're joking this time, right?"

"Maybe."

Emerson walked to the Knight memorial and knelt at the foot of a statue of a shrouded woman dressed in flowing robes, her face turned down in sorrow. Riley got out of the Civic and took a closer look at the statue. It was haunting and oddly erotic at the same time. A cold breeze rattled the leaves of a nearby oak tree, and Riley zipped her sweatshirt up to her neck.

"She's beautiful," Riley said, looking at the statue.

"Yes, that's my great-great-grandfather's mistress. Lamont senior commissioned this statue of her. He wanted it to be so beautiful that his wife would never visit his grave. That way, he said, he'd have peace in the hereafter even if he couldn't have it in this life."

"Maybe his wife would have been nicer to him if he didn't cheat on her with this sad lady here."

Emerson brushed some moss from the edge of a large flat piece of marble at the base of the monument. "I need to move this stone," he said.

Larry took one end and Emerson took the other. After a few moments of straining and pulling they were able to inch the stone back and expose a metal ring. Emerson tugged on the ring and the base of the monument dropped out, revealing a small fissure just large enough for a man to pass through.

"Meet us at the designated spot," Emerson said to Larry.

"I'll be there," Larry said. "You can count on me. And I'll put everything back in place here before I leave."

Emerson hung his rucksack on one shoulder, pulled a penlight out of his pocket, and pointed it at a dark stone staircase that disappeared under the monument. "Follow me."

"Down?"

"Of course."

"No way! Are you insane? God knows what's down there. Worms and spiders and dead people."

"And?"

"And I don't like any of those things."

"Pity. They're all rather interesting."

"Not to me," Riley said. "I'm staying aboveground."

"'Let us sit upon the ground and tell sad stories of the death of kings.'"

"That's Shakespeare, right?"

"So they would have you believe. My great-grandfather Lamont junior didn't, however. He spent a good deal of the fortune he inherited trying to prove that Edward de Vere was the real author of those plays. That and alcoholism were Lamont junior's main hobbies. He was an early version of what we would now call a conspiracy enthusiast. He believed, among other things, that the world was hollow and that the city of Atlantis still thrived there, controlled by the Freemasons who were infiltrating society and trying to take over the world."

"In other words, he was a nut."

"Perhaps. He also believed, against all rational thought—this was in 1910, mind you—that the government was going to prohibit alcohol consumption in all forty-six states. So he built this tunnel."

"He was a bootlegger?"

"Not in the least. He merely wanted to maintain his supply. And to have an avenue of escape when the lizard people took over."

"So this tunnel leads to your house?"

"Presumably. I've never actually used it. Care to find out? We'd be like urban explorers, only more subterranean."

An odd choking sound escaped from his lips. Riley guessed it was a laugh.

"Is that you joking?" she asked.

"I have my lighter side."

"Just warn me before you use it, okay? And why do you have to go to your house?"

"I have money there. And supplies. Since I'm fairly certain the house is being watched, we have to get in surreptitiously."

"How about you go to the house and I wait here?"

"I'm afraid that would ruin my plan. The timing would be off. I would have to leave you behind, and you know what would happen then."

"Rollo would find me and kill me?"

"Possibly, but I was referring to the fact that it's beginning to rain and you would get wet."

Riley looked up at the thick cloud cover. Yup, she thought, it was definitely beginning to rain. She pulled her sweatshirt hood over her head and narrowed her eyes at Emerson.

"You'd better know what you're doing," she said.

"Indeed," Emerson said, descending into the stygian darkness of the underworld.

The tunnel was surprisingly large and in surprisingly good shape for a little-used secret passage. They walked rapidly along the smooth, dark surface toward an unseen end, their way lit only by Emerson's little flashlight. Their footfalls echoed off the moist tunnel walls. The smell of damp earth clogged Riley's throat.

Just keep going, she thought. It has to lead *somewhere*. She stepped on something that squeaked and scurried away. She put her hand to her heart and bit into her lower lip.

"Crap on a cracker," she whispered.

"Such a colorful expression," Emerson said. "Keep walking."

"I'm going to get you for this," Riley hissed at Emerson. "I don't know what I'll do, but it will be something horrible."

"I shall look forward to it," Emerson said. "Life is an adventure." He paused for a beat. "Will it be sexual?"

Riley struggled to find her voice. "Why on earth would you think it would be sexual?"

"I don't know," Emerson said. "It just popped into my head."

"Would you like it to be sexual?"

"I might," Emerson said. "That would be interesting."

"Crickey!" Riley said.

• • •

They reached the end of the tunnel and looked up at an overhead grate. Emerson pounded on it a few times and the grate popped free, showering bits of rust down on their upturned faces. They pulled themselves out, and Riley looked around in the dim light.

"Where are we?" she asked Emerson.

"In the basement of Mysterioso Manor. I recognize the Egyptian sarcophagus on the far wall."

Riley's eyes widened. "Is there a mummy in there?"

"If rumor is to be believed," Emerson said. "I've been meaning to check but it will have to wait. Come along."

Riley trailed after him up a flight of stairs, through a closed door, and along a vast hallway. They ran into Aunt Myra on the second floor.

"For goodness' sakes," Myra said. "This is a nice surprise. Have you had lunch? I could make sandwiches."

"No time," Emerson said. "We're preparing to go off the grid. And you aren't supposed to be here. I texted you and told you to go back to Harrisonburg and wait for word."

"Good Lord, I don't read those text things. They're always Nigerian princes asking for money or some such."

"Fascinating, but not at all relevant," Emerson said, turning on his heel. "You've placed yourself in a dangerous situation. Everyone follow me."

"He sounds just like his father when he gets that tone," Myra said to Riley. "Authoritative. The Knight men have always been leaders. Of course, they were also philanderers and lunatics."

"A mixed legacy," Riley said, lengthening her stride to keep up with Emerson.

"Yes," Myra said. "There's a bit of scoundrel in the bloodline. The jury is still out on Emerson."

Emerson pulled up at the end of the hall, where a narrow winding staircase led to the tower room. "I haven't yet reached my full potential," he said, looking back at Riley. "The Knights are late bloomers. It's likely that in a few more years I'll be a rutting bastard." He motioned her through the door. "Be careful on the stairs."

Riley was pretty sure this was Emerson having a sense of humor . . . but then maybe not.

The staircase ended at a small landing and a single closed door. Emerson opened the door and crossed to a large freestanding safe that looked to Riley as if it belonged in a mob movie. The room itself was a round turret with windows on three sides and a stunning view of D.C. and the surrounding park. With the Washington Monument and the Capitol off in the distance, it looked like a picture postcard. The furnishings were rustic Victorian. She could picture Mark Twain sitting at the rolltop desk, eyeing intruders into his lair with an expression of disapproval.

"This reminds me of my granddad's office, but the view is much better," Riley said.

"This was my father's hideaway," Emerson said, working the dial on the safe.

"His hideaway from what?"

"My stepmother," Emerson said.

The lock clicked and Emerson swung the door open and removed a large duffel bag.

"What's in the bag?" Riley asked.

"Money," Emerson said. "Rainy-day money. Plus some off-the-grid essentials."

"Where are we going?"

"'Over the mountains of the moon,'" Emerson said.

"The obscure literary quotes are getting old," Riley said.

"It's Edgar Allan Poe. 'Eldorado.' I've been thinking about Poe a lot lately. 'The Gold-Bug,' of course. And *The Narrative of Arthur Gordon Pym of Nantucket*, where the hero descends into the Hollow Earth. That's rather ironic, don't you think?"

"Yeah, ironic."

As if her life wasn't bad enough she had to be saddled with Emerson Knight, Riley thought.

"It's 'The Purloined Letter' that I keep coming back to," Emerson said. "You remember the story."

"Remind me. Quickly."

"Auguste Dupin, the very first fictional detective— a lot more impressive than that poser Sherlock Holmes—is tasked to find an incriminating letter. The room has been searched thoroughly but no letter has been found. Do you know where he finds it?"

"Right out in the open. Stuck on a mantel."

Emerson looked impressed. "You've read it?"

"My father was a county sheriff. All us kids read it."

"It's been staring us right in the face. The Grunwalds and McCabe. They've been stealing gold. Perhaps they've been stealing it for years. But no one noticed. Until I came along."

"Until *we* came along," Riley said.

"That doesn't have the same ring to it, but okay. The point is, why have they been stealing the gold? They're already rich. They couldn't spend the money they already have in a hundred lifetimes. Why take this kind of risk?"

Riley shrugged. "Greed. Arrogance. Maybe it's just a game to them."

"No. It's got to be more than a game. They've diligently and painstakingly infiltrated themselves into the highest levels of our government. And, they're not limiting themselves to stealing from the Blane-Grunwald vault. They're stealing from the Federal Reserve, and the Chairman of the Fed is complicit."

"I met him in person when they were questioning me about you. He's taking orders from Werner. He's just one of their lapdogs, like Rollo."

"Interesting," Emerson said. "So they control both the world's gold supply and the Federal Reserve. They're trying to take control of the United States government."

"That's just a conspiracy theory," Riley said. "Our financial system isn't even based on gold anymore. It hasn't been since the seventies."

"Then what *is* it based on? It's based on trust. Belief in the United States government." He removed a dollar bill from his pocket. "It's printed right on all our money. *Federal Reserve Note.* It's only worth a dollar because the government says it is. You need to believe that the government will protect its value. Otherwise, it's just a worthless piece of paper. But what if that government responsible for safeguarding the money supply is exposed as incompetent? Or worse, what if the U.S. government is the one doing the stealing? Our currency would plunge overnight. It would be total and devastating financial chaos on a global scale."

Emerson's iPad was beeping inside his rucksack. He pulled it out, tapped in his security code, and the floor plans for Mysterioso Manor appeared on the screen.

"The flashing red dots indicate where the security has been breached," Emerson said.

"There are a lot of them," Riley said. "There are flashing dots all over the place."

"Yes," Emerson said. "We have visitors."

SEVENTEEN

─────※※─────

EMERSON CROSSED TO A FULL-LENGTH MIRROR set into the wall and pressed the palm of his hand against the glass. A clicking sound came from behind the mirror, which opened like Aladdin's cave.

"A fingerprint scanner?" Riley asked.

Myra shook her head. "You boys and your toys."

"It gets even better," Emerson said. "It's also a two-way mirror. When the salesman pitched it, I couldn't resist."

Everyone squeezed into the narrow space behind the mirror, and Emerson pulled the massive door shut. No one spoke, and in the absolute silence Riley's heartbeat rocked her body. She told herself she was safe behind the silvered sheet of glass, but she didn't believe it. Not for a moment. She saw the door to the tower room open and instinctively stepped back, bumping into Emerson.

Rollo entered the room accompanied by five men in assault gear, rifles held at their hips. He glanced briefly at the mirror, the high tower windows, the conical ceiling, and then his attention swung to the safe.

"The safe is open and empty," Rollo said, more to himself than to the men. "He's been here and moved on to another room." He turned to one of the men. "Stay here. You have a good view of the grounds should he try to leave the house."

Emerson tapped Riley on the shoulder and maneuvered her flat to the wall while he quietly lifted a trapdoor. Light was dim to nonexistent, but Riley could see the hint of a stairwell winding away from the opening. Emerson curled Riley's hand around his penlight and eased her forward.

"Take it slow. You're going to lead us out of here," he whispered, his lips skimming her ear.

Riley felt a shiver rip through her, the result of an unsettling mixture of absolute terror from their situation and pleasure from Emerson's touch. She cautiously lowered herself through the trapdoor and began creeping down the narrow stairs, fighting the panic of claustrophobia. The stairs had been set between the outer wall of the tower and the inner wall of the stairwell they'd originally climbed. Myra was directly behind Riley, and Emerson was behind Myra. Emerson had the rucksack over his shoulder and the duffel bag clutched to his chest, and Riley could hear the rucksack occasionally scrape the wall.

The stairs ended at a small narrow landing.

"Now what?" Riley whispered.

"It's a door," Emerson said. "There's a touch latch high on the right side."

Riley ran her hand up the door, found the touch latch, and the door opened into a long, windowless passage.

"This will take us to the garage," Emerson said.

"How did they know we were in the house?" Riley asked.

"I imagine they tracked me through my iPad," Emerson said. "I've turned it off and I'll destroy it when I get the chance."

They quickly traveled the length of the passage and came to another door with another high touch latch. Emerson opened the door and they walked into a large utility closet. He cracked the door of the closet, looked out, and jerked his head back in.

"There's an armed guard standing three cars down," Emerson said to Riley. "I can disable him but I need you to distract him."

Riley went wide-eyed. "How am I supposed to distract him? What if I startle him and he shoots me?"

"You're female," Emerson said. "Females distract males all the time. Just go out there and use your feminine wiles."

"I don't have any wiles," Riley said. "Harvard Law

didn't offer that course. I don't know how to distract men."

"Nonsense," Emerson said. "You distract me all the time."

"Good heavens," Myra said. "We're never gonna get out of here. Get out of my way. I'll distract him."

Myra let herself out and marched up to the guard.

"Hey," Myra said. "What are you doing here in Mr. Knight's garage?"

"Halt," the guard said, shouldering his rifle. "Who goes there?"

"Honey, you've been watching too much television," Myra said. "No one talks like that. I'm the Knights' housekeeper and I'm looking for their armadillo. The whole family is batty. They got a pet armadillo. Can you imagine?"

"I haven't seen it," the guard said. "You need to go back to the house."

"You remind me of my son. He has curly hair just like you. At least I think so. I don't see all that good with the cataracts. And I got a big speck of something in my one eye." Myra circled around the guard and pulled her eyelid up. "Do you see anything in there?"

"No, ma'am," the guard said, turning toward Myra, keeping her in his sights. "You need to go to the house."

"Well, it's killing me," Myra said. "There's something sticking in my eye! *Owww! OWWW! WOWWW!*"

In an instant Emerson was out of the closet and at the guard's back. Emerson put his hand to the guard's neck and the guard collapsed like a puppet whose strings had been cut.

Riley followed after Emerson. "Omigod," she said. "You killed him."

"Not nearly," Emerson said. "There are ninety-six *thodu varmam* points in the human body. Some points can actually reduce the number of days in a person's life. Some points just rearrange the *sara* and *kalai ottam*. The ancient Siddhars used *urakka kaalam* for anesthetic purposes to induce sleep when performing surgery. That's what I did. He'll be fine in an hour or so."

Emerson crossed to a '72 Jarama 400 GT Lamborghini. A four-seat beauty, all sky blue and sleek Italian perfection. "I believe this will do," he said to Riley. "You drive."

"You expect me to drive out of here?"

"Yes."

"The place is crawling with armed men."

"Most likely," Emerson said. "So you should drive very fast."

Riley pushed a stray strand of hair off her face. "Great. Give me the keys."

"The keys," Emerson said. "That's unfortunate."

"Why?"

"I don't have any. They're kept in a key closet in the kitchen."

"So hot-wire it," Myra said.

Emerson and Riley went blank-faced.

"Lordy," Myra said. "They don't teach you kids any skills these days."

She stepped over to the tool bench on the back wall, selected a small screwdriver, and used it to remove the panel covering the car's steering column. She disconnected the red wires from the ignition cylinder and used the screwdriver's tip to strip the ends from the wires, then twisted them together and dashboard lights came on.

"That's stage one," she said. "Here comes the tricky part. The starter." She isolated the brown wire from the tangle of cables, disconnected it, and carefully stripped the insulation off with the screwdriver.

"Get ready to rev the engine," Myra said. She took the brown wire, touched it to the exposed red wires, and it sparked. Riley hit the gas and the engine turned over.

Everyone jumped in, and Riley took off through the open garage door. A fleet of black SUVs clogged the driveway and blocked the exit.

"Go right," Emerson said.

Riley glanced over at him. "There's no road there."

"Is that a problem?"

Riley wrenched the wheel to the right, and the Lamborghini bumped over the lawn toward the conservatory. Riley checked the rearview mirror and saw the assault team running for their SUVs.

"Where am I going?" she asked.

"That way," Emerson said, pointing to the zebra enclosure.

"How do I get around the fence?"

"You don't."

Riley narrowed her eyes, leaned on the horn to warn

the zebras, and raced toward the chain-link fence. "Have air bags been installed in this car?"

BANG! The Lamborghini plowed into the fence, knocked a section to the ground, and rolled over it.

"No," Emerson said. "No air bags."

Riley sped through the pasture with the Lamborghini bucking and caroming over the rough ground.

"Are the SUVs gaining on us?" Riley asked.

"Not so much," Myra said. "They're having a tussle with the zebras, being that the zebras are through the hole in the fence and stampeding all over the place. So far one SUV has hit a tree and a second one's flipped over."

"What about the zebras?"

"The zebras are having a good time," Myra said.

Riley had a white-knuckle grip on the wheel. "We're coming to the end of the open pasture."

"The fence extends into the woods," Emerson said. "If you look carefully you'll see a narrow break in the trees where a path leads to an old stone-and-iron gate."

Riley slowed to a crawl and turned onto the path. She stopped at the gate, and Emerson jumped out and opened it. Riley drove to the other side and into an affluent suburban neighborhood. Emerson closed the gate, pitched his laptop into a small pond that backed up to the gate, and got back into the car.

"That gate looked a lot less substantial than the chain-link we demolished. Couldn't we have just knocked it off its hinges?" she asked Emerson.

"Yes, but that gate's almost a hundred years old,"

Emerson said. "I wouldn't want to destroy it. And it keeps the zebras out of the neighborhood swimming pools."

Riley drove to Fourteenth Street and parked a block away from the Columbia Heights metro stop.

"Now what?" she asked Emerson.

"Now we take the yellow line train to Virginia," Emerson said.

"I don't mean to talk out of school," Myra said, "but shouldn't we be going to the police?"

Emerson shook his head. "We're dealing with corruption at the very highest level and we have no idea how it trickles down. At the very least we would be detained and remanded to involved authorities."

Myra raised an eyebrow. "Do I want to know what the heck is going on?"

"It's the NSA," Riley told her.

"It's not the NSA," Emerson said. "If it was the NSA they would have caught us leaving the estate. They would have had helicopters and a fleet of cars all through the neighborhood to track us down no matter what we did. As it was, the operation at Mysterioso was limited to a small number of men."

"That's comforting," Myra said, rolling her eyes.

"It *is*," Emerson said. "It means that the U.S. government isn't behind this. Just an incredibly powerful cabal *within* the U.S. government."

"This is about the blog, isn't it?" Myra asked.

They had reached the train platform and Emerson pulled up. "You read the blog?"

"Of course," Myra said. "It's just about like having a son and a nephew on television. You're almost famous."

"Astonishing," Emerson said. "I rather like that."

"And I can always tell when you're the one writing the blog," Myra said. "You use more words than Vernon, and sometimes I have to look them up."

"I have a superior vocabulary," Emerson said. "In fact, it's superior in four different languages."

Riley cut her eyes to him. "You only speak four languages?"

"At a superior level," Emerson said.

The yellow line train glided into the station, and Emerson, Riley, and Myra stepped on board and found a near-empty car. A half hour later the train crossed the Potomac into Alexandria.

"This is our stop," Emerson said, rising as the doors opened at Huntington Station.

Everyone shuffled off the train, and Larry met them on the platform. "I had a feeling you'd be on this one," he said. "I'm parked in the lot."

"So Emmie's got you mixed up in this too," Myra said.

"Just like old times," Larry said. "Not too many dull moments when you work for the Knights."

"What sort of car do we have?" Emerson asked Larry.

"It's a nice big sedan. A Cadillac. I borrowed it from my cousin. It'll be good for the trip."

"Trip?" Riley asked.

"We're taking Aunt Myra home to Harrisonburg," Emerson said.

"Let me get this straight," Werner said to Rollo. "You knew where they were. You had them cornered. You went in with an entire unit. And you came out with nothing."

It was late at night and Werner and Rollo were standing on a shadowed, deserted street corner. Both men were armed, Rollo with a surgical knife, Werner with a semiautomatic that was neatly concealed by the line of his suit jacket.

"They weren't alone," Rollo said.

"I've already been briefed on your failure. They had a sixty-five-year-old woman helping them. You can't be expected to overcome odds like that."

Rollo's eyes were popped out even more than usual. Freakish glistening white orbs in his pale face.

"I'll get them," Rollo said. "You don't have to worry."

"You're the one who should be worrying," Werner said. "We're very near the completion of all our plans. If you fail me again and put the mission in jeopardy, I'll have you gutted and filleted like a fish. I'll do it myself and I'll use your personal knife."

EIGHTEEN

———❧———

LARRY AND MYRA CHATTED IN THE FRONT
seat. Their words were a monotone hum to Riley.
Emerson was in his zone. His body was warm and
masculine next to hers. She suspected his mind was on
a distant astral plane. It was black beyond the windows.
The road in front of them was illuminated only by the
Cadillac's headlights. Endless strips of white hypnotically
coming at them. The tedium of the drive was a narcotic,
and Riley drifted into sleep, waking when the car slowed
for a turn or stoplight, and then drifting off again
when the momentum returned.

She surfaced from her dreamless drifting and realized
the car had stopped. She sat up and squinted through
the windshield at a big black chunk of something and

blazing lights. Her head cleared and she recognized Vernon's RV.

"This is Harrisonburg?" Riley asked.

"I don't exactly live *in* Harrisonburg," Myra said. "I mostly live *close* to Harrisonburg. This here's Blue Ridge country."

Riley got out of the car and looked up. There were a lot of stars in the sky. More than she'd seen in a long time. Vernon's RV was parked just past some railroad tracks. A Blake Shelton song was playing somewhere inside the RV and spilling out the open door.

Vernon strolled over, coffee cup in his hand, and grinned down at Riley. "We got the RV all tuned up for you and it's ready to go."

"Go?" Riley said. "In an RV?"

"That's so you get to your destination in style and comfort," Vernon said. "And it's real secretive. You don't have to stop at a motel and give out your name. We even got it loaded up with food."

Riley had two thoughts. The first was that Vernon's grin was deadly good. And the second was that she had no clue where they were going. She was in whatever this was up to her armpits, and she wasn't being included in the decision-making process. Not acceptable.

"We need a word," Riley said to Emerson.

"Yes?"

"In private."

"In my experience, when girls get that steely eye look and use that tone it's never good," Vernon said to Emerson. "You must have done something bad."

"I can't imagine what it might be," Emerson said.

Riley leaned forward and poked him in the chest. "How about ruining my life?" Poke. "How about not consulting me on any of your nutso plans?" Poke. "And you didn't eat the sandwich I made for you."

"I don't like white bread," Emerson said.

"That's ridiculous," Riley said. "Everyone likes white bread."

"You're going into a land of hurt with this woman," Vernon said to Emerson. "She's pretty as all get-out but she's not dumb, and you're going to have to rearrange your thinking if she's a keeper."

"My thinking is perfect," Emerson said. "What do you mean . . . 'keeper'?"

Vernon hung an arm on Emerson's shoulder. "Son, you need to come with me. I got some homemade hooch in the RV that'll set it all straight."

Emerson followed Vernon into the RV, and Myra turned to Riley.

"Sometimes it's hard to tell who's the smart one," Myra said.

"Have they always been friends?"

"Ever since they were little boys. Emerson used to get shipped off to spend some of his summer with his 'country relatives.' We loved him dearly but he could be a trial. Even as a little boy he had a persistent personality."

"How did you get to be country relatives? You must have had the same privileged childhood as your brother."

"When I was four, my mother walked out on her marriage and left the Knight money behind. She took me with her. My brother, Mitchell, was fourteen and stayed with his daddy. When our father died, all the money went to him. It was just as well, because I've always been happy here in the mountains."

"I get the impression Emerson wasn't close to his father."

"Mitchell wasn't close to anyone. Not even his wives. Except for Bertram Grunwald. Mitchell and Bertram met at the University of Virginia and were instant chums. That's how they put it. Chums. After college they stayed chums. They shared a lot of interests."

"Such as?"

"Economics, poker, whores, and rockets. They used to fire them off from Rock Creek Park."

"The whores or the rockets?"

"Both, I think. This was before Mitchell and Bertram conquered the world. They never forgot how they started, though. Just two rich kids with a dream to get even richer. Though Mitchell was far richer to start with.

"They used to get together for poker games every Wednesday. Even when Bertram Grunwald was teaching at Harvard, Emerson's father used to fly up there for the game. That was how he gave Professor Grunwald his first million, by deliberately losing to him. It was their little joke."

"Emerson doesn't seem to be friends with the Grunwald boys."

"They never hit it off. And they didn't get to see much of each other. There was a big difference in age."

"Emerson's father must have been devastated when Bertram died."

"I suppose. Although it's rumored they had a falling-out shortly before Bertram passed. I don't know what that was about."

Riley looked around. "It's hard to see in the dark, but it looks like Vernon's RV is all alone here. Where's your house?"

"My place is down the road a bit," Myra said. "Vernon lives here in a cabin tucked into the woods. He likes it here because he's right on a good fishing pond. We've got a couple hundred acres of property between us. Most of it's uphill and downhill. Larry can stay in the RV and the rest of us can all stay in Vernon's little cabin tonight. I guess tomorrow you and Emerson will be taking off. I imagine he has a plan all laid out."

Vernon's cabin was half a notch above a man cave. Not a lot of frills but clean and comfortable, with indoor plumbing and a flat-screen television. Riley slept in the loft, where she was stuffed into a sleeping bag. Vernon and Myra had bedrooms, and Emerson slept on the sofa in front of the fireplace. Everyone was up early drinking coffee and eating Myra's pancakes.

"You know how to drive a Redhawk, right?" Vernon asked Riley.

"Not only can I drive it," Riley said, "I can change the oil and rotate the tires."

"Good to know she's gonna be taken care of," Vernon

said. "She's borrowed from my friend Andy Gattle. He's got a bunch of these old girls that he rents out to city people looking for a country experience. I gave him a jug of our special moonshine for it, and he brought it over at the crack of dawn all gassed up and everything."

"I thought we were taking *your* RV."

"No way," Vernon said. "You're going off the grid. You take mine and the feds will be on you like flies on a fruitcake."

They hiked a short distance in the chill mountain air, and Vernon handed keys over to Riley. "Your RV is the one next to mine. She's a beauty, right?"

Riley bit into her lower lip to keep from whimpering. It was a total hunk of junk. Rust everywhere. Nondescript paint job. She thought it might have at some point been painted with rainbow colors. Bumper sticker from Mama Jolene's Campground, and another advertising the NRA. Hula girl bobblehead on the dashboard.

"I know it looks a little over the hill," Vernon said, "but Andy keeps his girls tuned up and ready to roll. Plus you got an extra case of motor oil in the storage under your vehicle in case you need it."

Riley climbed into the driver's seat, and Emerson climbed in next to her. What few worldly possessions they had were stashed in the back, and Emerson had his rucksack at his feet.

Riley started the engine, slammed the Redhawk into reverse, and took out a lawn chair. She put it in park and leaned out the window. "Sorry about that, Vernon."

"Never mind that old chair," Vernon said. "I got three more."

Riley eased the Redhawk off Vernon's property, down the country road, and pointed it at the highway.

"Son," she said to Emerson, "we're going on a road trip."

"You sound like Vernon."

"I like Vernon. He reminds me of my brothers."

Emerson took a large fold-up map of the United States out of his rucksack and opened it. A bright yellow line had been traced across it with a highlighter.

"I'm guessing the yellow line is our route," Riley said. "What's at the end of it?"

"Nevada. When we were in Günter's office I showed you a note that said 'Shipments made to Groom Lake.' In light of all that's happened I feel it could be significant. Günter's office had been swept clean, but this note was handwritten on a yellow pad and overlooked."

"Groom Lake and Area 51 are all within Nellis Air Force Base," Riley said.

"Precisely. It's a top-secret government installation. People have theorized for years about what goes on there, but the NSA keeps them away."

"Everyone knows that aliens are kept at Area 51 along with all the *X-Files* and *Close Encounters* doodads," Riley said.

"Doodads?"

"That's the technical term."

"I suspect possibly a quarter of the world's gold

supply, some of which is mine, is being housed there along with the doodads."

"And you've reached this conclusion on the basis of five words written on a piece of paper?"

"Correct."

I'm hooked up with a fruitcake, Riley thought. The man takes the term "loose cannon" to a whole new level. He's a loose cannon with a bunch of nuts and bolts missing.

"I'd feel better about this road trip if you had something a little more concrete driving your gold theory," Riley said.

"Sometimes one must take a leap of faith," Emerson said. "Follow the yellow line."

Riley blew out a sigh and headed down Interstate 81. She hadn't driven a monster like the Redhawk in years, and she'd forgotten how cumbersome they were to maneuver. The reaction time was slow on the brakes and steering, and gusting wind rocked it side to side.

They stopped for lunch in Tennessee, and Riley studied the map while she ate her bacon cheeseburger. Emerson had chosen a southern route taking them through Nashville, Oklahoma, and the Texas Panhandle. They'd be passing very close to Bishop Hills, her hometown. It would be tempting to stop in and see her family, but Riley couldn't see it happening. They were supposed to be off the grid. She knew that included more than electronics. It included family. And most important, she didn't want to put them in jeopardy.

"What are we going to do when we get to you-know-where?" Riley asked Emerson.

"Look around."

"I am *not* breaking into any more gold vaults."

"I doubt the gold is kept in a normal vault," Emerson said. "That would be too obvious."

"I'm also not breaking into a high-security military installation," Riley said.

"We'll see."

"No! There's no 'we'll see.' People get shot doing things like that. And it's very against the law. What would the Siddhar think of that?"

"I haven't spoken to the Siddhar about it."

"Who is this guy anyway? Is he like Yoda?"

"He's more like Master Po. From *Kung Fu Panda*."

"Okay, but what is he like? Where does he come from? How old is he?"

"He's like himself. I don't know how old he is or where he comes from. He lives in a monastery outside Port Blair in the Andaman Islands."

"How did you meet him?"

"It was when I was sailing around the world. I dropped anchor at Corbyn's Cove in the Andamans. He was in the water. I saved him from drowning."

"Drowning? If he was so wise, why didn't he know how to swim?"

"Why don't I know how to drive? There are some holes in everyone's knowledge. The point is that I was lost. I was wandering. He saved me, as well."

"I can see that."

"He is still teaching me many things. The traditional medicine of the villages of Tamil Nadu. The *varmam* martial arts. The ultimate goal is to attain the *videha mukti*."

"What's that?"

"Leaving the body at the time of death. To attain an unbroken union with the divine and blend into the transcendent Self."

"That's heavy."

"I'm told at the time of death it feels quite light."

"Looks to me like you're a part-time student."

"I suppose that's true. I have responsibilities now. Perhaps that's not such a bad thing. The Siddhar likens my plight to the story of Kaubathar. Once upon a time, Pathanjali took the form of Adisesha and stayed in the Thillai forests for a long time. He wanted to teach the *vyagarana suthiram* to his disciples. However, Pathanjali was afraid that, since he was in the form of Adisesha, his disciples would be burnt to death when they came near him. So he made a partition between himself and his disciples. But the students were anxious to see the master's face. One student pulled the partition down. All the students were immediately burned to a crisp."

"Remind me not to have you tell my kids bedtime stories."

"One of the students, Kaubathar, did not attend the lecture on that day. Pathanjali was happy that one of his disciples was alive, so he changed his form to one less fatal and taught all his skills to Kaubathar."

"Is that the end? Is there a moral to that story?"

"Sometimes being away from your teacher is the best lesson. In a manner of speaking. I am here in body. There in spirit."

"That explains it."

"What?"

"A lot. And, by the way, I have no idea who Pathanjali or Adisesha are. I imagine Adisesha is something horrible, and Pathanjali doesn't sound like a treat either."

"I can drive, you know," Emerson said. "It's just that it's been a while and my license has lapsed. I imagine driving a car is like riding a bicycle. Once you learn, you never really forget. Of course, I never learned how to ride a bicycle, so I couldn't say if that's true."

"Maybe I'll keep driving."

NINETEEN

———— ❦ ————

Riley got off the highway at Jackson, Tennessee, and found a Walmart.

"We need necessities," she said. "Clothes and food."

"I asked Vernon to stock food for us," Emerson said.

"I looked through the cabinets and fridge. They're filled with beer and chips and beef jerky. Get some money out of the duffel bag. We're going shopping."

An hour later they had new sweatshirts and jeans, all of the basic food groups plus M&M's, and the RV tank full of diesel fuel.

"We can park here for the night," Riley said. "No one would think of looking for Emerson Knight in a Walmart parking lot."

. . .

Riley slept in a T-shirt and sweatpants in the cab-over bunk and Emerson took the queen bed in the back. Emerson slept like the dead, and Riley woke with every sound. A little before seven she stuffed her feet into her sneakers, zipped up her new sweatshirt, and shuffled off to Walmart. She returned minutes later with coffee and doughnuts.

"You made the morning news," she said to Emerson. "Me too. It's awful. They had the snack bar television tuned to a Washington station, and the news came on while I was waiting for fresh coffee. The conjecture is that you and an accomplice broke into my apartment and kidnapped me. They described you as an eccentric billionaire gone berserk. Anyone seeing either of us should contact the authorities immediately."

"Did they show pictures of us?"

"Yes. You were in a tux and you had a ponytail. I almost didn't recognize you. My picture looked like a mug shot. I think it was taken on my first day at Blane-Grunwald for my employment file."

"Did anyone recognize you?"

"Not that was apparent, but we should get on the road. A lot of people saw us yesterday while we were shopping and getting fuel. I'm sorry I made us go shopping. It was a bad idea."

"Not at all. We had to stop for fuel anyway. At least they don't know where we're going. Not yet, anyway."

Eight hours later Riley pulled into a KOA campground on South Choctaw Road near Oklahoma City.

"I can't keep driving," Riley said. "I can't sit anymore, and I'm having a hard time staying awake."

"This should be okay as long as we don't give them our real names," Emerson said. "There's no reason why anyone should suspect we're in this motor home."

"We should have gotten disguises and fake IDs," Riley said.

"That would be helpful," Emerson said. "I didn't anticipate television coverage."

Riley hadn't anticipated *any* of this. She could barely believe it was happening. When she'd woken up this morning her first thought had been to decide what she should wear to work. This was instantly followed by a mental reboot, because there was no work. At least not at Blane-Grunwald.

She eased the Redhawk into visitor parking and Emerson went into the office to register. Not a lot going on in the campground. It was off-season on a weekday. Mostly empty spaces. Emerson returned and directed Riley to a spot toward the back of the campground.

"Who are we?" she asked.

"Mr. and Mrs. Dugan."

"We're married?"

"It seemed appropriate."

"You don't intend to act married, do you? I mean, at night and all."

"Do you think I should?"

"No!"

"Then I guess I won't."

There was a long silence.

"Was that awkward?" Emerson asked.

"Yes."

"I could cloud your mind so you don't remember."

"Do *not* mess with my mind. Why did you pick the name Dugan?"

"I had a dog named Dugan."

"What kind of dog?"

"Brown. I don't remember him very well. I was quite young and we didn't have him very long. He bit my father, and my father replaced him with a giraffe."

"You had a strange childhood."

"Everyone's childhood is strange. It prepares you for the strangeness of adulthood."

Riley maneuvered the RV into its assigned space, and Emerson jumped out and plugged them into the electrical hookup.

"All the comforts of home," Emerson said, back in the Redhawk, settling into a swivel club chair.

"No television."

"Is that important to you?"

"It would be nice to get the news," Riley said.

"I get the news on my computer."

"We don't have one of those either," Riley said.

"The news is overrated anyway," Emerson said. "We tried listening to the news on the radio this morning and it was depressing."

Riley was pacing in the RV, trying to get some exercise without going out and showing her face. They didn't have any immediate neighbors, but she thought the campground might have security cameras. She was freaked out enough. She didn't want the Grunwald goon squad breaking her door down in the middle of the night.

"I don't see how this is going to end well for us," Riley said.

"I have a plan."

"Does it involve fleeing to a foreign country and surrounding ourselves with bodyguards?"

"I'm going to find the stolen gold and expose the Grunwalds. They'll be put in jail and we'll be heroes."

"How are you going to do this?"

"I haven't got the details worked out."

"You have no clue."

"Not at the moment, but I'm sure it will come to me."

"You think the gold is hidden on the air force base."

"Yes. Or in the vicinity."

"Are you familiar with the air force base? Do you have a map? Aerial photographs? Inside information?"

"No, no, no, and no."

"That's not the answer I wanted to hear."

"I've made arrangements for a guide," Emerson said.

Riley nodded. "I guess that could work. It's someone reliable, right? Knows the area in and out?"

"I really don't know. Vernon made the arrangements."

"Oh boy."

"You grew up in Texas," Emerson said. "Groom Lake was practically in your backyard. You must have some familiarity with it."

"Nope. Just the usual urban legend. When we took

a vacation we opted for Six Flags. Groom Lake wasn't in the running. It's actually about a twelve-hour drive."

Riley was back on the road after another restless night. The sky was a brilliant blue and the air was crisp. Emerson was silent in the seat next to her. Her second cup of coffee of the day was in the cup holder. She was on Interstate 40 and in six hours they'd reach Amarillo. If she took loop 335 she'd be home in Bishop Hills.

Ten years ago she'd been the country girl going off on a great adventure, anxious to leave Texas. She loved her family but she'd wanted independence. She'd wanted to experience a larger world, to make her mark. And now here she was heading back to Texas under strange circumstances. Not the triumphant return she'd hoped for. And she wouldn't be taking the loop road this trip either. Too dangerous.

"I need to find a way to contact my parents and tell them I'm okay," Riley said.

"Understood. I'm sure I can find a way to make an untraceable contact when we get to Vegas."

He's on the hunt, Riley thought. He's stimulated by this. She could see it in his eyes and in his posture. She could feel the energy radiating off him. He wasn't the hunted. He was the hunter. And that's where they differed. She felt hunted. She was numb with disbelief that her life had taken this turn. She was going through the motions of putting one foot in front of the other and moving forward, but her heart wasn't in it. She was in survival mode, and Emerson had become the Caped Crusader. Okay, she admitted to herself, Emerson has probably *always* been the Caped Crusader. The man has no fear. It's all like a game to him.

The ache in her chest started an hour before they reached Amarillo. She was homesick. The road and the landscape were familiar and she could feel the pull of family. She hadn't been home since Christmas. Too long, she thought. If she somehow made it through this she'd visit more often.

They motored along without speaking, Emerson lost in his own thoughts, Riley not trusting her voice. They were on the outskirts of Amarillo, and Riley felt the ache begin to lift. The road was forcing her to look forward. They were approaching the no-man's-land between Amarillo and Tucumcari, New Mexico, now. One of those stretches where it seemed like the white lane lines went on forever and never seemed to reach human habitation.

She checked her side mirror and saw a vehicle approaching from the rear. It was a red Jeep traveling at high speed. In moments it was on her, passing her, and swerving back into her lane ahead of her. The Jeep instantly slowed to a crawl and Riley had to stomp on the brakes to keep from plowing into it. Riley pulled left to pass and the Jeep veered in front of her, blocking her.

"How odd," Emerson said, sitting up straighter in his seat.

"There's a second car on my back bumper," Riley said. "It's a black SUV."

PING! PING! PING! A bullet took out the side mirror.

"They're shooting at us," Riley said.

She slammed the brake pedal to the floor, the Redhawk fishtailed to a stop, and the black SUV crashed into the back of the motor home with a loud *BANG!* Riley pulled forward and stuck her head out the window. The entire front of the SUV was crumpled, and steam spewed out from under the hood.

The red Jeep came to a stop several car lengths in front of the Redhawk. The driver's door opened and Rollo jumped out and opened fire.

"Holy crap!" Riley said.

Emerson narrowed his eyes. "Ramming speed, Mr. Sulu."

Riley floored the gas pedal, ducked behind the steering wheel, and aimed for Rollo. Rollo continued to shoot, peppering the windshield, registering surprised horror only an instant before Riley bounced him off the front of the Redhawk and sent him airborne. She put the Redhawk into reverse and backed into Rollo's Jeep, pushing it off the road and into a ditch.

"Just in case he's not dead," Riley said.

Emerson raised an eyebrow. "This is a new side to you."

"I might have gotten carried away what with being shot at and all."

"I'm actually quite turned on."

"You're a very strange man."

"Thank you. I have my moments."

Rollo was a crumpled heap alongside the road, and the

man in the black SUV was on his feet and limping away from them. A car traveling in the oncoming lane pulled over and stopped. A good Samaritan looking to help.

"Do you suppose the hit-and-run rules apply when you've run over someone who tried to kill you?" Riley asked.

"I imagine it's a gray area."

A second car came to a stop in the oncoming lane. The drivers of both cars were out and running toward Rollo.

"We're not needed here," Riley said, pulling away from Rollo's car and easing the Redhawk back onto the road.

"I agree," Emerson said. "Time to move on."

Riley squinted through a small clear patch of glass in the windshield. "It's amazing that we're alive, considering how many rounds he pumped into this RV."

"The impact glass helped," Emerson said. "And he was sighting high."

"We're going to have to abandon the Redhawk. And it would be best if it wasn't found. I don't want to implicate Vernon's friend in this."

"I've instructed Vernon to say that the Redhawk was stolen, if anyone should ask. This won't reflect badly on him or his friend. We can leave the beast on the side of the road. Our larger problem will be getting to Nevada without it."

"We've got a ways to walk," Riley said. "And we're going to have to do it off-road, but I know where we can find a ride."

TWENTY

———∞∞∞———

DWAYNE MOON ALMOST CHOKED ON HIS Twizzler when he saw Riley walking toward his patrol car. He got out with his hand on his holstered Sig. The hand on the Sig was more muscle memory than thought.

"Riley? What are you doing here? We heard you were kidnapped." Dwayne cut his eyes to Emerson. "Is this the guy who kidnapped you? Should I shoot him?"

At twenty-nine, Dwayne Moon was a year older than his sister Riley, but she always thought of him as her baby brother. It was Riley who had taught Dwayne how to ride a two-wheel bike and a skateboard, not the other way around. She helped him with his homework. Taught him cursive handwriting. The multiplication tables. Spanish grammar. And how to nail a grasshopper at a hundred feet with their dad's old Smith & Wesson. Later, Riley taught him to drive a manual transmission.

For the past six years, Dwayne had been a highway patrolman. He spent most nights like he was spending this one, happily waiting in his speed trap under the Washington Street Bridge on I-40, radar gun at the ready.

"I wasn't kidnapped," Riley said. "This is my boss, Emerson Knight."

"Well, damn," Dwayne said, "I *told* Mom you weren't kidnapped. Why didn't you call her this week? She's been worried sick." He hauled back and studied Riley. "Are you sure you're not kidnapped? Maybe you got a case of what do you call it when you get a crush on your kidnapper? Stockroom syndrome?"

"It's called Stockholm syndrome, and I don't have it. And I didn't call Mom because we're off the grid. I don't have a phone." Riley sniffed at Dwayne's uniform. "I smell burger and onion rings."

"I just ate the burger, but I got onion rings left. You want some? I even got ranch dressing." He looked toward Emerson. "The three greatest contributions the United States made to world culture are jazz, rock and roll, and ranch dressing."

They all piled into Dwayne's patrol car, and Dwayne passed the onion rings around.

"You can use my phone to call Mom and Dad after I call you in," Dwayne said.

"You don't need to call us in," Riley said. "I'm fine. I wasn't kidnapped. There was no crime committed."

"The feds have a BOLO out for you. I got to bring you in."

"No, you don't."

"I'm a law enforcement officer, sis. I got responsibilities. How did you know I'd be here anyway?"

"You have to make your monthly quota. I figured you'd be at your favorite speed trap. How's it going?"

"For crap. Nobody speeds anymore. Gas prices are too high." Then he added, "You're looking good, sis."

"Thanks, so are you."

He nodded toward Emerson. "This guy treating you all right?"

"Yes, I am," Emerson said. "She's my amanuensis."

"I oughta punch you right in the mouth," Dwayne said.

Riley did an eye roll. "It means 'assistant.'"

"So I'm guessing you're off the grid because the feds are looking for you and you don't want to be found," Dwayne said. "I get why they're looking for you. They thought you were kidnapped. The big Q is why don't you want to be found?"

"Without going into a lot of detail, we're looking for some of Emerson's inheritance," Riley said. "It's . . . missing."

"Oh man, does this have to do with that missing gold scam?"

"How do you know about that?"

"Lowell won't shut up about it. He keeps going on about Miss M. and Mr. K." Dwayne's eyes opened wide and he gave a bark of laughter. "Hot damn! That's you isn't it? Miss M. The M stands for 'Moon.' Am I right? Am I right?"

"Perhaps I should cloud his mind," Emerson said.

"Too late," Riley said. "That ship sailed."

"Are you really that Mysterioso guy?" Dwayne asked Emerson.

"Sometimes," Emerson said. "Other times, no."

"Could I have your autograph?"

"No," Emerson said.

"We were following a lead on the gold when we had a transportation mishap," Riley said to Dwayne. "I was hoping I could borrow the GTO. Without Dad knowing about it."

"You mean you want to steal it?"

"Did I say 'steal'? No, I did not. I said 'borrow.'"

"What do I say when he finds out it's missing?"

"Tell him you took it to Jimmy to get serviced. Tell him the check oil light was on."

"He does all that himself. He doesn't trust Jimmy."

"Then tell him I stopped around and *borrowed* it and there was nothing you could do to stop me. And you can tell him I'm okay."

"He's gonna yell at me. I hate when he yells at me. And then Mom's gonna be mad because you didn't stop there and she's gonna cut me off from dessert. And tomorrow is meatloaf and chocolate cake. You owe me for this one. I might not even help you except it's not every day I get to meet a celebrity like Mysterioso. Wait until I tell Lowell. He's gonna poop himself."

• • •

Dwayne dropped Riley and Emerson off at Motel 5 on Interstate 40 and promised he'd be back in the morning. A week ago Riley would have thought twice about sharing a bed with a strange man, but now she was too tired to care. And she was thinking that Emerson was strange in a nonthreatening way that was sort of charming. One room for the two of them was okay with her. If the NSA or FBI broke down the door she'd rather not be alone.

So here she was at one A.M., wide awake with Emerson's arm casually thrown across her, his body radiating heat, his breathing even. They'd watched some television, crawled into bed with most of their clothes on, and Emerson had fallen asleep without incident. She was struggling. She was especially struggling for the last half hour when the arm curled around her. Crap on a cracker, she liked it! How horrible is that?

She finally found sleep somewhere around two A.M. When she woke up at six-thirty Emerson was showering. An hour later they checked out of the motel and walked across the street to a gas station convenience store to wait for their rendezvous with Dwayne. Riley had a Coke Slurpee and nachos, and Emerson ate three granola bars.

"Wow, three granola bars," Riley said. "Do you know how many calories you just swallowed?"

"I have a high rate of metabolism," Emerson said.

"And I probably consumed less than you did with those nachos."

"No way," Riley said. "The cheese is fake. There's almost no food value in the nachos and hardly any calories."

"Then why do you eat it?"

"It tastes good. And they didn't have any hot dogs."

"You would have a hot dog for breakfast?"

"Only if there weren't any cinnamon rolls."

The Pontiac GTO pulled into the parking lot. All thirty-five hundred pounds of it, growling the low rumbling sound that used to be the mating call of the American automotive industry.

Dwayne swung the heavy door open and climbed out, tossing Riley the keys. "It's all yours, sis. Don't scratch the paint."

"Did you tell Mom and Dad it was for me?"

"Yeah. Mom's stompin' around in a state. Dad says for you to be careful. He said to give you this." He handed Riley a heavy brown paper lunch bag.

Inside was their dad's old Smith & Wesson.

Riley teared up and nodded. "Tell him thanks. Can we drop you somewhere?"

"No. Freddie Schmidt is gonna pick me up and then we're going to the all-you-can-eat buffet at Big Bob's."

Emerson sat in the passenger seat, holding the gun awkwardly in his hands while Riley drove the GTO. "Is it loaded?" he asked.

"It's loaded."

"It belongs to your father?"

"Yep. My father used to be a sheriff."

"I remember. Was that difficult for you?"

"Not at all. He taught me how to use a gun. He also taught me right from wrong. I always wanted to grow up and help people. Somewhere in college I decided the best way to do that was to safeguard their money."

"That's what you're doing now," Emerson said. "On a global scale."

Riley hoped that was true.

They passed Albuquerque and Flagstaff and drove in silence. They stopped only for the occasional bathroom break or fast food drive-through, until twilight, when they saw the ambient light of Vegas in the distance.

Riley felt a stir of excitement in her chest. She loved Vegas. She loved the lights, the fountains, the size of the fakery, and the noise of the casinos. Most of all, she loved that she could soon get out from behind the wheel and into a comfy hotel room.

"We can't walk through a crowded hotel lobby," Emerson said. "Someone might recognize us and call us in. We need to find a motel where I can register us and you can go straight to the room."

"Are you going to cloud the clerk's mind when you register?"

"I doubt it will be necessary. I think I'm sufficiently disguised."

Riley agreed. He didn't look like the photo that was displayed by the news media. No more ponytail.

No perfectly tailored tuxedo. His hair now fell across his forehead and curled over his ears, and he had a three-day beard. He looked more like a pirate than a billionaire.

A half hour later Riley pulled into a budget motel five miles from the Strip. Emerson registered and they trudged up the stairs to their second-floor room. Riley threw her backpack on one of the two queen beds, and Emerson dumped his duffel bag and rucksack on the floor.

"Home sweet home," Riley said.

"They have complimentary coffee in the morning."

"And television and flush toilets."

"One really doesn't need much more than that," Emerson said.

"It's not the Carlyle."

Emerson looked around the room. "No piano."

Riley fell asleep halfway through a sitcom rerun and didn't wake up until seven the next morning.

"I smell coffee," Riley said, sitting up, swinging her legs over the side of the bed.

"Interesting," Emerson said, handing Riley a cardboard container of coffee. "You slept through the fire alarm but you woke up when I entered the room with coffee."

"There was a fire alarm?"

"At five-thirty. I didn't feel threatened so I ignored it. When I went down for coffee they said someone accidentally set their wastebasket on fire, but no damage was done."

"I don't suppose they had food down there?"

"Vending machines. Nothing suitable for breakfast. We can get something once we're on the road."

Riley took a fast shower and got behind the wheel with her hair still damp. The sun was bright but the air had some chill to it. She followed Interstate 15 north to U.S. Route 93, leaving Vegas behind. The road had a steady uphill climb.

"I think my ears just popped," Riley said. "How high are we?"

"Groom Lake is a salt flat at an elevation of 4,462 feet. It's in a high-desert environment. I believe Route 375 will be coming up shortly. You need to go left on 375."

Riley paused when she reached the two-lane road. "The sign says EXTRATERRESTRIAL HIGHWAY."

"I fear Groom Lake has become a theme park."

"Do I keep going?"

"By all means. We'll be meeting our guide at a diner on this road."

"Does it have a cross street? A mile marker? A name?"

"No, no, and I don't know, but I'm sure you'll recognize it when you get there."

Riley thought that was an unjustified vote of confidence.

"It's lunchtime and I'm getting hungry and there's nothing out here," she said after several miles. "Are you sure there's a diner? One that actually sells food?"

"I have no reason to think otherwise." Emerson sat forward. "I believe it's just ahead of us."

Riley squinted against the sun and saw a silver double-wide shimmering in the distance. A couple one-room bungalows and several small campers and trailers had been arranged behind it. The sign on the double-wide said EARTHLINGS WELCOME. She supposed it meant them, because there were no other earthlings in sight. The diner was in the middle of freaking nowhere. A dusty pickup truck, an even dustier Chevy Volt, and a dented and Bondo-patched Volvo station wagon were parked in the lot in front of the double-wide. A small hand-painted sign stuck into the hard-packed dirt advertised OUT OF THIS WORLD FOOD.

"Clever," Riley said.

"More sarcasm?"

"Astonished disbelief."

Riley shrugged out of her hoodie, wrapped the gun securely inside, shoved the bundle under the seat, and got out of the car.

Inside the double-wide was a jumbled display of alien kitsch. T-shirts, mugs, and shot glasses lined shelves, all bearing images of bulging-eyed gray aliens and glowing spaceships. A counter ran along one wall. A few barstools that had been patched with duct tape lined the counter. Behind the counter, a hard-faced waitress with a pink apron and a lot of teased-up hair gave Emerson the full body scan. A large American flag hung on the wall behind the counter.

"Patriotic," Emerson said.

Riley nodded. "It reminds me of the bars back home."

They sat at one of the Formica-topped tables and looked at the plastic-encased menu. The waitress ambled over with coffee.

"What'll it be, hon?" she asked Emerson.

"Grilled cheese," Emerson said.

"Go figure," the waitress said. "I had you figured for a carnivore."

"I'm the carnivore," Riley said. "I want a bacon cheeseburger, fries, and a Coke."

The waitress walked off, and a weathered forty-something woman left her seat at the counter and approached Riley and Emerson. The woman was wearing a flak jacket with a military insignia over the pocket, her long blond hair was going gray, and her eyes were hidden behind mirrored aviators.

"The migrating birds fly low over the sea," she said to Emerson.

Stupid, stupid, stupid, Riley thought. Should have brought the gun with me. This woman is a nut.

Emerson looked up at the woman. "The toothless tiger rules the restless jungle."

"Oh boy," Riley said.

"That was our countersign," Emerson said to Riley. "If I'm not mistaken this is our guide."

The woman pulled a chair up to the table, sat down, and leaned in close. "Yep. I'm your guide, all right. I'm Xandy Zavier. That's Xandy with an 'X.' My real first name is Amy, but screw that." She focused on Riley. "Who are you?"

"I'm Riley Moon."

"Cool. What's your real last name?"

"Moon," Riley said.

"Oh, I thought, 'Moon,' you know . . ." Xandy made a whistling noise and looked around. "There's a lot of whackos here."

Riley looked at the military insignia above Xandy's pocket. It was an image of an alien wearing a lobster bib and holding a knife and fork with the words TO SERVE MAN above it. Yeah, Riley thought, a lot of whackos.

"So who are *you*?" Xandy asked Emerson.

"Emerson Knight."

Xandy took her aviators off and focused her pale blue and bloodshot eyes on Emerson. "*The* Emerson Knight? Better known as Mr. Mysterioso?"

"Technically, I suppose, I am Mr. Mysterioso," Emerson said.

"And you do the blog," Xandy said. "That blog changed my life. Before I read it I was just an average dental hygienist. That blog gave me the courage to follow my bliss."

Riley raised her eyebrows in question.

"Following UFOs, of course," Xandy said. "Wait a minute, how do I know it's really you?"

"You don't," Emerson replied.

"That is such a Mr. Mysterioso thing to say," Xandy said, her voice dripping with admiration. "You know you're wanted by the police, right?"

"Does that bother you?" Riley asked.

"Hell, no," Xandy said. "I've got a few traffic tickets in my background too, if you know what I mean."

"How does this diner stay in business?" Riley asked Xandy. "It's in the middle of nowhere."

"A fair number of tourists and UFO trackers show up on weekends. There's another diner down the road a ways that's a famous UFOlogist watering hole. This place gets the overflow. If you're trying to stay off the grid this is the place to hang."

"We need to get to Groom Lake," Emerson told Xandy.

"No problem," Xandy said. "I'm your girl."

The waitress returned with the food plus the apple pie and coffee that Xandy had left on the counter.

"Eat up and I'll take you to the back gate," Xandy said.

TWENTY-ONE

❈

T HEY LEFT THE GTO AT THE DINER AND TOOK Xandy's beat-up Volvo down a narrow road that wound through scrub desert. Xandy stopped at a black-and-white-striped gate that was bordered on either side by towering metal poles bristling with floodlights and video cameras. A sign said WARNING: MILITARY INSTALLATION. NO TRESPASSING. PHOTOGRAPHY OF THIS AREA IS PROHIBITED. USE OF DEADLY FORCE AUTHORIZED. There was a guard shack with a Ford F-150 parked beside it, and armed sentries lounged against the shack, soaking up sun. A chain-link fence stretched as far as the eye could see.

"Intimidating," Riley said. "How are we going to get through this?"

"We aren't," Xandy said. "I just wanted you to see

it. We're going to sneak in at night going over hill and dale where the Cammo Dudes can't see us."

"The Cammo Dudes are the guards?" Riley asked.

"You got it," Xandy said. "Around here we call them the Cammo Dudes." Xandy pulled a U-turn and headed away from the gate. "We can hang out at the inn and rendezvous at twenty-one hundred."

"How are we going to get over the chain-link fence with the razor wire?" Riley asked.

"The fence stops at some point," Xandy said. "You can just walk into the restricted area."

"And no one's going to shoot at us?"

"Hard to say," Xandy said.

Emerson rented one of the tiny bungalows behind the diner and retreated into it with Riley. The thin blinds were drawn against the blazing sun and the air conditioner hummed to keep the temperature down to a crisp eighty-five degrees. A full-size bed with a sagging mattress took up most of the room. A small wooden table and two ladder-back chairs hugged one of the walls. The bathroom contained a vintage toilet, small sink, shower stall without a shower curtain, and two large roaches that were sneakers up.

Riley gingerly sat on one of the ladder-back chairs. Emerson stood in the corner, folded his arms across his chest, and closed his eyes.

"What are you doing?" Riley asked him.

"Communicating."

"Communicating with whom?"

"The universe and beyond."

"Are they talking back?"

"At the present moment you're the only one talking back."

Riley blew out a sigh and looked around. No television. No radio. No phone. No computer. No magazines or books.

"I haven't got anything to do," Riley said.

Emerson didn't answer. He was at one with the universe.

The sun was low in the sky when Emerson opened his eyes and unfolded his arms.

"Did you talk to any aliens while you were in the zone?" Riley asked. "We seem to be in the neighborhood."

"Nothing specific," Emerson said, "but it was a refreshing trip."

Riley thought it was a good thing one of them had had a refreshing trip. It for sure wasn't her. She was terrified that if she closed her eyes a roach would crawl up her nose.

"Do you think they have room service here?" Riley asked.

"Doubtful, but I can fetch something from the diner. What would you like?"

"Surprise me."

Emerson returned with meatloaf sandwiches, a bag of chips, a box of wine, and a bag of Skittles.

"Impressive," Riley said. "You even thought to get dessert."

"It turns out that one of the campers is actually a bar and a convenience store."

Riley peeled the wrapper off the meatloaf sandwich. "I'm worried about tonight. Do you think we can trust Xandy?"

"I trust she knows how to get into the restricted zone. Beyond that we're on our own."

"What are we going to do once we get into the restricted zone?"

"Look around."

"That's it? We're just going to wander around and keep our eyes peeled for your gold?"

"More or less."

"What's the more?" Riley asked.

"The more is a question mark. It acknowledges the future unknown."

The slivovitz brandy sloshed back and forth in Werner's tumbler as he looked through the little window at the clouds and the landscape far below. Were they passing over Kansas? Missouri? What was the difference? Both flat, dull states, meant to be flown over.

He looked over at his brothers. Manny was relaxed, watching a movie on his iPad. Hans was going over paperwork.

"I don't see why we all needed to make this trip," Werner said to Hans. "We have people to take care of security breaches. Security is *your* area."

"This is more than a security breach. This is a potential disaster," Hans said. "And it's family."

"We aren't even certain of their plans. For all we know they could be going to Vegas to shoot some craps," Werner said.

"Hans is right," Manny said. "This is family and we need to take equal responsibility for what must be done. We all know they aren't going to Vegas for a night on the town. They're in Nevada to destroy us, and we have to make sure that doesn't happen. We should have taken care of this when we first recognized the problem, but we're all a bunch of softies."

This got a laugh out of all three of them. Truth is, they weren't soft. They'd underestimated the enemy.

"Do you really think Günter is working with Emerson?" Werner asked.

Hans shrugged. "No way to know for sure, but it would make sense. Either way, if they're a team or working separately, they need to be stopped. Permanently."

"And you think they're in Nevada?" Werner asked.

"I know they're in Nevada," Hans said. "My men have seen them."

They all looked toward the back of the plane. The door to the rear compartment was closed. It was the old man's private lair. He and his nurse. He was along for the final kill.

At precisely nine o'clock, Xandy showed up at the door to the bungalow and loaded Riley and Emerson into her

Volvo. She drove them several miles down a very dark road, parked behind a piñon tree and a rock formation, and passed out night vision goggles.

"Are these so we can spot Cammo Dudes?" Riley asked.

"Mostly they're so you don't step on rattlers," Xandy said.

They left the Volvo and set out on foot over the uneven ground, following Xandy through the Tikaboo Valley. There was barely a sliver of moon in the sky, and Riley was happy to have the goggles. Snakes aside, it would have been difficult to travel without assistance.

They'd walked for a little over an hour when Xandy pulled up. "If you look straight ahead you can see the surveillance towers on the next ridge."

"I imagine they support cameras and lights," Riley said.

Xandy adjusted her goggles. "That's what they'd like you to believe." She lowered her voice. "The cameras are decoys. They look like cameras but they have special technology that can fry your brain. You get too close and *Zzzzzzt*, your brain leaks out your ears and you're left with nothing in your head."

"That would be unfortunate," Emerson said.

"Yeah," Riley said. "I bet you hate when that happens."

"The ridge marks the perimeter of Nellis Air Force Base. Beyond that you're in Area 51. We're close enough now that I'm sure the Cammo Dudes are watching us.

I'll swing to the northwest and draw their attention. Then you can cross over."

"What will they do to you?" Emerson asked.

"Nothing. Just point their guns at me, make a lot of threats, and then send me on my way. We've done this dance before. They think I'm a harmless nutjob alien hunter."

Emerson adjusted the duffel bag on his shoulder. "I'm sure you're not harmless," he said to Xandy.

"Thank you," Xandy said. "That means a lot coming from Mr. Mysterioso."

Riley and Emerson watched Xandy trudge off to the right and continue trudging until she was a small figure on the horizon. Suddenly she turned and raced toward the AFB perimeter screaming like a banshee. Within seconds a Ford F-150 truck zoomed over the hill toward Xandy, headlights blazing. Men in camouflage spilled out and rushed around her.

Emerson and Riley took off running and scrambled to the top of the ridge, past the cameras, the motion detectors, and the brain liquefiers. Headlights from a distant truck swung in their direction and the truck sped toward them.

"*Incoming!*" Riley said, catching sight of the truck.

Emerson spun her around and pushed her toward the higher ground of Groom Mountain. "*Run!*"

Riley ran flat-out, reached the upward slope, and kept going. Rocks shifted under her feet, and she stumbled but pushed on. The goggles weighed her down so she ripped them off, tossed them aside, and kept moving, crawling up the hillside, judging the ground by the feel of it under her shoes and hands.

She lost all trace of Emerson in her mad rush. When a floodlight beam cast from a Cammo Dude's truck swept up and across the mountainside, Riley pressed herself into the ground, wrapping her arms around the base of a juniper tree. She quieted her jackhammer heartbeat and willed herself inside the rough wood. I am the tree, she thought. Be one with the tree!

The beam of light passed over her, but she didn't move. She saw the light sweep the mountainside again, the blood pounding in her ears. The light blinked off, and she strained to hear the sound of the engine. When all she heard was the whisper of wind in the juniper she lifted her head and looked around. The truck was gone. Or maybe it had just extinguished its lights. The landscape was barren. No sign of Emerson. She hadn't heard shouting or gunshots. She told herself that was a good sign and that Emerson was most likely as safe as she was. As safe as anyone could be alone in a desert at night in a top-secret military installation.

She didn't think going back was an option. They would be looking for her. From her vantage point she could see headlights crisscrossing the desert floor in the distance. The only way is up, she thought. Climb to the top of the ridge and look around. She supposed Emerson was doing the same. He was looking for his gold. She just wanted to find a way out. She climbed as carefully and as quietly as possible. She didn't have the night vision goggles to help her find her way, and her hands were raw from grasping at bristlecone branches and pawing over rocks. Periodically she would stop and listen for the sound of someone else slipping on gravel or breathing heavy. No sound carried back to her.

A pulsing glow, like the vibration from a neon light, was coming over the top of the ridge in front of her. The diner had featured a satellite photo of Area 51 on the wall behind the counter. It had shown the salt flat and the airstrips and the various buildings. Riley thought the pulsing light most likely was coming from the airstrip.

She heard the drone of an approaching plane and saw its lights in the night sky. The lights drew closer, dipped below the hill, and disappeared.

Riley reached the rocky knob of the summit and lay there catching her breath, feeling the wind on her face. It was colder up here, but at least the earth was even and she didn't have to worry about falling backward. And she could see what they didn't want her to see.

She carefully walked to the edge of the ridge and looked over. Far out across the desert floor, there it was. Groom Lake. A salt flat of almost blinding whiteness, lit by a cascade of floodlights. It was illuminated like a football field, but there were no spectators, no players. No one at all. It was eerie, and Riley could see how the sight would give rise to thoughts of flying saucers and extraterrestrial vehicles. The plane that had just landed was parked at the end of the runway, close to a cluster of hangar-type buildings.

She pulled back from the edge and turned at the sound of a footfall. Something was moving toward her.

Difficult to see in the dark. Her first thought was bear, but then she realized it was a man crouching down in an attempt to be less visible. Not Emerson. This man was unsteady.

She had her father's gun tucked inside the waistband of her jeans, rammed into the small of her back, but she didn't want to use it. She didn't want to put a bullet into a body, human or otherwise. Even more, she didn't want to give herself away with a gunshot.

"Stop where you are," Riley said. "I have a gun."

"You've come for me, haven't you?" the man said. "I didn't think it would be you."

Riley squinted at the man. His hair and clothes were unkempt and he had a beard. "Günter?"

"You might as well shoot me," he said. "I don't want to face what lies ahead for me when you bring me in."

"I didn't come looking for *you*," Riley said. "I'm here with Emerson. He's looking for the stolen gold."

Günter managed a humorless smile. "He's come to the right place."

"Why are you on the run?"

"To stay alive. There was a time when that seemed to matter, but I'm not so sure anymore."

"Your brothers say you stole six hundred thousand dollars."

Günter gave a snort of disgust. "They said that? They actually said that? The bastards!"

"So, it's not true?" Riley asked.

"Of course it isn't! I stole much more than that," Günter said.

TWENTY-TWO

⊗⊗⊗

T HERE WAS THE SOUND OF AN OBJECT BRUSHING
against a piñon tree, and Riley and Günter turned
toward the sound. Something or someone was creeping
uphill following the route Riley had taken to get to the
summit. Riley and Günter dropped to the ground, and
Riley quietly drew her gun. A man appeared in the near
total darkness. Riley recognized the silhouette. A tall,
lean man wearing night vision goggles with a duffel bag
hooked over his shoulder. She stood and tucked the gun
back into her jeans.

"I was worried about you," Riley said to Emerson. "I
didn't know where you were."

"I was just below you when they swept the hillside
with the spotlight. I had the benefit of the goggles, and
I knew there were men left behind. I stayed hidden until

the men were picked up and the truck drove off. Then I followed your trail of dislodged rocks and broken branches."

"Did the Siddhar teach you tracking skills?" Riley asked.

"I didn't need tracking skills. It was like a herd of buffalo had rushed uphill," Emerson said. "Is that Günter Grunwald?"

Günter stepped forward and extended his hand. "Please excuse my appearance. This has been a trying experience."

Emerson shook Günter's hand and looked beyond him over the rim of the bluff.

"Area 51," Emerson said. "Easy to imagine aliens down there. The salt flat is quite impressive."

Riley nodded agreement.

"I've been down there and I didn't see any aliens," Günter said. "Unless you count Rollo."

"Why are you here?" Emerson asked Günter.

"Good question. I don't have a good answer. I'm trapped. I can't get out of the country. I don't have a passport. I can't get help from law enforcement. I don't know whom to trust. My brothers are hunting for me, and they'll kill me if they find me. I guess I would like to do something to expose what's going on here, but I haven't a clue how to go about that. So I hang here and watch."

"How did you get into this mess?" Riley asked him.

"Did either of you know Yvette Jaworski?"

Emerson and Riley shook their heads no.

"You wouldn't have liked her," Günter said. "No one did. She was not a likable person. She was disagreeable, negative, argumentative, opinionated, and belligerent. And I don't say this just because she was a strong woman. If she'd been a man, people still would have called her a jerk.

"But there was something about her that touched me. Maybe it was that despite how intensely unpleasant Yvette was, all she really wanted was to be liked. To have friends. She just didn't know how to go about it.

"So when she came back from Munich with a wild story about the gold trade being compromised, people didn't pay attention, not only because the tale was wild and unbelievable, but because no one wanted to listen to anything Yvette Jaworski said.

"I was assigned by my brother to deal with her. He always gave me the bad jobs. It was his way of reminding me that I was lower on the totem pole than he was. What he didn't understand was that I didn't want to be higher on the totem pole. I didn't want to be on the totem pole at all. I just wanted to make enough to live comfortably. And collect gold.

"I loved gold. Not money. Gold. I loved its history and its luster and its pure chemical makeup. I loved the stories of buried treasure, real or imagined. 'The Gold-Bug' by Poe. *Treasure Island* by Stevenson. *The Sign of Four* by Conan Doyle. And the real ones. The money pit in Oak Island. The Beale ciphers in Virginia. Mosby's treasure. I never thought of finding them. I just loved that they were out there, so tantalizingly close and yet so far.

"And Yvette, she was a goldbug like me. So when I went to talk to her, we at least had that in common. We could trade stories of treasures and treasure hunting. In fact, she once gave me a replica of the gold bug from the story. It was quite beautiful. You should see it."

"We have," said Emerson.

"You've been to my home?"

"Yes."

"How was my wife?"

"Coping. She's thinking about selling the house."

"Is she?" Günter was silent for a beat. "Is my boat still there?"

"It was at the dock when we visited last week," Emerson said.

"That's good," Günter said. "I love that boat."

"What was Yvette's wild story?" Riley asked.

"Oh. Yes. It was the Germans that started it. When they began to talk about repatriating their gold."

"Why did they want to do that?"

Günter shrugged. "It was their gold, and I guess they just wanted to see it."

"Precisely," Emerson said. "One should be able to see one's gold."

"In fact, a lot of nations have started talking about getting their gold back," Günter said. "Switzerland. The Netherlands. Venezuela moved its gold to Brazil. Think of it. Venezuela thought *Brazil* was a safer place to store their gold than America.

"Maybe that was what started it. Plan 79. That crazy idea my brothers had. Maybe it started way before that." Günter removed a gold coin from his pocket and showed it to Emerson and Riley. "My brothers have been minting these for years. From the stolen gold."

Riley took it from Günter and held it in her hand. "Why coins? Isn't it easier just to keep the gold in bars?" She handed the coin to Emerson.

Emerson examined the coin closely. "You can't very well go to the grocery store and pay for a loaf of bread with a thirty-pound gold bar. The coins are meant to be used as currency."

"Why does it have an image of Lord Voldemort dressed up like Julius Caesar on it?" Riley asked.

Günter looked a little embarrassed. "It's difficult to see in the dark but my father's face is engraved on this coin."

"And," Emerson continued, "Caesar was the first of the Roman emperors. The man responsible for ending five hundred years of democracy in the Roman civilization."

Günter nodded. "I guess. My father never had much respect for democracy. Always said it was nothing more than mob rule. Anyway, I just discovered the coins by accident. My brothers never bothered to tell me about them or what they were intended for. It kind of hurt. They've excluded me from the family for my entire life."

Emerson returned the coin to Günter. "Well, every form of currency needs a name. All the good ones, like

Drachmas and Dinars are already taken so let's call them Grunwalds."

Günter looked appalled. "That sounds ridiculous. It makes them sound like some sort of funny money you'd get at Disney World to pay for souvenirs."

"Well, your brothers should have thought of that before they put a picture of Lord Voldemort on the coins," Emerson said. "Really, they have nobody to blame but themselves."

"So, you began stealing coins?" Riley asked Günter.

"Yeah. They were kept in a vault in the D.C. office. I took just a couple at first. When no one said anything, I took more. I filled my briefcase with them. I guess I liked the idea of stealing from my brothers. I guess it was my way of getting back at them for all the times they'd slighted me over the years.

"I had to hide them somewhere, for safekeeping. In the beginning I put them in plaster statues of Saint Nicholas and buried them in my yard."

"For Christmas?" Riley asked.

"Hardly," Günter said with a sad smile. "Saint Nicholas is also the patron saint of thieves."

"Of repentant thieves," Emerson said.

"I guess I didn't read the fine print."

"Your wife said the gardener found some of them. She was in the process of exhuming one from a flower bed when we went to visit her."

"I mostly buried them in the flower beds because it was easier digging. Not a lot of them. Maybe ten or twelve. It never occurred to me that at some point a bush would get replaced. When the first one got dug up I tried to find the others, but I was like a squirrel burying nuts. I couldn't remember where I put the stupid things. I even went over the yard with a metal detector one night but obviously didn't find all of them."

"What about the rest of the gold?" Riley asked Günter.

"Underwater," Günter said, putting the coin back in his pocket. "It was fun stealing from my brothers and hiding the . . . Grunwalds. It stopped being fun when two executives from Blane-Grunwald were tasked with calming the Germans down. Lawrence Tatum and Daniel Ferguson."

"Those are the two men who committed suicide last month," Emerson said.

Günter nodded, grim-faced. "The Germans were insisting on repatriating their gold. Not only that, but they were insisting that it not be recast. Gold has a fingerprint. By using a battery of techniques to look at the relative amounts of impurities, including platinum, palladium, lead, thallium, and bismuth, it's possible to tell one horde of gold from another. But once it is melted down and recast, the print is erased.

"The Germans not only wanted the same amount of bullion they had deposited back in the 1950s, they wanted that precise gold.

"To the U.S., this seemed like an unreasonable demand. We dragged our feet. We returned only a paltry amount of gold. Tatum and Ferguson tried to persuade the Germans that everything was fine, that the gold would be returned to them eventually. Unfortunately for Tatum and Ferguson, they requested a visit to the Federal Reserve so they could personally assure the Germans that all was well.

"Two weeks later, they both 'jumped' out of the windows of office buildings, one in London, the other in Tokyo. That was when my friend Yvette got involved.

"She was in Munich, on another matter, when she heard about the suicides. She knew that the Germans were unhappy, but like everyone else, she thought Germans were *always* unhappy. She didn't believe in conspiracies. Not at first. Then she began to investigate.

"By the time she came back to Washington, she was a full-fledged convert. And like any convert, she wanted to spread the word. The Federal Reserve was being looted, she said. And it may have been going on for the last twenty years.

"Everyone was used to tuning Yvette out, so nobody paid any attention. I was given instructions to listen to her calmly and shut her up. To humor her. So I did. I even went to New York, to the Fed, just to show her she was wrong.

"Sadly, she was right. She was right about everything. The gold was being stolen and replaced by tungsten bars. On a massive scale. I found out about Plan 79."

"Why '79'?" Riley asked.

"The nucleus of the gold atom has seventy-nine protons. It must have seemed like a good code name for the operation. A plot by a cadre of nefarious central bankers working with the Federal Reserve, hoping to corner the gold market and control the world's finances.

"I rushed back to Washington to tell my brothers what I'd discovered. I even brought fake gold bars with me, as evidence. I thought they'd be shocked. I thought I'd have a hard time convincing them of the truth. Instead, they listened very calmly. And then they congratulated me on figuring it out. Werner laughed. Hans said it took me long enough. And Manny just patted me on the head.

"Then I told them I knew about the coins. That got their attention. And I told them that I'd stolen forty million dollars' worth. They really sat up and took notice then. Six hundred thousand, my ass!"

"What did they say when you told them?" Emerson asked.

"What could they say? I had the gold. I either kept quiet or talked. And if I tried to talk, I knew they'd shut me up. Permanently. But I didn't need to tell anyone. I knew the secret. I was like the hero of 'The Gold-Bug,' who'd figured out the key to the treasure. It was a glorious feeling. That was enough for me."

"So what went wrong?" Riley asked.

"Yvette went wrong. She couldn't let it go. I told her to walk away, but she wouldn't listen. We both knew where they were sending the gold. They were sending it to a place where no one could look for it. Where secrecy was paramount. Where the crazies had built up another myth entirely. Groom Lake. Area 51. When

Yvette suddenly disappeared, I knew she'd gone to Groom Lake to snoop around, so I went after her."

"Why?" Riley asked.

"Another good question without a good answer. I was afraid she'd screw everything up. I was afraid she'd find the gold and blow the whistle on all of us and finally someone would believe her. It wasn't like I was innocent in all this. I had millions in bootlegged gold coins hidden away. Anyway, I thought I might be able to find her in time and persuade her to abandon the hunt."

"And?"

"I found her but it was too late. At least it was too late for her." He looked over at the salt flat. "There's a whole network of caves underneath the salt flats. People think extraterrestrial spaceships and alien bodies are hidden down there. I wish they were right."

"You've been in there?" Emerson asked.

"Yes. It's incredible. There's more gold than you can possibly imagine. God, I'm sick of the stuff."

"But no alien corpses," Riley said.

"No. Just Yvette's. With her head smashed in. When I saw her I couldn't believe it. It was horrible. It had just happened. And I was almost next. Rollo was there with his scalpel. He came after me and I panicked. I grabbed a gold bar and threw it at him and caught him on the side of his head. I don't know how I managed to hit him. I was so scared, my vision was blurred. He staggered back and I hit him with another bar. Square in the forehead. Right between his eyes. I turned and ran and I've been running ever since."

"This place is a fortress," Riley said. "How did you and Yvette get in?"

"She told me she had an access pass. I think it was bogus but it got her in."

"And you?"

"I'd done some research online. I'd studied satellite photos of the area and I'd eavesdropped on Werner and heard him talking about tunnels. I knew about the mining operation. Lead and silver were discovered in the southern part of the Groom Range in 1864. There are still entrances into those tunnels. I made a good guess based on my eavesdropping and chose the tunnel that led me to the gold. It turns out that security is high aboveground but lacking below. Some of the tunnels are randomly patrolled, and some not at all. There are cameras in the area close to the gold stash but they look rusted out. I'm not sure they're maintained. Although Rollo did know Yvette was in the gold vault. And he also knew I was there. So some of the security cameras must be functioning."

TWENTY-THREE

———✦———

"I'M BEAT," GÜNTER SAID. "HAS ANYONE GOT food?"

Emerson pulled granola bars out of his duffel bag and passed them around.

"How have you been eating?" Riley asked Günter. "Where do you stay?"

"I've been hiding out in an abandoned cabin not far from one of the mine entrances. For whatever reason, the guards don't seem to patrol that patch of the Tikaboo Valley. I have to be careful, but I can pretty much come and go without being seen. I have some money stashed away but it's not going to last forever."

"I saw you at Fletcher's Cove," Riley said.

"I was trying to help Maxine. She'd had an affair with Werner but he kicked her to the curb when she turned thirty. If that wasn't bad enough, he demoted her and gave her to me. The whole office knew. It was humiliating for her. I think she lived to get even. In the end, she didn't live at all.

"When I realized I had to disappear, I gave her a bar of gold to hide. And not just any bar of gold. It happens to have a serial number that identifies it as belonging to the German government."

"That bar's worth about half a million dollars," Riley said. "You trusted her not to just disappear with it?"

Günter smiled. "The one in my safe was a counterfeit and worth a hundred times more, at least to my brothers. It happens to have the same serial number as the German bar I gave Maxine."

Riley shook her head. "If it was ever discovered, it could implicate the Grunwalds."

"Bingo. I told Maxine she should get hold of the bar in my safe and turn both bars over to the press if anything bad should happen to me."

"Like death?" Riley said.

"Yes. Like death. Unfortunately, Maxine didn't wait for news of my death. She got into my safe and switched the two bars. Then she went to Fletcher's Cove and showed it to Werner. She was trying to broker her own deal. To get some measure of revenge. She didn't know what she was getting into. If only I could have reached her in time to stop her."

"How did you know she had the fake bar?" Riley asked.

"We would talk once a week. Just a short conversation

keeping me informed. She told me she was going to get the bar and blackmail Werner. I told her not to do that, but she wouldn't listen. It was the last conversation we had. She wouldn't answer my calls after that so I returned to D.C. to try to stop her. I didn't dare go to her house but I suspected she would attempt the transfer at the cove. Werner went fishing there every Wednesday. It was a safe way to meet with his brothers and other partners in crime. Needless to say, I didn't succeed in making contact with Maxine."

"And then you came back here?"

"I can't explain it. I feel safe here. It's like I'm hiding in plain sight. Or maybe I'm waiting for Werner to visit his gold and I'll sneak in and choke him while he sleeps."

Riley cut her eyes to him. "You're kidding, right?"

"No," Günter said. "I'm quite serious. I would like to kill Werner."

"Okay then," Riley said. "Good to know."

"I'd like to see the gold and get a sample," Emerson said to Günter.

"The nearest tunnel entrance is over an hour's walk from here," Günter said. "Ordinarily I couldn't do it in the dark but I can find my way if I use your goggles."

"How did you know we would be here?" Emerson asked Günter.

"I didn't," Günter said. "I come here when I want to spy on the airfield. I saw the landing lights go on a couple hours ago so I hiked over. Seeing Miss Moon standing there was a shock."

"I heard a plane fly in when I was halfway up the mountain," Riley said.

"I got here just after it landed," Günter said. "I was too late to see the passengers disembark, but I've seen Hans fly into Groom Lake in a similar plane."

"Does he come here often?"

"Almost never," Günter said.

Riley was walking on autopilot. The day had been too long. She was wearing the wrong shoes and she was thirsty. She wanted a mojito.

"How much farther do we have to go?" she asked.

"Not much farther," Günter said.

"I heard that three hours ago."

"We've only been walking for two hours," Emerson told her.

"So we should be there, right?" Riley said. "Remember how this magical tunnel entrance was over an hour away?"

"It's slower going in the dark," Günter said.

"What happens when we find the tunnel?" Riley asked. "Is it attached to a Ritz-Carlton?"

"It's just a tunnel," Günter said. "We need to find a big creosote bush. I wouldn't have a problem in daylight or even bright moonlight, but everything looks weird with these goggles."

"There are creosote bushes all over the place," Emerson said. "And bushes that *aren't* creosote bushes *look* like creosote bushes in the dark."

"This is a big one," Günter said. "And it has a hole mostly hidden under its branches. Don't step in the hole."

Riley and Emerson fanned out and combed the scrub.

"Are you sure we're in the right area?" Riley asked.

"More or less," Günter said.

"Found it," Emerson said. "How stable is the ground around this?"

"Very stable. It's actually the beginning of a cavern."

Emerson found a stone, dropped it into the hole, and counted. "I calculate that the floor of the cavern is thirty-six feet below us."

Riley peered down into the hole. "How do you figure?"

"Physics. All you need is a rock, a stopwatch, and a simple equation derived from Newton's Laws of Motion."

"So how fast is the rock going when it hits the ground?" Riley asked.

"Its terminal velocity is about twenty-five miles per hour," Emerson said.

Riley took a step back. She didn't like the idea of disappearing down the hole and reaching terminal velocity. It sounded . . . terminal.

Emerson turned to Günter. "You've used this entrance?"

"Not exactly. I accidentally dropped a flashlight into it trying to see the bottom. I decided it was inaccessible and went back to using my original tunnel entrance. Two days later I found the flashlight while I was exploring underground. If you can get down there it's a shortcut to the gold repository. Otherwise we need to keep walking. There's an easier entrance about five miles from here."

Riley looked at the hole in the ground. "Thirty-six feet is a long way down."

"Fortunately this duffel I've been carrying not only contains emergency cash and granola bars but also emergency rappelling equipment," Emerson said.

"You expected you'd have to rappel?" Riley asked.

"The bag has been in the safe for several months. I originally packed it when I thought I might go on a mountaineering adventure. The adventure never materialized and the bag remained in the safe."

Emerson unzipped the duffel and pulled out a couple tight coils of rope, some clamps, a hammer, and a small headlamp attached to a headband.

"I have the bare minimum equipment here but I think it will do the job," he said.

"Do you always take wads of money when you go mountaineering?"

"The adventure involved a possible ransom situation. Fortunately it resolved itself without my intervention."

"How much money do you have in the bag?" Riley asked.

"Just short of two million. I've been paying cash for our motel rooms."

Riley considered hitting him with the hammer. She'd been scrimping along trying to save money on cheap motels and he had millions in his duffel bag.

"You have that look," Emerson said to Riley.

"What look?"

"Squinty eyes, jaw clenched, shoulders hunched. I've seen that look on women before and it's never turned out well."

"Have any of the women with this look ever hit you with a hammer?"

"No," Emerson said.

Riley made an effort to relax and unsquint her eyes. "There's always a first time."

Emerson hooked clamps and anchor plates onto the rope and hammered the anchor plate into an outcropping of rock close to the creosote bush.

"That should do it," he said, dropping the free end of the secured rope into the hole.

"I didn't hear it hit bottom," Riley said.

"Nevertheless I'm sure it did. By my calculations we have more than enough rope. Have you done any rappelling?"

"No. None."

"I didn't pack a harness so we'll have to make do."

Emerson found a smaller length of rope, wrapped it around Riley's waist, tied it in a knot, and passed it between her legs.

"How do you feel?" Emerson asked her.

"Like I'm wearing a rope thong."

"That's an erotic comparison," Emerson said. "I like it."

"You've done this harness thing before, right?" Riley asked. "You know what you're doing?"

"I was into rope bondage for a while in Japan. They

call it *kinbaku-bi,* which means 'the beauty of tight binding.'"

"You're joking, right?"

"If it makes you feel more comfortable, then yes." He bound the ropes together in a big loop at her waist and attached a carabiner with a spring-loaded gate onto it, then fed the rope through a large, intricately designed hook with a lever on the side.

"This device is called a descender," he told her. "Grab the lever and it will control your rate of descent."

"Couldn't they come up with a more ominous name for it?" Riley asked. "Maybe a 'drop into hell machine'?"

"You're using humor as a defense. Very good."

"Will it defend me against falling to my death?"

"No. Put these on," he said, handing her leather gloves and the headlamp. "Turn the headlamp on once you're fully in the cavern."

"Wait a minute. What about you?"

"I can manage with less equipment. When you reach the bottom give me a signal so I can descend."

"You're going to send me down *first*?"

"I thought you would want to go down first."

"I want to go down *never.*"

"It would be easier for me to help you get started if you go first."

Riley looked over the edge of the hole. "What's the big deal? You just jump in, right?"

"More or less," Emerson said.

"I'll go down first," Günter said. "I did my share of mountain climbing when I was younger. I can do it."

"I don't have enough equipment to make a harness for you," Emerson said. "I only packed one descender and one headlamp."

"No problem," Günter said. "I'll be fine."

"At least take the second pair of gloves," Emerson said. "Go down as slowly as possible."

Emerson eased Günter over the side of the hole. Günter wrapped a leg around the rope and swung off into space.

"Eeeeeeeee," Günter screamed. *WUMP!*

Emerson and Riley looked into the hole.

"Günter?" Emerson stage whispered.

"Unh," Günter said.

"Are you okay?"

"No. The rope is too short."

"I was certain I calculated correctly," Emerson said. "Perhaps I underestimated the time it took for the stone to hit bottom."

"I think I broke my leg," Günter said.

"I'm going next," Emerson said, hooking the duffel bag over his shoulder. "I need to assess the situation."

"Sure," Riley said. "Bon voyage. Happy landings."

Emerson slipped over the side, and even in the almost total blackness Riley could see that he was controlling his descent. Emerson was toned muscle on a lean frame. And he was skilled on the rope. She heard him drop to the cavern floor, heard a murmured conversation between him and Günter.

"Riley, you're next," Emerson called from below. "Pull the rope up and attach it the way I showed you.

Remember to switch your headlamp on when you go over the edge and begin to drop."

Riley looked into the hole. "Over the edge" had new meaning. "Over the edge" was freaking scary. She pulled the rope up and worked it into the descender. She inched closer to the hole and sat with her legs dangling.

"Anytime now," Emerson called up to her.

"You can do this," Riley said to herself. "The rope is secure. Emerson is on the bottom. You have a job to do. You need to help Emerson find the gold and see that justice is done. This is what you've always wanted to do. This is your chance to make a difference. This is your opportunity to be brave."

"Riley," Emerson called, "who are you talking to?"

"Myself."

"Could you hurry it up?"

"I'm going to be brave," she said.

"Just jump in and get it over with," Günter yelled up at her. "I'm not getting any younger."

Riley sucked in some air, held her breath, closed her eyes, and pitched herself forward into a free fall. She squeezed the descender, the ropes caught, and she hung, swinging in the vast blackness of the hollow earth.

She switched the headlamp on and saw bats clinging to the side of the cave inches from her face. Someone whimpered. She supposed it was her. She switched the lamp off and played out the rope, dropping more slowly, trying to control the whimpering.

"What happened to the light?" Emerson asked her.

"I shut it off. I don't want to see where I'm going. You didn't tell me there'd be bats."

"Well, of course there are bats. It's a cave."

"I hate bats."

"Think of them as pigeons. Pigeons of the night."

Riley wasn't too crazy about pigeons either. Even in the daylight.

She turned the headlamp back on and looked down at her rope. Not much left. She looked beyond the end of the rope at Emerson. There seemed to be a lot of empty space between the end of the rope and Emerson.

"Um, Emerson?" she said. "I've reached the end of my rope."

"Release the descender and let yourself drop the rest of the way."

"No way. It's too far!"

"I'll catch you."

"Not gonna happen."

"At the risk of seeing *that look* again I'd like to remind you that you were going to be brave."

"There's a difference between brave and stupid."

"I could cloud your mind and minimize the difference."

"No! Jeez Louise. On the count of three. One, two, two and a half . . ."

Riley released the descender and dropped like a sack of cement, knocking Emerson flat on his back with his arms wrapped tight around her.

"Got you," he said.

Riley was breathless, sprawled on top of him. "I need a moment."

"No problem."

"Maybe you two should get a room," Günter said. "Has anyone noticed I'm in a lot of pain with a broken leg?"

"Do you know anything about broken legs?" Riley asked Emerson. "Like what to do for them?"

"I've read a few articles."

Riley rolled off Emerson. They got to their feet and stood over Günter.

"I need a knife," Emerson said.

"I don't have a knife," Riley said, "but I have a gun."

"A gun isn't going to help me," Emerson said. "I don't want to kill him. I want to slit his pants leg."

"I have a Swiss Army knife," Günter said. "It's in my pocket."

Emerson found the knife and cut Günter's pants leg off above the knee. The leg was swollen and turning purple.

"There's no bone sticking out," Emerson said. "I think that's a good sign."

"We should make a splint," Riley said. "What have you got left in your bag?"

"Money."

"Get me on my feet and I'll see if I can put weight on the leg," Günter said.

They pulled him up and he winced in pain.

"I'm not going to be able to walk," Günter said. "Leave me here."

Emerson took the headlamp from Riley and handed her the duffel bag. "I'll carry him," Emerson said. "We can't afford to stay here much longer. If the security force patrols this area they might see the rope and come down after us. And we can't leave Günter here. We need him to take us to the gold."

Riley nodded. The adrenaline rush from the fall had worn off and she was running on empty. "Understood."

TWENTY-FOUR

———— ✺ ————

E MERSON SLUNG GÜNTER OVER HIS SHOULDER, and Günter grunted and moaned and told them to go to the right side of the cave.

"Look for the tunnel opening," Günter said.

They crossed the cave and moved into what was clearly a man-made mining tunnel. Emerson's hair skimmed the overhead support beams, and dust sifted down in the light from his lamp.

They trudged on for what seemed like an eternity to Riley. If this was the shortcut, she didn't want to see the longcut. They reached an intersection, and Emerson stopped and looked around.

"Which way?" he asked Günter.

"Through the wall," Günter said.

Emerson set Günter down on the tunnel floor and gave him the headlamp. "Show me."

Günter played the light across the rock face and found a small fissure. "There."

"I see it," Emerson said. "I thought it was just a shadow until you put the light directly on it."

"I found it purely by accident," Günter said. "The fissure goes on for about thirty feet and takes you to the secret vaults."

"I'm barely going to squeeze through there," Emerson said to Günter. "I'm going to have to leave you here."

"I'll be fine," Günter said. "As long as I don't move my leg, the pain is down to a dull throb. Get some gold and return through this same fissure. It's the safest way out."

"Does this fissure open directly into the vault?" Emerson asked.

"Not directly. You'll come out to another tunnel. Go left for about fifty feet and hope no one's there. Take the headlamp. If the lights are on in the vault it means the guards are patrolling. Wait until the lights go off to come out in the open."

"Stay here with Günter," Emerson said to Riley. "It'll be easier to sneak around the vault if I'm alone."

Riley was sure that was true. She was exhausted and no longer operating at peak brilliance. And she wasn't confident that she could navigate the fissure without a total freak-out panic attack.

She watched Emerson fit himself into the small space and silently disappear from view. She told herself he would be okay. After all, he was Emerson. He could cloud minds and endure pain. And he was fearless and strong. And he was sort of smart, in a weird way. She sat down beside Günter with her back pressed against the cool rock wall of the tunnel and willed herself to stay calm.

"He's going to be okay," she said to Günter.

"Yes," Günter said.

"All he has to do is find the gold and bring some of it back, right? And then he can turn it over to the press or the authorities or whoever and all this will end."

"More or less," Günter said.

Riley looked over at him. She was beginning to hate that phrase. "More or less?"

"The gold has been recast. It no longer bears the stamp of its origin. Emerson will need to find Dr. Bauerfeind. He's a German chemist who has developed a technique for reading the fingerprint of gold even after it has been melted and re-formed. Yvette was in contact with him. She was going to use him to try to trace the gold from the German mint. It has a very distinctive combination of palladium and thallium."

"So if we can get our hands on some of that gold and give it to Dr. Bauerfeind, our case is made."

"We have to find him first," Günter said. "He went into hiding when Yvette disappeared."

"Piece of cake," Riley said, closing her eyes. "Easy-peasy."

• • •

Riley woke with a start, completely disoriented. There was a total absence of light. The air was cold and damp against her face. Someone was shaking her awake. Her mind cleared and confusion was replaced with fear.

"Günter?" she asked.

"Yes."

"I must have fallen asleep."

"I heard what sounded like gunshots from the other side of the crevice," Günter said. "It was faint but distinct."

Now Riley heard them. Two more shots. She was on her feet, arms outstretched in front of her, feeling for the wall. She reached the wall and found the crevice.

"I'm going to help," she said to Günter. "If I don't come back—"

"Not an option," Günter said. "You have to come back."

Riley sidestepped into the crevice. She was squeezed between two rock surfaces, but it was no darker than it had been in the cave with Günter. Total dark is total dark. She moved as fast as she could, shuffling inch by inch. She felt the change in the air and saw a hint of light and knew she was close to the end of the fissure. She paused when she came to the edge and listened. She heard nothing. Not significant, she thought. Nothing short of a freight train would be heard over her beating heart. She stepped out and squinted into the darkness. It was light enough for her to know she was in the tunnel. Too dark to make out details. The light was coming from the left and she knew the left led to the vault. She drew her gun and cautiously walked toward the light, hugging the wall. She turned a corner and the light was suddenly blinding.

She was in a cavernous space with a high vaulted ceiling studded with stalactites, stretching as far as she could see, lit by bright fluorescent work lights. The huge vault was filled with more gold than Riley could possibly have imagined. Stacks and stacks of gold bars lined up like walls of a city built by King Midas. The golden ramparts zigged and zagged, forming a giant maze. A maze that didn't need to lead to a treasure because it was made of treasure.

She remembered what Günter had told Emerson. If the lights are on, the guards are patrolling. No surprise, since she'd heard gunshots. She didn't see any movement. No shadows. Didn't hear anyone walking or talking. She quietly moved to the closest wall of gold bricks. She crept to the end of the wall and peeked out. Nothing but wall after wall of gold.

"Mr. Knight?" a voice called out.

It was Rollo speaking in his calm, silky voice.

"We can keep this game up for hours but you know what the outcome will be," Rollo said. "There's no way out. After all, this isn't your mansion, riddled with hidden doors. We're bound to catch you in the end."

Relief swept through Riley. Emerson was all right. Not killed. Not captured.

"Oh, I know, you think if you drag this out for as long as possible, something will come up," Rollo said.

"Someone will come in to help you. Someone like that girl hiding behind stack number 55."

Security cameras, Riley thought. The place was probably lousy with them.

"Come out right now and I won't hurt her," Rollo said.

I have just six rounds of ammo, Riley thought. I have to make them count. She was a good shot. The best in her family. She hunted with her dad and her brothers. Ducks, deer, wild pigs. This was different. This time she was the hunted as well as the hunter. This time she would be firing at a human being. Not something she thought she would ever do. She'd have to sight and fire fast, and retreat. She took a quick look and saw that Rollo was walking directly toward her, limping slightly. He was maybe five stacks away. He had a big Band-Aid on his forehead, a Band-Aid over his nose, and a black eye. And he had a gun in his hand.

"Miss Moon," Rollo said. "It doesn't look like Mr. Knight is going to sacrifice himself for you. That leaves me no choice but to shoot you. Perhaps you would be so kind as to step out into my field of vision again."

Showtime, Riley thought. Take him down. She took a calming breath, sprang out from behind the stack of gold, imagined a bull's-eye over Rollo's heart, and fired. His eyes went wide with surprise and he fell to the floor. Riley put her hand to the wall of gold for support. Breathe, she told herself. *Breathe!*

Emerson rounded the corner of Stack 55, ran the

length of it, and reached out and yanked Riley behind the wall.

"Holy cats," Riley said. "Holy cow!"

"There's a freight elevator halfway down the room on the far wall," Emerson said. "Run for it."

Riley ran flat-out with Emerson inches behind her. They reached the elevator, and Emerson lifted the gate and got in.

Riley hesitated. "Where does this go?"

"Somewhere else," Emerson said.

He pulled her in, slammed the gate closed, and punched the UP button. The elevator rumbled and began to move.

Riley felt a hot flash of panic. "We're going down!" she said. "*Do something*. Make a mind cloud. Make us go *up*."

"I haven't yet mastered *up*," Emerson said.

Their descent was long and jerky and very fast. They were rocked back on their feet as the car came to an abrupt stop.

"I suspect you're not going to be able to shoot your way out of this," Emerson said to Riley. "You might want to drop the gun just in case we're met by a platoon of nervous guards."

Riley dropped the gun, the gate opened, and a half dozen Cammo Dudes moved forward with their XM29 rifles trained on Emerson and Riley. Riley looked beyond the guards and saw that Günter was trussed up on a hand truck like a trophy waiting to be stuffed. Riley couldn't tell if he was unconscious or dead.

Riley and Emerson were pulled out of the elevator and the elevator was sent back up. A couple minutes later the elevator returned and Rollo stepped out. He had a hole in his suit jacket and looked like he was in pain.

"I'm going to have a nasty bruise, thanks to you," he said to Riley. "You're an excellent shot, but you need to aim higher if you want to kill someone wearing a Kevlar vest."

Emerson and Riley were escorted down a dimly lit hallway. Günter was rolled along behind them. Rollo limped behind Günter. No one spoke. The procession stopped in front of a door. A Cammo Dude unlocked it and motioned Emerson and Riley inside. The door was closed and locked behind them, and Riley heard the hand truck continue on down the hall.

They were in a storage room that was lined with crates with stenciled labels reading GROOM LAKE and NELLIS AIR FORCE BASE. Xandy was sitting hunched in a corner with her arms wrapped around her knees.

"Sorry we dragged you into this," Riley said to Xandy.

"It was bound to happen sooner or later," Xandy said. "Damn aliens."

"I assume the Cammo Dudes brought you here?"

"They didn't let me go, like they always have before. They brought me here and questioned me about Mr. Mysterioso."

"I hope you told them what you know," Emerson said.

"Well, I spent the first couple of hours pretending I didn't speak English. Then that creepy Rollo guy came in and showed me his knife. After that, I told him everything. I even made up some stuff. Hope you don't mind."

"Not at all. I hope what you told him was interesting."

"He seemed to think so." She leaned forward and whispered, "You know what I think? I think that Rollo dude is an *alien*, that's what I think. Those big bug eyes. That weird smile. And he's all beat-up like he crash-landed."

In a manner of speaking, Riley thought. Rollo face-planted on the highway.

"Did they probe you yet?" Xandy asked Riley. "They always get around to probing you. That's what the other abductees tell me, anyway."

"I wasn't abducted."

"Denial is the first stage," Xandy said. "How did you get here if you weren't abducted? Did you walk through the front door?"

"You're right," Riley said. "I was abducted."

Emerson sat down against the wall and leaned back on a crate labeled NEVADA TEST AND TRAINING RANGE, closing his eyes.

"Are you actually going to sleep?" Riley asked.

"What else is there to do?" Emerson said. "Might as well be rested and refreshed for what's coming up."

"For torture? I'd rather be a little blurry-eyed for torture."

Xandy leaned forward and nodded toward Emerson. "He's an alien too, right?" she whispered.

"Definitely," Riley said.

The door opened and Rollo stepped in. "They want to talk to you," he said to Emerson. "Come with me."

Riley thought he sounded like a little boy whose Christmas had been postponed.

Emerson got to his feet and turned to Riley. "After you, Riley."

Rollo shook his head. "No. Not her. Just you."

"I'm afraid I must insist," Emerson said. "Miss Moon is my executive assistant."

"They don't want to see her. Just you."

"I don't care what *they* want. I don't even know who *they* are. I go with Miss Moon, or I don't go at all."

Rollo turned on his heel and went out, slamming the door behind him.

"See if it's locked," Riley said to Emerson.

Emerson tried the door, the door opened, and a guard pointed his gun at Emerson. Emerson closed the door. "Not locked," he said.

"Maybe you shouldn't be making Rollo angry," Riley said.

"It passes the time," Emerson said. "But I really shouldn't get such pleasure from it. I'll have to take a long look at that."

"Yeah, you can do that while he's torturing you with his medical instruments."

"It will, as I say, pass the time."

"Why is it so important that I go with you?" she asked Emerson.

"It's not. But it's very important that you don't stay here."

"Uh-oh," Xandy said. "What's going to happen here?"

"Rollo is going to have time on his hands," Emerson said.

Xandy went pale. "He's going to probe me, isn't he? I don't suppose I could be your other executive assistant? Or your assistant's assistant? Really, I could help around the house. Look after your pets?"

"You don't want to do that, trust me," Riley said.

"Don't worry," Emerson said to Xandy. "Rollo doesn't have any history with you. You should be fine."

"'Should' doesn't cut it," Xandy said. "Besides, who's to say I don't have a history with him? I've had a lot of past lives. I've done some crazy doo-doo."

TWENTY-FIVE

⊷⊶

T HE DOOR OPENED AND ROLLO GESTURED TO
Emerson. "Miss Moon can come with you."

Emerson stepped out into the hall and Riley trudged
after him in awe of his stamina. He was unsmiling and
serious but completely focused. She could practically
hear his mind crackle with energy. She, on the other
hand, was struggling to stay alert. They walked to the
end of the hallway and were shown into a conference
room. The table was typical high-polish boardroom. The
chairs were black leather, rolling on wheels. The walls
were lined with flat-screens. The flat-screens had video
links showing live shots of Area 51. Some of the screens
rotated with interior views of the gold vault.

Günter had been pushed up to the table. He was
still strapped to the hand truck but it looked like he'd

had medical attention. His head drooped but his eyes were open and fully dilated. Some drool escaped from the side of his mouth. He had a soft cast and brace on his leg.

"They're on their way," Rollo said. "Make yourself comfortable."

Emerson walked to the head of the table, pulled out a chair, and sat down. There was a console of controls in a panel on the table in front of him. He flicked a couple switches and the images on the giant screens went black.

"Do you think you should be messing with that?" Riley asked.

"Why shouldn't I?"

"They might get angry."

"I think they're already angry."

"The Grunwalds?"

"Yes," Emerson said. "The Grunwalds."

Günter made an effort to raise his head. "Am I dead yet?" he whispered.

"No," Riley said. "I think you're just drugged."

"That's good to hear. Because I feel confused. On the positive side, my leg's not hurting. And I can smell colors."

There was the sound of men marching down the hall, and Werner Grunwald strode into the room. He was followed by William McCabe in his dark custom-tailored suit and Hans Grunwald in his uniform. Manny Grunwald entered last, pushing a sick older man in an oxygen-equipped wheelchair. The man was dressed in a white knit shirt and navy V-neck sweater. His white hair was neatly combed. His slippers were fleece-lined. He was sucking hard on his oxygen, his skin was the color of wet concrete, and one eye was closed, but the other eye was focused on Emerson like a laser beam.

Emerson smiled at the old man. "I thought you were dead. Interesting to see you've still got one foot out of the grave, Bertie."

"Bertie?" Riley asked.

"Let me introduce the elder Grunwald," Emerson said to Riley. "This is Werner's, Manny's, Günter's, and Hans's father. Recently risen from the grave. In my house he was known as Bertie."

At the mention of his father, Günter struggled to open his eyes and see through his haze of narcotics. He turned to Emerson and whispered hoarsely. "I see dead people. They walk around like regular people. They don't see each other. They only see what they want to see. They don't know they're dead."

"Isn't that what that little kid said to Bruce Willis in *The Sixth Sense*?" Riley said to Emerson.

Bertrand gave his son a disgusted look. "Günter, you incredible nincompoop. I'm not dead."

Günter was undeterred. "That's exactly what a dead person would say."

Werner moved to take his place at the head of the table and pulled up short when he realized Emerson had already claimed it. He stood for a couple beats with his eyes narrowed and his lips pressed tight together while everyone else shuffled around finding a seat.

"Sit down, Werner," Bertie said on a gruff rush of expelled oxygen. "*Anywhere.*"

"Can we offer you something to drink?" Manny asked Riley and Emerson.

"Water," Emerson said.

"Water for me as well," Riley said.

"And you, Günter," Manny asked. "What would you like?"

"Gin. With a side of rainbows."

"We'll make it ice water," Manny said, pleasantly, and nodded to an aide in a gray suit standing by the door.

"Get on with it," Bertie said.

Riley raised her hand. "Question," she said. "When you put the men in this room together, you run one of the biggest banks in the world, you run the Federal Reserve, you run the NSA, and you're about to have a voice on the Supreme Court. You're already running the country. What more do you need?"

"We need to own it," Werner said. "Soon we'll have everything in place and we'll set McCabe to printing massive amounts of currency, devaluing the U.S. dollar. Then we shut off the money spigot from Blane-Grunwald and the other mega-banks will follow. It will be a complete collapse of the dollar and probably every other major global currency. Our gold will be worth a hundred times what it's worth today."

"In fact, if you have your way, your gold coins will be the only surviving currency in the world." Emerson looked to Riley. "You have to admire the elegance of it.

They're not just out to steal the world's gold. That would make them simple thieves. They want to simultaneously destroy all other forms of wealth. Essentially, they make themselves even richer by making everyone else poorer."

Bertrand sucked another breath of oxygen. "Sometimes you have to burn the field down so new crops will grow."

"Impressively ambitious," Emerson said. "What do you want from us?"

Hans pressed an icon on his iPad and one of the flat-screens flickered to life. The opening page of the Mysterioso website came up, the smoky letters drifting into view and looking eerier in wide-screen high definition.

The image went to static for a moment then was replaced by a video feed. Looking like it was made on a laptop computer, the image was all fish-eyed and high contrast, but it was clearly Emerson in the turret room. There were stacks of money on the table next to him, and he addressed the camera.

"Hello, this is not Mr. Mysterioso, but ... okay, this is Mr. Mysterioso. And I need your help. As I'm sure you're aware, I have stumbled onto something of a hornets' nest. I'm going to go underground for a bit. Underground. If you don't hear from me by the twenty-eighth of September, remember this. Two. Eighteen. Thirty-five. One. One. Zero-zero."

There was a sound of knocking on the door behind him and Riley could hear Aunt Myra's voice, calling out sweetly, *"Emmie, are you there?"*

Emerson reached out toward the screen and the image went black.

Hans leaned forward and spoke with military authority. "We only have one question for you, Mr. Knight. What does 'two, eighteen, thirty-five, one, one, zero-zero' mean?"

"I think your father can explain that," Emerson said, gazing at the old man in the wheelchair. "Can't you, Bertie?"

Bertie sucked in oxygen and glared at Emerson with his single seeing eye. "You have your father's guts, young Emerson," he said. "Too bad you don't have his sense."

Riley didn't attend church, but her mom was a good Christian woman who'd worked hard at instilling Christian values in her children. Kick that to the curb after today, Riley thought. She'd just tried to kill a man and now she was thinking very un-Christian thoughts about the elder Grunwald. She was thinking he was in a state of decay and that he had the putrid gaze of a zombie. It brought to mind a Bible quote her grandmother favored. *But if thine eye be evil, thy whole body shall be full of darkness.*

"February eighteenth, 1935, was the date of one of the most infamous series of decisions ever returned by a U.S. Supreme Court," Bertie said. "*Norman v. Baltimore & Ohio Railroad. United States v. Bankers Trust. Nortz v. United States. Perry v. United States.* This was during the dictatorship of Franklin Delano Roosevelt. He illegally packed the Supreme Courts with Communists."

Werner pressed his lips together and gave his head a small shake. Hans looked like he wanted to bang his head on the table. Manny did an eye roll. And McCabe looked like a heart attack waiting to happen.

"He did!" Bertie said. "He closed every bank in the country. Illegally."

Riley raised her hand again. "We were in the middle of the Great Depression."

"A minor economic correction," Bertie said, wheezing and gasping for air. "Hoover had the right idea. The market will regulate itself. But Roosevelt had other plans. He issued an executive order requiring the surrender of all gold coins, gold bullion, and gold certificates by citizens of these United States to the government by May 1, 1933, in exchange for their value in U.S. dollars." Bertie furiously sucked oxygen. "Congress, his lapdogs, also passed a resolution canceling all gold clauses in public and private contracts."

The aide arrived with water for everyone, took in the climate of the room, quickly deposited the water, and left.

"People tried to fight it," Bertie said. "Their cases went to Roosevelt's Supreme Court, where all four were decided in favor of the government's position. Gold couldn't be owned by the people anymore. The government had stolen it all for itself."

"President Ford signed a bill in 1974 legalizing the private ownership of gold coins, bars, and certificates," Emerson said.

"Yes. I saw to that," Bertie said. "But he didn't repeal

the gold clause resolution! That clause still stands as an affront to every citizen and a threat to every private fortune."

"Until Manny takes his seat on the Supreme Court and overturns it," Emerson said.

Werner nodded in affirmation.

"So," Emerson said, "to follow Grunwald reasoning, you are not stealing the gold. You are returning it to private hands. Where it belongs."

"Precisely," Werner said.

"It must have taken years to amass all that bullion," Emerson said.

Werner again answered for the family. "We were cautious."

"And this has been going on since the turn of the century," Emerson said. "January 1, 2000. One, one, zero-zero."

"Very good," Bertie said. "It seemed an appropriate time to begin the new order."

"And your sons are following in your footsteps?"

"All but one," Bertie said.

"Why did you fake your death?" Riley asked.

"There was going to be a congressional investigation. Some talk of unlawful activity. I decided it would be better to die. The outpouring of affection from powerful people would drown out the inquiry."

Bertie was laboring to breathe, his chest expanding and collapsing with each word. Everyone at the table was pitched forward as if that would help the man speak.

"So your dream is almost a reality," Emerson said.

"You'll soon be firmly in control of all the world's wealth and, hopefully, be positioned to install yourselves as the leaders of the new order."

The Grunwalds exchanged glances.

"That's overstating it a bit, but yes," Werner said, "that's our plan in a nutshell. Very good. Now what we need you to do is to post another video on your website. An update. To let your viewers know you're all right. And to explain those numbers away in an innocent fashion."

"I see," Emerson said. "And why should I do that?"

"If you don't cooperate I'll have to turn you over to Rollo and allow him to flay the skin from your bones."

"And if I *do* cooperate?" Emerson asked.

"I'll have him kill you quickly."

Riley reached for her water, realized her hand was shaking, and quickly withdrew it and put it in her lap.

Emerson shook his head. "I'm sorry, that isn't enough of a carrot. I *know* I'm going to die. Everyone's going to die. A few hours, more or less, makes little difference. You have to offer me more than that."

Hans looked up the table at Emerson. "I don't think you understand the situation here. We hold all the cards."

"On the contrary. To continue your analogy, I think you have a very bad hand. I hold all the aces. You want me to make a recording. Ergo, I make the recording or I don't. It's all up to me."

"You're our prisoner."

"I'm no more a prisoner here than I am anywhere

else. Whether I feel free or not is entirely up to me. You can beat me. Torture me. It won't make me any more likely to do that recording. And it will make the video rather suspect, don't you think, if I appear black and blue, with my lips swollen and my nails ripped out?"

Hans leaned forward. "And what will be more likely to make you do the video willingly, Emerson?"

"That's simple," Emerson said. "Gold."

"You want gold?" Werner asked.

"Yes," Emerson said. "I have some gold. I want more. Is that so hard to understand?"

"That's bullshit," Bertie said. "You never gave a hoot about your family business. You only wanted to be a rock-and-roll drummer or a Tibetan monk or whatever would piss your dad off the most."

Emerson shrugged. "So I've changed. I've put away childish things. I want in on Plan 79."

"How much do you want?" Werner asked.

"Oh, a round number. Say, a thousand Good Delivery bars."

Werner gave him a blank stare. "That's ridiculous. We're not giving you a thousand bars."

"It's a drop in your infinitely larger bucket. Well worth it, don't you think? To have Mr. Mysterioso cover your tracks?"

There was an exchange of glances among the Grunwalds, and Werner smiled at Emerson. "If you'll give us a moment?"

Werner, Manny, and McCabe stood in unison and

left the room, with Manny once again pushing his father's wheelchair.

"You were bluffing, right?" Riley whispered to Emerson. "When you told them you wanted all that gold. You were just playing for time, right?"

"I was playing for whatever I could get. Which I don't think is very much."

The door swung open and Werner stepped in. "Two hundred gold bars," he said.

"I shouldn't accept it, but I'm feeling agreeable," Emerson said. "Two hundred gold bars it is."

"Come with me," Werner said. "We have a recording to make. Miss Moon will stay here."

TWENTY-SIX

◆◆◆

T HE DOOR CLOSED AND RILEY LOOKED OVER
at Günter. He was taking a nap. There were no
windows in the room. The television screens had all
gone black. The air filtration system hummed in the
background. She felt herself nodding off and jerked
herself awake. If she was to be drugged or killed, she
wanted to see it coming. She didn't want to be killed
while she was asleep.

As the minutes dragged on she became increasingly
worried. She didn't trust the Grunwalds. They were all
psychopaths, and she was sure they were capable of the
most terrible torture. A wave of nausea slid through her
stomach at the thought of Emerson alone with them.
When Werner said Rollo would flay Emerson alive,

she didn't think it was a threat. She thought it was a promise.

She went to the door and looked out. Armed guard.

"I thought I'd go for a walk," she said.

He drew his sidearm, and Riley popped back into the room and closed the door. Fifteen minutes later the door opened and Emerson walked into the room, followed by Werner.

"We're free to go now," Emerson said to Riley.

"What about Günter and Xandy?"

"They're free to go as well," Werner said. "Rollo will escort you out."

Riley stood and made a pretense of looking relieved. She knew Emerson was playing the game, waiting for his moment. She'd play along too. She'd wait for the moment. She hoped the moment happened soon, because she knew Werner couldn't allow them to walk away. It had gone too far for that. Werner had to kill them. It was just a matter of how and when. Riley figured Werner wanted them off the military base so he wouldn't be implicated. That was a good thing. It gave them more time to find the moment.

There were six armed guards plus Rollo waiting in the hall. Xandy was with them, looking like she might bolt and run at the first chance. One of the guards collected Günter and rolled him out of the room, and everyone walked en masse to the freight elevator. Rollo pressed the button to summon it.

"One last thing," Emerson said to Werner. "How will I get my gold?"

"Oh, that. You won't be getting that," Werner said.

"I won't?"

"No, no," Werner said.

"So you lied to me?"

"Yes, we lied. We do that. We've been lying for years. Frankly, I'm surprised you didn't see that coming."

"I considered the possibility."

Werner turned to Rollo. "Take them out and kill them. Make it look like suicide."

"A group suicide?" Rollo sounded skeptical.

"Yes, I see the problem," Werner said. "Murder-suicide then. Emerson killed them all, then killed himself. Make it colorful. Emerson is such a colorful character."

Werner took a step back and everyone else got into the freight elevator. Xandy's eyes were darting around like the little steel balls in a pinball machine. Günter looked like he was still smelling rainbows. The six guards were stoic. Rollo was smiling.

They stepped out of the freight elevator onto a loading platform where a large panel van was waiting. Günter was rolled in first and laid flat. Emerson, Riley, and Xandy were handcuffed with plastic ties and herded in next. One of the guards got behind the wheel, and Rollo took the seat next to him. Two of the remaining guards came on board and closed the back doors.

It was early Friday morning and the sun was blazing over Groom Lake. The air shimmered over the salt flat and neighboring runways. The sky was azure. The van was white and utilitarian with no seats in the cargo area. Emerson, Xandy, and Riley sat on the floor with their backs resting against the side panel. If they looked forward between the two front seats they had a glimpse of sky and whatever lay ahead of them.

After a half hour on the road, Riley had exhausted all her hopeful anger and was left with such deep and debilitating sadness she could barely breathe. She knew she was supposed to be waiting for the moment, but honestly she didn't have a lot of faith that the moment would save them. Her life was going to be cut short. She'd never again sit down at the dinner table with her parents and her brothers. She wouldn't have a family of her own. No more sunrises and sunsets. No chance to use her education to help people solve their financial problems.

She looked over at Emerson. His eyes were closed and he was gently rocking with the motion of the van. He didn't look sad or scared. He looked peaceful. Of course he's not worried, Riley thought. He's been working on his karma. He's already got one foot out the door for a better afterlife. He'll probably move on to some astral plane for superior souls. My fate isn't so rosy. I just tried to kill a man . . . twice. And I haven't been to church in ten years. I could end up coming back as a snail.

Rollo had instructed the driver to head for Vegas. He had four people to kill and he needed a location that would draw attention away from Area 51. Even more troublesome was the fact that he'd been instructed to make it look like a murder-suicide. He'd like to think he could put a gun in Emerson's hand and get Emerson to shoot the two women and stupid Günter, but he didn't think that would happen. And he couldn't shoot them himself and blame Emerson, because the gunshot residue wouldn't show up on Emerson's hand during the postmortem examination. Damn *CSI* shows, he thought. They'd spoiled murder for everyone.

Emerson opened his eyes and turned to one of the guards. "I'm curious about you," Emerson said. "What's your story? How did you get here? Why do you do this?"

The guard didn't respond.

"I assume from your uniform that you're one of the nonmilitary personnel assigned to base security. As Xandy would say, you're a Cammo Dude. So why do you do it? Are you in it for the money?" Emerson asked.

No response.

"You're killing four innocent people for the money? That's interesting. It must be a lot of money. How much?"

No response.

"Do you get health benefits too? Retirement? Dental?"

"Enough talking," the guard said.

"What's your name?" Emerson asked him.

"I told you to shut up." The guard turned to Riley. "Tell him to shut up or I'll shoot him."

"He doesn't listen to me," Riley said. "I'm just his amanuensis."

"You're his *what*?"

"Amanuensis."

"My sister had that when she was pregnant," the guard said. "They wanted to see if the baby had anything wrong with it."

"That's different," Riley said. "That's amniocentesis."

They went south on Interstate 15, past Vegas and into the desert. The driver turned right onto a little two-lane blacktop road that led off into the back of beyond. After a couple miles they pulled over and parked at an abandoned service station.

"Is this it?" Xandy asked. "Is this where they're going to kill us? It's because we know about the aliens, isn't it? At least we're not going to get probed."

Riley looked over at Emerson, and Emerson shrugged.

"Why are we parked here?" Riley asked Rollo.

"We're waiting," Rollo said.

There was the sound of a car approaching from the rear. The guard driving the white van acknowledged the car with a wave of his hand. He put the van into gear and pulled back onto the road. They followed the winding road toward the base of a mountain. The van stopped, and Rollo got out and opened a small gate. He returned to the van, and the van lurched forward and bumped over a rough dirt trail that zigzagged uphill.

"This is Mount Potosi, isn't it?" Emerson asked.

"Very good," Rollo said.

"Carole Lombard's plane crashed right about here," Emerson said. "I always liked Carole Lombard." He turned to Riley. "She was a movie star in the thirties. Did you ever see *My Man Godfrey*? *Nothing Sacred*? *Twentieth Century*?"

"I've never seen *Twentieth Century,*" Riley said.

"I'll set up a screening," Emerson said. "Are you free next Wednesday?"

"I'll have to check my schedule," Riley said.

"You see," Emerson said, "I do like some popular culture."

"Just pre–World War II popular culture?" Riley asked him.

Emerson smiled. "I like to wait to see if it will last."

"You don't seem to be worried about, you know . . . dying," Riley said.

"Worrying is an unproductive activity," Emerson told her. "And it's pointless. I prefer to be in the moment."

"Or at least *waiting* for the moment," she said.

"In this case, yes. Anticipation is key."

The van finally chugged to a stop, and Rollo and the driver got out. The cargo door was opened and Rollo looked in.

"Okay, people," Rollo said. "This is the end of the road. Everyone out."

They were at the top of the mountain. It was studded with transmitting towers and satellite dishes, and off in the distance Vegas was visible, surrounded by a deadly desert under a smoldering haze. Riley thought it looked like something that had survived a nuclear apocalypse. She turned her attention to the car that had followed them, and a chill ripped through her. It was her dad's GTO.

"I know how it's going to happen," she said to Emerson. "They're going to send us off the cliff in the GTO."

"It *is* a colorful ending," Emerson said. "Kudos to Rollo. It won't work, of course, but it was a good idea all the same."

"Why won't it work?"

"We won't let it. We borrowed your father's car in good faith. We need to return it to him."

"Not to mention me."

"Goes without saying," Emerson said.

"Put Günter in first," Rollo said to the guards. "I want him strapped into the backseat."

Günter was rolled over, taken off the hand truck, and stuffed into the car. There was some screaming involved when they removed the brace and bent his leg to fit into the backseat, but the task was accomplished. Xandy was put in next. She was in the back beside Günter. She was babbling about the space-time continuum and her grandmother's blue crystal. Her handcuffs were removed and she slapped herself.

"Wake up," she said. "Wake up!"

"I know you're not in favor of worrying," Riley said to Emerson, "but I'm feeling some apprehension."

"No problem," Emerson said. "I have a foolproof plan."

"Great. What is it?"

"I had a small camera in my pocket. I took pictures of the gold, then took the memory card out of the camera and swallowed it. So when they find my body and do an autopsy, the pictures of the gold will be there."

"*That's* your plan?"

"It's more of a backup plan."

"Is there one that doesn't involve us dying?"

"Yes, but that one's a little sketchier."

Rollo walked over to Riley. "Guess what. You're next. You get to go in front so you have a good view on the way down."

Riley looked at Emerson. "Um . . ."

"Wait for it," Emerson said.

"Wait for what?" Rollo asked him.

"*It*," Emerson said.

"Cut them loose," Rollo told the guard. "We want them clutching at each other and screaming. We want drama."

The guards had sidearms and automatic rifles. Rollo had Riley's S&W.

"Get in the car," Rollo said to Riley. "Get in the car or I'll shoot him. Nothing serious. After all, he has to drive you off the cliff. Still, I could cause him pain. Shoot off a toe or a finger."

Riley slid onto the passenger side seat, and Rollo closed the door.

"Now you have a choice," Rollo said to Emerson. "I'll

give you a chance to end this pleasantly. I'll let you shoot your friends. One clean bullet to their heads. Over and done with. Otherwise, they're going to go off this cliff in this car. They're going to be broken and mangled. Probably burned alive in the wreckage. It's an ugly way to go. Spare them that. You can even finish yourself off the same way, when you're done."

"I don't feel comfortable with that," Emerson said. "I'm not actually a gun person."

"Guns don't kill people," Rollo said. "Pontiac GTOs being pushed off mountains kill people."

Riley reached across the gearshift and honked the horn. Rollo turned to look, and Emerson kicked out with his foot, landing a sideways blow on Rollo's midsection. One of the guards drove the butt of his rifle at Emerson's chest. Emerson moved with it, grabbed the rifle, and threw it off the cliff. The remaining two guards ran to subdue Emerson, and Riley used the opportunity to jump seats and get behind the wheel. She cranked the engine, slammed the car into reverse, and floored it.

The dirt road was narrow and carved into the side of the hill, and the white panel van blocked her way. Riley hit the brakes, and Günter screamed as his leg banged against the seat in front of him. Riley speed-shifted into second and drove forward toward Emerson. He was in a no-win situation with three armed guards and Rollo. She saw him get thrown to the ground and go still.

"No," she whispered, slowing to a crawl with nowhere to go. "No, no, no."

Emerson was lying in a heap on the ground, Rollo

poking him with his foot. The driver's door to the GTO was wrenched open and Riley was yanked out of the car by a guard.

"Emerson?" she asked.

"Dead," the guard said.

TWENTY-SEVEN

───∞∞∞───

RILEY WALKED TO WHERE EMERSON WAS lying. She dropped to her knees and put her hand to his chest. No heartbeat. No sign of life. His eyes were open and fixed. A trickle of blood oozed from the corner of his mouth.

"This is a real pain in the ass," Rollo said. "He was supposed to die in the car wreck, but he insisted on fighting us and hit his head on a rock."

"Let us go," Riley said. "Let me take him home so his Aunt Myra can say goodbye. We aren't going to make problems without Emerson."

"No can do," Rollo said. "The boss man wouldn't like it. And it wouldn't be any fun." He gestured to one of the guards. "Get her back into the car, and this time tie her in."

Rollo got behind the wheel, put the car into gear, and drove close to the cliff's edge. He put the car into neutral and got out. Emerson's body was loaded in behind the wheel and the seat belt was fastened around him to keep him upright. Riley could see the bloody wound on the back of Emerson's head. The desert dust had mixed with Emerson's blood to form a thick mass in his black hair.

"What's the matter with him?" Xandy asked.

"He's dead," Rollo said as he leaned in to make sure the brake was off. "Say a prayer for him. And throw one in for yourself."

Rollo slammed the door closed and ran back to the van. The van pulled up to the rear bumper of the GTO and nudged the car forward. Riley strained against the rope restraints.

"I can't get loose!" she said. "Xandy, get up here and help me!"

"Not necessary," Emerson said. "I think I can do this."

Riley felt like her heart might explode. He was alive!

Emerson gave the GTO some gas and moved about twenty feet forward to the very edge of the cliff. He threw the car into reverse and plowed into the front of the white van, knocking it back.

"I thought he was dead," Günter said.

"He g-g-got over it," Riley told him.

She was sobbing uncontrollably, gulping in air, tears running down her face and soaking into her shirt. She had no knowledge that she was crying. She was swallowed up by the horror of the moment and the relief that Emerson was alive.

Emerson ground through a couple gears and took off. The car skidded out along the edge of the cliff. Emerson turned back onto the road, cut around the van, and slammed into its left side.

He put the car in reverse, backed up, put it into what was left of first and slammed into the van again. The van slid sideways and Emerson put his foot to the floor and shoved the van and all its occupants over the edge of the cliff.

No one said anything. Everyone just sat there breathing. Hard to believe the horror was over. Hard to believe they were alive. Riley kept looking at the spot where the van had disappeared. She was blinking tears away, waiting for Rollo to climb back up, like a hockey-mask-wearing killer in a cheap horror movie. But Rollo remained out of sight. The monster didn't rise again.

"The Siddhar's not going to approve of this," Emerson said. He rested his forehead on the steering wheel. "Is there something wrong with my head? I have a splitting headache."

Xandy reached around and untied Riley. "We need to leave before the aliens return," she said.

Riley shrugged out of the ropes, got out of the car, and walked to the edge of the cliff with Emerson. They looked down at the white van. It was upside down at the bottom of the mountain. It was far away but they could see that it was smoking. There was an explosion, and the van was consumed by a fireball. Black smoke billowed off the van and was carried away on the air currents.

Emerson wrapped his arm around Riley, hugged her into him, and kissed her on her forehead. "Crap on a cracker," Emerson said.

Riley got behind the wheel and gripped it hard to keep her hands from shaking. She put the car into gear and very carefully drove down the mountain. She got to the highway and turned to Emerson.

"Now what?" Riley asked.

"I don't mean to complain," Günter said, "but I'd really like to see a doctor. Or at least get some more of those drugs. I'm in agony here. Sorry."

"We'll get you help soon," Emerson said. "I'd like to get out of the area first." He turned to Riley. "Take the Saint Rose Parkway exit and turn right on Executive Terminal Drive."

Riley looked over at Emerson. "You have a plane?"

"Yes. Of course."

"Why didn't we use it to get to Nevada in the first place?"

"Aunt Myra needed it. Dr. Bauerfeind was in seclusion in Vancouver, and Aunt Myra was kind enough to pick him up in my absence. I suppose I should consider getting a backup plane, but I've never needed one before."

"But the plane is here now?"

"Hopefully. I suspected we might need a fast getaway

so I asked Aunt Myra to hop down here and wait for us once she secured Dr. Bauerfeind.".

Riley followed Emerson's directions to the airport and looked at Xandy in the rearview mirror.

"What about Xandy?" Riley asked.

"I'm going home," Xandy said. "Put me in that fancy plane of yours and drop me off in Des Moines. The hell with aliens. I'm going back to being a dental hygienist."

Henderson Executive Airport had twin runways, a tower straight out of the 1940s, renovated like a museum piece, and a state-of-the-art sleek modern traffic control center.

There were several hangars and a fleet of corporate jets sitting out on the blacktop. Riley parked at the private terminal, and they loaded Günter onto a rolling luggage rack and followed Emerson inside. Emerson found his pilot and they were escorted out to the plane, leaving everyone in the terminal open-mouthed in shock at the bedraggled, blood-splattered group.

Emerson owned a G550 configured to comfortably seat twelve. It flew with two pilots and a flight attendant, a stocked galley, a pleasant lavatory, and a fully functioning office. The interior had high-gloss wood trim and soft cream-colored leather seats and couches. The exterior of the plane was gleaming white with a majestic royal blue "M" that swooped along the sides like an eagle flying in for the kill. The guest towels in the lavatory were also monogrammed with a royal blue "M."

Aunt Myra was in the open doorway of the G550,

smiling at them like she was welcoming them to a barbecue.

"Well, there you are!" she said in her Appalachian drawl. "I was getting ready to send out the bloodhounds."

"We were delayed," Emerson said. "We've sustained some injuries, I'm afraid."

A couple baggage handlers hauled Günter off the luggage rack and carried him up the stairs to the plane. Aunt Myra got him settled onto one of the couches and buckled him in.

"We'll sit you up for now," she said. "After takeoff we can lay you down and make you more comfortable."

"Alcohol would help," Günter said.

"We got plenty of that," Myra said. "Pick your poison."

"I'd kill for a martini."

"I'll pass it on to Margie. That's the flight attendant."

Myra turned to Emerson. "If you don't look a wreck. We've gotta get you some better people skills. Were you in another one of them bar fights?"

Riley's eyebrows raised an inch. "Bar fight? Emerson?"

"I swear, him and Vernon were a trial when they were younger, and they aren't much better now."

An older man with coarse gray hair and bushy eyebrows was sitting in a single seat toward the back of the plane.

"Dr. Bauerfeind," Emerson said. "Nice to see you again. Sorry about my appearance. We had some problems getting out of the gold vault."

"Understandable," Bauerfeind said. "I had some

problems as well. Fortunately Myra came and rescued me just as the Grunwalds' henchmen were breaking down my door."

"There were only two of them," Myra said, "so it wasn't much of a problem."

"She kicked one of them in the privates," Bauerfeind said. "And then she sucker-punched the other in the throat."

"Yeah, and then we ran like the dickens and jumped into the car and took off for the airport," Myra said.

"Tell the pilots that the first stop is Des Moines," Emerson said. "After that it's back to D.C."

"Sounds like a plan to me," Myra said. "Everyone take a seat and buckle up. Soon as we're in the air, Margie will get you all something to eat and we can take a look at the hole in the back of Emmie's head."

They were an hour out of Des Moines when Riley woke up and looked with longing at the iPad on the console next to her.

"Are we still off the grid?" she asked Emerson.

"Not effectively," he said. "I'm sure they're tracking my plane. Although it might take some time to determine exactly who was incinerated in the van."

"I'd like to tell my family I'm okay."

"I'd prefer that you wait until we're on the ground in D.C. It would spoil my plan if we were met by armed guards at the airport."

"You have a plan?"

"Of course."

"Does it involve the memory card?"

"Not directly. The photographs are worthless without a gold sample. Unless we can trace the gold back to the Federal Reserve, we can't prove any wrongdoing."

"What about the fake gold that's *in* the Federal Reserve?"

"I doubt they're going to open the vault to us, and the chances of breaking in again are slim to none. However, there is another source of recast gold."

They simultaneously turned and looked at Günter passed out on the couch.

"I think I'm seeing your plan," Riley said.

"How many martinis did he have?" Emerson asked.

"Too many," Riley said.

"I can get the information I need verified by Vernon," Emerson said. "He's babysitting the house."

Vernon was in the kitchen when he answered his phone. "Em," he said. "It's like you read my mind. I got the zebra pen repaired and rounded up all the zebras, but one of them wandered into the house and I can't get him out. He's looking at me like I'm an idiot. I swear he's giving me the evil eye. I offered him a carrot and some alfalfa and a can of cat food, but he's not having any of it."

"That's Willie. He's harmless. He just talks a good game."

"You named him Willie?"

"Yes, after Willie Sutton. He was a convict. The zebra has stripes. It makes sense."

"If you say so, cuz."

"Give him a salt lick and he'll be happy."

"I don't know where you keep the salt licks," Vernon said. "He's gonna have to be happy with potato chips. I got a big bag of those."

"Whatever," Emerson said. "I need you to do something for me first."

"I'm on it. What do you need?"

"Go into the library and find the plaster statue of Saint Nicholas."

"Okay, but Willie's gonna follow me. He's been following me all over the house."

"Yeah, he'll do that. He doesn't know he's a zebra. Call me back on the plane number when you get the statue."

Vernon called back ten minutes later. "I got it," he said. "Now what?"

"Break it open."

"Whoa. Isn't that sacrilegious? I mean, busting a statue of Saint Nick? Wouldn't that put me on the naughty list?"

"The naughty list is a myth, Vernon."

"So you say. I'm not taking any chances."

"Vernon, break the statue. I'll suffer the consequences."

"Does it work that way? How will Santa know?"

"I'll write him a letter."

Emerson and Riley listened on the other end of the line as Vernon hit Saint Nick with a meat mallet.

"Is there anything inside it?" Emerson asked.

"Yeah, a little bag. With coins in it."

"Gold coins?"

"Uh-huh, with pictures of some guy that looks like Magneto from *X-Men* on it."

Emerson glanced at Riley, who nodded. "That would be Bertie," she said.

"How many coins?" Emerson asked.

Vernon took a second to count. "Ten."

"Thanks, Vern," Emerson said. "Give Willie a hug for me."

"So Günter was telling the truth about the coins," Emerson said. "Let's hope his wife didn't find the mother lode and cash it in."

TWENTY-EIGHT

⬤⬤⬤

I RENE GRUNWALD GOT UP EARLY EVERY MORNING to work out. And by "work out" she meant have a pitcher of sangria while lying in a lounge chair in her backyard and watching the sun rise over the river.

She hardly thought about Günter at all nowadays. Oh, sometimes she woke in the middle of the night and was glad for the extra space in bed. But other than that, he had disappeared from her world like the memory of an annoying summer song. One minute it had been going through her head endlessly, the next minute she couldn't even recall it.

Of course, she knew he'd given her all she had, and she was grateful for that, after a fashion. The house here on the Potomac. The house up on Cape Cod. The stocks and bonds.

She spread a towel on the lounge chair on the patio and looked out at the river as the sky turned the deep blue that meant the sun was coming up. She'd miss this place when she moved. But that wouldn't be for a while. She would hold out for the best offer on the house. And then she'd be moving to Paris or London, where Washington, D.C., would be a distant, hazy memory.

The sky lightened and she realized her view had changed. The boat was missing. Günter's boat should be at the dock. The boat had been stolen. Damn. Günter had paid more attention to that boat than he had paid to her. Oh, well, it was insured, she thought. Now she didn't have to go through the annoyance of selling it. She could simply collect the insurance.

Riley, Emerson, and Vernon cruised up the Potomac, past Reagan National Airport on the left, and got ready to branch off to the Anacostia River, heading to the District Yacht Club. Vernon was down belowdecks. Emerson was at the wheel, the wind blowing his shaggy hair around his face.

Riley tried to keep her red curls out of her eyes, but the breeze kept whipping them back around. "I still think we shouldn't have stolen this boat," she said.

"We aren't stealing it. We're retrieving it for Günter."

"Yes, but we retrieved it in the dark without telling Mrs. Günter."

"It was simpler."

Riley was sure that was true.

"I'm not much of a sailor but I'm surprised it can float, considering the weight it's carrying," Riley said.

"It's riding low," Emerson said. "I noticed it when we went to Günter's house that first time. The boat sat far too low in the water for a craft of this size. It bothered me, but I didn't make too much of it. Until Günter told the story of stealing the coins and hiding them."

"You guessed they were in the boat even before he told us?"

"When he first talked about the coins he said they were underwater. It was a very good clue. He has buckets and buckets and buckets of gold in the ballast. Thirty thousand one-ounce coins. Almost a ton of gold. Hidden under the murky water."

Bertie Grunwald gazed out at the view of the Capitol. Most people looked at the blinding white dome and felt a rush of patriotism. Bertie saw it and thought only of obstruction and procrastination. Oh, the things he could have accomplished in the years he was running the Fed, if it weren't for this damned democracy.

He probably wouldn't live to see things put right. Of course he'd been thinking he was at death's door for years now. He just refused to walk across its threshold. Death would come soon enough, and when it did he would be blessed to know that his sons would carry on for him.

Hans was the strong one. Manny was the clever one. He'd figure out all the legal niceties to make the coup seem constitutionally sound. Werner, he was the hungry one. Werner was ruthless enough to make things happen.

Bertie thought of Günter for a second, involuntarily. Then he pushed the thought away. Günter had been a constant disappointment from his childhood on, and in the end he had relinquished his right to be a Grunwald. Günter was no longer his son. Especially since he was most likely dead. The final report wasn't back from the coroner's office, but Bertie felt confident of the results. There were several people in the van, but they were burned beyond recognition. Ashes and a couple molars. Rollo and his guards were also missing. Bertie assumed something went wrong and they went over the cliff with their prisoners. Not a large loss. Rollo was a screwup. Good riddance.

Bertie was sitting in his wheelchair on the eighteenth floor of the Blane-Grunwald building on Constitution Avenue. The floor above the seventeenth floor. The floor above everything and everybody, he thought. As it should be.

He turned his chair toward the television monitor on the wall. C-SPAN was covering the Red Mass, the Catholic ceremony blessing the Supreme Court and its newest member-to-be, Manfred Grunwald. Tomorrow was the first Monday in October, when the Supreme Court convened its new session. Then the new order would begin.

The dignitaries were arriving in their black limousines at the front steps of the Cathedral of Saint Matthew the Apostle on Rhode Island Avenue. The redbrick building wasn't as big as Saint John the Divine in New York or Our Lady of the Angels in Los Angeles, but it made up in style what it lacked in size. From its Romanesque Revival architecture to its Byzantine mosaics, it looked like an Eastern Orthodox church transplanted from Istanbul to Washington.

Rhode Island Avenue was entirely blocked off by Secret Service agents who stood in strategic locations, their black suits bulging with unidentified weaponry. News stations were outside the church, focused on the arriving celebrities, trying desperately to find an unpredictable story in the most preplanned ceremony of the calendar year.

One by one the movers and shakers of America made their way out of limos and up the steps into the church. The Supreme Court justices. The cabinet officials. Members of the diplomatic corps. Prominent lobbyists. Leaders of the Senate and the House. The vice president. And three Grunwalds.

The doors to the cathedral were closed and C-SPAN cut inside. For the first time, the ceremony itself was going to be broadcast to the entire world. Or as much of the world as watched C-SPAN.

Inside Saint Matthew's, the Byzantine motif was even more pronounced. Red marble arches framed the mahogany pews, separating the transepts from the central nave. Statues lined the aisle in front of the apse like monumental guardians. On the floor in front of the altar, set in a circle of black marble, were the words

HERE RESTED THE REMAINS OF PRESIDENT
KENNEDY AT THE REQUEIM MASS,
NOVEMBER 25, 1963, BEFORE THEIR REMOVAL
TO ARLINGTON, WHERE THEY LIE IN AN
EXPECTATION OF HEAVENLY RESURRECTION.

Bertie had been teaching at Harvard when the assassination occurred and was as shocked by it as everyone else. When he moved into the circles of power in the seventies, he occasionally made an effort to find out what had happened and who had been behind it. It was a source of constant disappointment to him that he had never found any concrete signs of a conspiracy.

The archbishop of Washington began his march down the aisle wearing the startling blood-red vestments that symbolized the tongues of fire that the Holy Spirit gave to the apostles during Pentecost. He followed a priest in blindingly white robes carrying a golden cross, and another very tall one swinging a censer filled with smoking incense. A flock of cardinals in scarlet frocks with tall white miters on their heads came trailing behind him. The whole effect reminded Bertie of the circuses of his youth. He half-expected a lion tamer to come in next, followed by acrobats and tumblers and a tiny car full of clowns.

The solemn procession passed under the red and gold dome, and sunlight streamed down. This was old-school majesty at its finest, Bertie thought. He was an atheist, but he approved of the sentiment and pageantry. Blind the people with ceremony, circuses, and red robes.

Keep them happy and distracted. Power brokers like him could do whatever they wanted.

The choir sang and the organ played and the ceremony began. There was much standing and sitting and kneeling by the congregation, and a reading from the Acts of the Apostles by a junior priest. Bertie had begun to nod off before the actual homily began. He took a sip of green tea to try to wake up. God, he hated green tea.

Bertie stared at the flat-screen. He could see his sons sitting in the front of the church. Like the three wise monkeys. Except they could see, hear, and speak all manner of evil, Bertie thought with a laugh that shook his whole body and brought up some phlegm.

Werner shifted uncomfortably in the hard wooden pew. He couldn't wait to hear the bishop say "Go in peace" so he could get out of there and go back to Blane-Grunwald. He glanced next to him where Hans sat ramrod straight, with no expression on his stony face, chest thrust forward to show off all his medals, as if he were in combat and shouldn't show fear.

Manny, on the other hand, looked like he was enjoying the hell out of the show. Since he was joining the Supreme Court tomorrow, Manny considered himself the guest of honor, as if this whole ceremony was being put on solely for his amusement.

Archbishop Aberrai stepped up to the pulpit, and Werner sighed as Aberrai began to speak in his soothing

Ethiopian accent. Keep your eyes open and look awake, Werner thought. The old man was watching C-SPAN and there'd be hell to pay if he caught one of his sons nodding off.

"I have thought long and hard about the words of the reading for today," Aberrai said. "In this city, we all seem to speak in different languages, don't we? It's a bit like the Tower of Babel, isn't it?"

Blah, blah, blah, Werner thought. What the hell was the idiot talking about? He looked around. If this was his property he'd put in a cash bar. Maybe a Starbucks. God, he could really use a Starbucks.

"Why can't we speak so that each of us hears the other in his own native tongue?" Aberrai said. "Why can't we—"

The lights went out.

The church wasn't plunged into darkness, exactly. There were stained glass windows high up on the walls letting in colored light, and glowing beams streamed down from the opening in the dome. Werner supposed the best way to describe what happened was that the church was plunged into dimness.

Riley looked down into the church from high up in the dome. She could see the nave of the cathedral and watched as the congregation reacted to the sudden loss of illumination with quiet disinterest.

"Well," Archbishop Aberrai said. "I guess this is a sign from above."

The congregation laughed and the archbishop continued. It was an easy crowd, Riley thought. They were going to love her little slide show. She touched an icon on her iPad, and images were projected from remote cameras scattered around the church. The images were ghostly but clear. Images of gold. A freaking maze of the stuff. The gold hoard in Area 51.

The tall priest holding the censer of incense stepped forward. "You're looking at images of the world's gold," he shouted. "Gold that's been stolen from the Federal Reserve vault and recast and repositioned in Nevada."

Werner leapt to his feet. "That man is an impostor. He's not a priest. That's Emerson Knight! He's a wanted man! And he's insane. Security!"

"Let him finish," the archbishop said. "I rather like the slide show."

"Thank you, Alex," Emerson said to the archbishop. "The gold is at Nellis Air Force Base. It's being stored in tunnels and caverns under what is commonly called Area 51."

Hans signaled his aide to stop Emerson and cut off the C-SPAN feed. Manny popped a Rolaid. Werner looked to see where the nearest exit was located.

"Werner Grunwald, Hans Grunwald, Manfred Grunwald. He who covers his sins will not prosper," Emerson said, dodging a Secret Service agent and bolting for a side altar lined with a series of confessional booths.

Emerson yanked open the door to the first confessional. Gold coins spilled from the tiny room, rolling and clattering and shimmering and spinning on their edges before rattling to rest on the tile floor.

"But whoever confesses and forsakes them shall have mercy," Emerson said, opening the doors to the other booths and freeing still more coins into the church. Thirty thousand of them in all.

There was stunned silence for ten seconds, and then there was bedlam. Everyone had their phones out, taking selfies and video. C-SPAN clicked back on. Security locked arms to keep people away from the coins. The network news trucks returned to the cathedral and jockeyed for position. And Werner vomited all over the floor of the men's room.

Bertie Grunwald threw the remote at the flat-screen but it fell short. Fucking modern televisions, he thought. Too damn far away.

TWENTY-NINE

<hr />

RILEY HAD BEEN IN THE INTERROGATION room for six hours. For most people, this would have been a terrible hardship. Even a few weeks ago, Riley herself would have seen it as a nightmare.

Now she just thought it was a nice place to sit down and take a rest. After all, she wasn't climbing down a rope into a dark cavern or getting pushed over a cliff, tied up in a car. True, the agent was asking her all kinds of questions, but he didn't have any type of surgical instruments on him at all. And on top of that, he was kind of cute.

Besides, answering his questions was nothing more than relaxing. Because she simply had to tell him the truth. How hard was that?

"Where did the coins come from?" he asked.

"Günter Grunwald's boat. He had them hidden there."

"Why did he do that?"

"Because he didn't want anyone to know that he had them. Because he stole them from his brothers. Because they stole gold from the Federal Reserve and made the coins from that. But I'm sure Günter's telling you all about this."

"Is he?"

"Come on," Riley said. "Knock it off. You know that as well as I do."

Günter and Dr. Bauerfeind had met up with Riley and Emerson when they were being escorted out of the cathedral. Günter and Bauerfeind had to talk their way into the paddy wagon. Eventually they convinced the Secret Service that they were a part of this madness. Now they were somewhere in this building on L Street being questioned. It was one big happy family.

"Dr. Bauerfeind will be able to tell you the origin of the gold in the coins," she told him. "Much of it will be from the Deutsche Bundesbank in Frankfurt, Germany, by way of the United States Federal Reserve."

"How did you get into the cathedral? The Secret Service had it cordoned off."

"We brought the coins into the church before the Secret Service arrived. Emerson did a favor for Archbishop Aberrai a couple years ago, and the archbishop returned the favor by letting us into the church. Now it's my turn," Riley said. "What's your first name? Where'd you grow up? Who's your favorite Batman?"

"I'm not the one being questioned here."

"Am I under arrest?"

"No." He blew out a sigh. "I hate when they have me interrogate people with law degrees."

"So?"

"Jordan. Atlanta. Kevin Conroy in *Batman: The Animated Series*," he said.

"I agree, isn't he the best?" Riley stood and stretched. "I'd like to go home now. I've told you everything you need to know."

"By your own confession, you broke into the Federal Reserve vault in New York, you trespassed onto restricted Air Force property in Nevada, and you disrupted a Roman Catholic liturgy in Washington, D.C. And there's more. Do you want me to go on?"

"Not necessary. There were circumstances. You're dealing with the biggest gold theft in the history of forever. And everybody knows about it. It was on television. You can't make us disappear, because too many people saw us. People are going to have to know the truth. You cannot just make this go away. And if all that isn't enough, I'm pretty sure I saw Bill O'Reilly in the audience at the church."

Riley sat opposite Myra at the kitchen table. When Emerson's father had been in residence, the table had been used by household staff. When Myra took over, the table became the heart of the house. The only time the large formal dining room table was used was when the iguana climbed up and tried to eat the candles.

"They made it all go away," Riley said to Myra. "*Poof!* Swept under the carpet."

"Have another cookie," Myra said, pushing the brown bear cookie jar over to Riley. "You accomplished what you set out to do. Em got to see his gold. And no one's trying to kill you anymore. It's all good."

"I suppose that's true. Although Emerson's gold now has Bertram Grunwald's face on it. At least Blane-Grunwald was able to gather it all together for Emerson to see."

"I imagine they'll melt it down and Bertie's face will go away," Myra said.

"Eventually. Fortunately Dr. Bauerfeind's technique was able to determine ownership of most of the gold."

"So everybody will get their gold back."

"I've been told that the process of discreetly reshaping and removing the gold from Nellis Air Force Base and transporting it back to the Federal Reserve vault in New York will take several years to complete. But yes, everyone should ultimately get their gold back."

"And the Grunwald boys disappeared and Bertie went back to being dead."

"Except for Günter," Riley said. "He was rewarded with a clean record and temporary stewardship of the firm of Blane-Grunwald."

"Are you going to work for him?" Myra asked.

"I haven't decided."

Vernon walked in and took a handful of cookies from the cookie jar.

"Hey, Rye," he said. "You're looking pretty today. Did you see the new RV Emerson got me? It's totally sweet. Got a shower and everything in it. It's even got my name embroidered on the bedspread. The old Redhawk was an okay babe magnet, but this one's a killer."

"What happened to the old Redhawk?" Riley asked him.

"I gave it to Andy, since his got sort of beat up and abandoned."

Riley ate a cookie and looked at her watch. "Emerson said he'd meet me here an hour ago. Where the heck is he?"

"You know Emmie," Myra said. "He runs on Emerson time."

"I saw him a while back," Vernon said. "He was in the greenhouse talking to that yogi guy."

Riley took one last cookie and went to the conservatory. She wandered along the overgrown paths, keeping a watchful eye out for snakes and spiders, finally stumbling into Emerson. He was sitting cross-legged by a small lily pond. He saw her and rose.

"You're an hour late," he said to Riley.

"I was waiting for you at the house."

"Yes, but I'm not at the house."

"How was I supposed to know that?"

"I'm sure I told you," Emerson said.

"No."

"Well, it's insignificant because here you are and here I am."

Riley supposed that was true.

"I have a business proposition for you," Emerson said. "I've decided that we should be a team and embark on a great adventure."

"What adventure would that be?"

"I don't know. That's what makes it an adventure. It will involve detective work. I think we're very good at doing detective work."

"We're *terrible* at detective work. We almost died!"

"Yes, that part was exhilarating."

"You must still have a concussion."

Emerson touched the back of his head. "Perhaps, but I feel fine."

"I'll have to think about it."

"There's nothing to think about," Emerson said. "It's the chance of a lifetime."

"Would I get paid?"

"Is that important to you?"

"Yes."

"Would you like a zebra?" Emerson asked her.

"No. I'd like money."

"Well, then, it's not an issue. I have lots of money."

"Tempting."

Emerson raised a single eyebrow and smiled slyly. "I rather like the idea that I might tempt you."

CHAPTER ONE

———⊗⊗⊗———

I t was a little after one in the morning when Riley Moon stopped struggling to make sense of the spreadsheet in front of her. She scraped her chair back from her desk, stood, and gave up a sigh. She was in a small room in a large mansion in Washington, D.C., and she was surrounded by boxes, laundry hampers, and black garbage bags that were filled with official papers. She'd been hired to untangle the complicated financial affairs of the Knight family, who for generations had been brilliant at making money and pathetic at keeping records. Riley had been on the job for almost two months, and she'd reached the conclusion that it would be best for everyone if she set the office on fire and destroyed every available document.

Her curly red hair was a rat's nest from the recently

acquired habit of raking her fingers through it. Her blue eyes felt bloodshot. She thought a martini would fix everything, but she didn't have the energy to make one. She had two degrees from Harvard, a cute nose, a nice family back in Texas, and no social life. The closest she came to having a man in her life was her boss, Emerson Knight, a man known far and wide as an "odd duck." True, he was rich, brilliant, and a totally hot-looking guy, but that didn't alter the fact that he was quackers.

Emerson was the latest heir to the Knight fortune, and he had no interest in either making more money or keeping better records. He simply wanted to get his family's affairs in order so that he could keep their many charitable trusts operating while he pursued a life of investigation.

Their backgrounds were worlds apart, Riley thought. Her father was the sheriff of a small, dusty town in North Texas. Her mother was a second grade teacher. Her childhood home was modest. It had unfashionable, comfortable furniture, a small backyard that was fenced for the family dog, a kitchen table that seated seven, and a dining room table that seated a tight ten but was only used for Thanksgiving dinner. Growing up she had to compete with her four brothers, so she knew how to shoot, throw a punch, hit a hardball, and cuss.

Riley glanced at her office's small window and considered her options. She could traipse downstairs, get into her black-and-white Mini Cooper, and drive home to her apartment on Monroe Street in the Mount Pleasant section of Northwest D.C., or she could select one of the many guest bedrooms just down the hall and sleep here at the Knight mansion, Mysterioso Manor.

"The answer is obvious," Emerson said, standing in shadow on the far side of the room. "It would be more efficient for you to stay here."

"Crap on a cracker!" Riley said, whipping around, hand over her heart. "You just scared the heck out of me. How long have you been standing there?"

"That's an interesting question. On a quantum level, either always or never."

"And on the level we all live on except you?"

"About twenty seconds. I was checking the security monitors and I saw your office light was still on."

"I can't reconcile money spent through your animal rights charitable trust with money received. You seem to have too much money, but I don't know where it came from."

"Is that a dilemma?"

"Yes!"

Only one of many, Riley thought, looking at her boss. He had a peculiar intelligence that set him apart from other brilliant people she'd met. He was good at connecting the dots even when half the dots were missing. Unfortunately, he was also a charmingly annoying enigma with just the right combination of charisma and resourcefulness to convince her of just about anything. And if that wasn't enough of a problem, he looked like a model for a romance novel cover. He was six feet two inches tall, with a lot of wavy black hair, smoldering dark eyes, and a hard-muscled, lean body. The dark hair and eyes he'd inherited from his Spanish mother. The muscle was the result of years of martial arts practice.

Riley agreed with Emerson that it would be most efficient for her to spend the night here. Problem was, the guestrooms were creepy. In fact, the whole mansion was creepy. It was a massive gray stone Gothic-Victorian architectural disaster with a wraparound porch, multiple chimneys, hidden passages, gargoyles, turrets, and lancet windows. It was filled with priceless bric-a-brac, elaborate woodwork, uncomfortable antique furniture, and heavy velvet drapes with gold tassels. Previous generations of eccentric Knights had lived in the mansion and filled it with their collected treasures, wives, and mistresses.

Riley was about to choose comfort over efficiency when Emerson's house security alarm screamed out *Intrusion, intrusion, intrusion.*

"What the heck?" Riley said, clapping her hands over her ears.

Emerson tapped a code into his smartphone. The noise stopped, and images from the house's security cameras appeared on the phone's screen. "Follow me," Emerson said. "The game is afoot."

"Really?" Riley said. "Someone just broke into your house and you're quoting Sherlock Holmes?"

"It popped into my head. It seemed appropriate."

"Hiding in the closet and waiting for the police seems *more* appropriate."

"We would have a very long wait. The alarm system

isn't connected to the police. I have my own top men who handle these sorts of problems."

"Who?"

"Vernon."

Vernon was Emerson's cousin from West Virginia who'd taken up semi-permanent residence in a monster RV he kept parked behind the mansion. He was a big, good-natured guy who had a way with the ladies and preferred fishing to thinking.

"If there was any danger, Vernon would be here," Emerson said. "He has *unagi*."

"*Unagi*?"

"It's a state of total awareness. Only by achieving true *unagi* can you be prepared for any danger that might befall you."

Riley followed Emerson to the stairs, arming herself with a massive two-handed sword she'd appropriated from a suit of armor guarding a bedroom.

"First, Vernon doesn't have *unagi*," Riley said. "And second, there's no such thing as *unagi*. You heard about it on an episode of *Friends*. An episode we watched together last night!"

"If there *is* an intruder I'll use my powers to cloud his mind so he won't see me," Emerson said.

"Awesome. Great plan. And what about me?"

"You have a big sword."

Riley mentally acknowledged that she did indeed have a big sword and that Emerson did have an uncanny talent for sneaking up on people.

They stopped on the second-floor landing and looked

over the railing at a little man standing in the foyer below them. Bald head. Short. Asian ancestry. Orange monk's robe. Jesus sandals.

"Hello, Wayan," Emerson called down to the little man.

The man raised his eyes and smiled. He put his palms together, fingers up, and bowed his head slightly in greeting. Emerson repeated the palms-together greeting and went down the stairs to meet him.

"This is Wayan Bagus," Emerson said to Riley. "He's the Buddhist monk I studied with during my voyage of discovery."

"I thought your mentor was Thiru Kuthambai Siddhar."

"There are many paths to enlightenment," Emerson said. "The Siddhar was also a mentor." Emerson turned to the little monk. "How did you get here?"

"I walked," Wayan Bagus said.

"From Bali?"

"I walked onto a boat. Then I walked onto a plane. Then, when the plane landed in Richmond, I walked some more."

"Richmond is more than a hundred miles from here," Riley said. "How long did it take you?"

Wayan Bagus smiled politely. "Buddha tells the story of a granite mountain that reached many miles into the sky. Every hundred years it was wiped with a silk cloth held in the mouth of a bird until the mountain was worn away to nothing. So, not so long."

Riley suppressed a grimace and managed a tight

smile. She didn't want to be rude, but criminy, wasn't it bad enough she had to endure this philosophical baloney from Emerson?

"I suppose everything is relative," Riley said to Wayan Bagus. "Still, it had to have been a long, difficult trip. And how did you manage to get into the house once you found it?"

"The universe provided a way. Also, the door was unlocked." He turned to Emerson. "I need your help. The island I was using as a hermitage is missing. I think it was stolen."

"Define 'missing,'" Emerson said.

"Gone," Wayan Bagus said. "Vanished without a trace. Although I did find a few coconuts bobbing on the waves. And a wooden bowl I used for my morning meal."

"Islands normally don't go missing," Emerson said.

"Nevertheless, it is missing just the same," Wayan Bagus said.

"Fascinating," Emerson said. "Where exactly did you see it last?"

"It was right where I'd left it. About two hundred miles north of Samoa."

"And what makes you suspect it's stolen and not just lost?"

"For the love of Mike, Emerson," Riley said. "You can't steal—or lose, for that matter—a whole island."

"That's exactly what makes it so intriguing," Emerson said.

"Last month some men appeared on my island and

told me I had to leave," Wayan Bagus said. "When I objected they forcibly removed me and placed me on a different island. By the time I found my way back, my island was gone."

"What did these men look like?" Emerson asked. "Did you know any of them? Were they Samoans?"

"They were wearing khaki shorts and funny hats. Only one man spoke to me, and he spoke in English. Another man gave me an injection, and I woke up hours later."

"Was there anything special about your island?" Emerson asked.

"I know of nothing that would be of extraordinary value. It was typical of the hundreds of uninhabited, unmapped islands around Samoa. It had a mountain and beaches and rainforests. It was a very nice place for a hermitage, except for the volcano."

"I'm quite fond of volcanoes," Emerson said.

"They are interesting," Wayan Bagus said, "but I find the energy can be disruptive to meditation."

When Wayan Bagus was comfortably settled in a third-floor guest room, Emerson and Riley made their way to the library. It was an enormous room with an intricate parquet floor, hand-carved oak bookshelves, and a second-level balcony. Newspapers and magazines were neatly stacked on the floor, and half a dozen whiteboards were scattered about. The whiteboards were covered with Emerson's cryptic notes. Some of the notes were devoted to the tangled estate left behind when Emerson's father had died under mysterious circumstances the previous year. Most notes were simply concerned with whatever sparked Emerson's imagination, ranging from quantum physics to tarantula crossings. A weather-beaten Coleman tent had been erected in front of the massive stone fireplace. Buddhist prayer flags hung from a line stretched between the tent and the fireplace mantel.

Emerson crossed the room, climbed a rolling ladder, and inched his way along, clearly looking for a specific book in the science section.

"It's almost two in the morning and the crazy little monk is asleep in bed," Riley said. "Why are we here in the library?"

"Wayan Bagus is many things," Emerson said. "Crazy isn't one of them. His mental and emotional acuity are superior. If he says his island is missing, then it is most certainly missing."

"And?"

"And we're going to help him find it."

"We?"

"I'm changing your job description to amanuensis so you can assist me in the search. You served as my amanuensis once before, and the results were excellent."

"We were almost killed!"

"The key word is 'almost.' We survived and, you have to admit, it was exhilarating. This will give us an opportunity to once again marry our abilities."

"It wasn't exhilarating. It was terrifying. And I don't know about the marry thing."

"I'm using the term 'marry' in the broad sense of the word, as in 'join together.' I'm brilliant and intuitive and you're practical and have a driver's license. We're the perfect team."

"Of course."

Emerson continued his search. "I thought I should clarify," he said over his shoulder, "because I recently read a book about body language and nonverbal cues, and I decided you find me irresistible."

"*What?* I don't think so. If anyone is irresistible here it's me."

Emerson paused, seeming to have found what he was looking for. "The two aren't mutually exclusive, but we need to maintain the sanctity of the amanuensis-client relationship despite our deepening physical attraction."

"Aha! So you *do* find me irresistible."

"Not at all. 'Irresistible' would indicate a lack of control, and I have control in spades."

Emerson reached for a book, his shirt rode up, and Riley sneaked a look at the bared skin and perfectly toned abs. She narrowed her eyes slightly and thought that she had pretty good control too. Otherwise her hands would be all over those abs.

"Look through this book for the section on Samoa," Emerson said, passing to Riley a copy of *National Oceanographic and Atmospheric Administration Nautical Maps of the Pacific*. "I'll be right down."

By the time Emerson joined Riley at the desk, Riley had found the chapter. It was page after page of detailed maps, with information about water depths, latitudes and longitudes, natural and manmade hazards, currents, and anything else you would need to know if you wanted to navigate by boat through the Samoan island chain.

"As your amanuensis, I have to tell you this is insane. A bunch of men wearing khaki clothes stole an island? I mean, who's your prime suspect? UPS?"

Emerson flipped through the pages. "We would have to consider UPS. They're always *losing* things."

"What of yours have they lost?"

"Ice skates. A volleyball. A sculpture I'd created."

"And they never found any of it?"

"To be honest, Tom Hanks did personally deliver the sculpture to my house, but that was seven years later."

Riley smacked her forehead. "You couldn't possibly be confusing your life with the movie *Castaway*, could you?"

Emerson stopped flipping. "That explains a lot. I always thought it was weird that Tom Hanks would just randomly show up at my front door and give me a package."

"You're a very strange man."

"My Match.com profile says I have a quirky sense of humor."

"You have a Match.com profile?"

"Actually, no," Emerson said. "I just have a quirky sense of humor."

Riley stared at him for a couple beats thinking it was a good thing he had great abs because he wasn't going to get far with the quirky humor. She turned her attention to the book in front of Emerson. It was opened to a map of the Pacific Ocean, showing an area about two hundred miles northeast of Samoa.

"There must be at least a hundred islands," Riley said. "Any one of them could be your monk's island."

"And those are just the mapped islands. There are probably a hundred more that nobody's ever bothered to survey."

"It's like trying to find a needle in a haystack," Riley said.

"Then let's find the needle."

"You don't find the needle," Riley said. "It's a metaphor for an unsolvable problem."

"Ah, but the problem isn't unsolvable," Emerson said. "When Wayan Bagus told me he was going to spend a couple years living in solitude on a deserted island I sent him an emergency satellite transponder. Fortunately he brought the transponder with him, and he gave it to me before he went to bed."

Emerson pulled from his pocket a small orange device that looked a little like a walkie-talkie.

Riley turned the transponder to the ON position. This one had more bells and whistles than the ones she'd used hiking the Texas backcountry with her father and brothers, but it operated on the same basic principle: to send out a beacon signal with GPS coordinates so that first responders could locate you.

"What am I looking for?" she asked.

"The data history. We should be able to use it to

track Wayan Bagus's movements over the past couple months."

Riley read off the first set of GPS coordinates, and Emerson plugged them into his laptop.

"That one is Rock Creek, Maryland," Emerson said. "Mysterioso Manor, to be more precise. They're in reverse chronological order. Skip backward until you find a period of time where he was in just one place for a while. We can assume anything else is him traveling to America."

Riley scrolled through the data. "He was at 8° 24' 34.2648" south and 115° 11' 20.1084" east for a couple weeks."

"That's a small island off the coast of Bali," Emerson said. "That's where he went after he was evicted from his stolen island. How about before that?"

"He was at 11° 3' 36.3544" south and 171° 5' 39.2232" west for six months."

"Bingo," Emerson said. "That's in the middle of the ocean, about two hundred miles from Samoa. He was either floating around in the Pacific for half a year or that's his deserted island hermitage."

Riley put the transponder on the desk and traced her finger down the map in the book to 171° west, looking to see if there were any islands in the approximate area. "Here! There's a little unnamed island, labeled with those exact coordinates."

"Odd," Emerson said. "This island had obviously been surveyed at the time of the book's publication ten years ago, but the image from Google Earth shows nothing but ocean at that location."

"Not surprising," Riley said. "Google Earth also shows an empty field where my parents live. Everybody knows it's just a compilation of various satellite images and still photographs. It's notoriously inaccurate when it comes to rural and unpopulated areas."

"Perhaps," Emerson said, accessing the National Oceanographic and Atmospheric Administration website onto his iPad. "Let's check out the most current nautical maps. These were revised last year."

Riley looked over Emerson's shoulder as he found the set of online maps that corresponded to page 233 in the book.

"There's nothing at 11° 3' by 171° 5'," she said. "In fact, there's not even anything close to that location, except water. It doesn't make sense. The island was there five months ago. Wayan's emergency transponder proves that. And the NOAA mapped it more than ten years ago. So why isn't it on the most current NOAA maps?"

Emerson smiled. "There's only one explanation. Someone erased the island from the NOAA database."

"Why would someone do that?" Riley asked.

"For the same reason a murderer hides the body," Emerson answered. "To cover up a crime. Someone stole Wayan Bagus's island. Tomorrow we're going to hunt it down."